The French Pyrenees

The French Pyrenees

JOHN STURROCK

faber and faber

LONDON · BOSTON

First published in 1988
by Faber and Faber Limited
3 Queen Square London WC1N 3AU

Photoset by Wilmaset Birkenhead Wirral
Printed in Great Britain by
Richard Clay Ltd Bungay Suffolk
All rights reserved

British Library Cataloguing in Publication Data

Sturrock, John
The French Pyrenees.
1. Pyrenees – Description and travel –
Guide-books   2. France – Description and
travel – Guide-books
I. Title
914.4′8904838   DC611.P983

ISBN 0-571-13741-5
ISBN 0-571-15137-X Pbk

Contents

CONTENTS

List of Illustrations

between pages 110 and 111

Maps drawn by Chris New

List of Maps

Acknowledgements

Various people, in England and in France, gave me help and advice in the making of this book. But I must single out Paul Bahn, prehistorian, who read the whole of the manuscript, saved me from error and supplied some fine illustrations.

J.S.

Introduction

The earliest writers to mention the Pyrenees, Diodorus of Sicily and the Greek geographer Strabo, both believed that they ran from south to north, and said so with such authority that it was the seventeenth century before anyone seems to have noticed any differently. It is a mistake one can sympathize with, because we very much like mountain ranges to run either straight up and down or straight across the map. Many mountain ranges do so: the Andes, the Rockies, the Alps, the Himalayas, all seem to know the rules. But the Pyrenees don't: they run at an angle, from north-west to south-east, a necklace around the broad throat of the Iberian peninsula. This slanting course can be confusing when it comes to writing about them, because one may easily want to say that this place or that is 'north' of the Pyrenees, meaning only that it is deeper into France, or north-east from the watershed. In this guidebook, I have tried to be pedantic and keep all the compass bearings as true ones, rather than trust false impressions born of the mountains' own obliqueness.

This is a book strictly about the French Pyrenees, with only the barest digressions over the top into Spain. It suits me very well to be thus one-sided, because I find the French Pyrenees more interesting and hospitable than the Spanish. The two sides of the chain are remarkably different. In France, the Pyrenees rise up with a spendid suddenness as you drive towards them, especially if you have come across the flatnesses of Aquitaine and the region of the Landes. The transition from plain to mountains on the French side is quick and surprising, and on clear days the spread of high peaks can make a stunning horizon from towns such as Pau, themselves only a few hundred feet above sea level. On the Spanish side the mountains take longer to flatten out and the eventual plains are quite high anyway, so that the heartening sense of an abrupt elevation into the highlands is lost. There is simply more of the Pyrenees on that side than on the French; indeed, two-thirds of the 55,000 square kilometres which the mountains are estimated to cover are in Spain. And because the climate on the two sides is markedly different, so is the condition of the land; mountain greenness is for the most part to be had in France, where the rain falls, carried in plenty by the north-west winds. The Spanish side is contrastingly dry, a barer, tougher country, lending plausibility to the old romantic claim that Africa begins at the Pyrenees, as in a way it did during the prolonged Islamic occupation of the peninsula.

Many writers on the Pyrenees get to them apologetically almost, by way of the Alps, as if they were a next-best, a neglected stand-in, suitable for those who have grown tired of that better-known chain and who need a change. That is not the way I come to them; I shall not compare the Pyrenees with the Alps because I look on them as an end in themselves, and a profoundly desirable one. What is certain is that they are not so smart as the Alps, for they have never had the same cachet. They were not included on the Grand Tour in the eighteenth century and have not succeeded since, I am relieved to say, in equipping themselves for the satisfaction of luxurious vacationers. The Pyrenees have a great honesty about them. During the skiing season in winter, and in the summer season too, they remain a conspicuously modest region of France, and as a happy consequence of that a conspicuously cheap one in which to travel. If, as I do, you have a strong weakness for one- and two-star French hotels and the equivalent menus at dinner-time, then the Pyrenees are an incomparable region. It would be hard to spend great amounts of money there, or pamper yourself unduly, even if you wanted to. You could say that they are the democratic version of the Alps.

This guide to the mountains assumes that whoever travels there does so by car; it is organized very much by roads and by the roads between roads. There is, of course, no other rational way to get about in the Pyrenees; unless you are walking. There is a most respectable tradition of British pedestrianism in these mountains, culminating no doubt in the excursions of Hilaire Belloc and of his fellow romantic, J. B. Morton, better known as the humorist 'Beachcomber', who were still able to look on the Pyrenees as some kind of bulwark protecting Christian Europe from invasion by the infidels. Morton, writing in the 1930s, has vitriolic things to say about motor cars and those degenerate enough to arrive in them, and the reliable modern road network of the Pyrenees, with its multiple new passages into Spain, would have revolted him. His boisterous and reactionary way of travelling is not, I will admit, my own, but I conclude that even today serious walkers in the mountains will not want to be weighed down by an easy-going book like this one, which knows nothing of discomfort or danger, but seeks tamely to indicate where the ordinary pleasures of tourism are to be found.

The chief credential I can offer for writing it is an excessive liking for travelling in southern France, and a great liking for mountains. This is a guide written not, however, by some veteran steeped in the life and scenery of the Pyrenees, but by an irregular visitor who has never failed to enjoy them. This, I hope, is an advantage so far as reading or using the book goes, since those with a deep and private local knowledge of places may turn out to be less practical or accessible as guides to them than those who travel there in very much the same state of partial or complete ignorance as the average tourist. So my own account of the mountains remains deliberately within the perspective of the outsider. If it is mildly opinionated here and there, that is because I take the purpose of a guide such as this as being to say what is wrong with places as well as what is good. I have not included anything by way of reports on hotels or eating places, since that would have been foolish. I prefer to report only on what is more or less permanent, on buildings or landscapes, not on such mutable and emotive affairs as the quality of food or lodgings.

The book naturally covers the whole of the French Pyrenees, from the Atlantic coast to the Mediterranean, in a continuous journey of 250 miles or more. That is a journey that could, I suppose, be driven easily enough in a single day, provided your only aim was to get to the other end. But I do not imagine anyone wanting to visit the entire chain like this in one go. There are three distinct parts to the French Pyrenees: the Basque country, the central or High Pyrenees, and Roussillon or the Catalan Pyrenees; and each of these has quite enough that is beautiful or interesting in it to make it well worth a holiday in itself. This is a necessarily brisk guidebook then, to a large and magnificent tract of country; the last effect I would wish it to have would be to make anyone *rush* the Pyrenees. We may have lost the tradition of visiting them on foot, but we can still visit them slowly, as at their great age they deserve.

The Basque Country

Mountain ranges make sensible national frontiers and despite one or two kinks along the way, the Pyrenean watershed divides France neatly and conclusively from Spain. At the two ends of the chain, however, the border between nations is not a border between peoples. At the Mediterranean end, the inhabitants on either side of it are Catalans and very aware of the historical and linguistic bonds which transcend the national frontier; while at the northern, Atlantic end they are Basques, similarly aware of their distinctiveness as a people. In the 1980s the Basques have had much international publicity because of the passion and all too often the excesses of their campaign for separatism. But the politicking and the violence have nearly all come from the Spanish Basques; French Basques have remained relatively quiet. Ask a French Basque about the violent activities over the border in Navarre and he or she will in my experience be unsympathetic, not towards separatism as such but towards the sometimes murderous way in which it is being sought. French Basques seem happy to go on being French as well as Basque. And because the French Basque country, unlike the Spanish, is thoroughly rural, it is very much a tourist region; it would stop being so were terrorism to cross the frontier. A true separatist movement on the French side would be bad indeed for the local economy.

As a people, the Basques are the oddity of Western Europe, because of their language, the *eskuara* as it is called, which is one

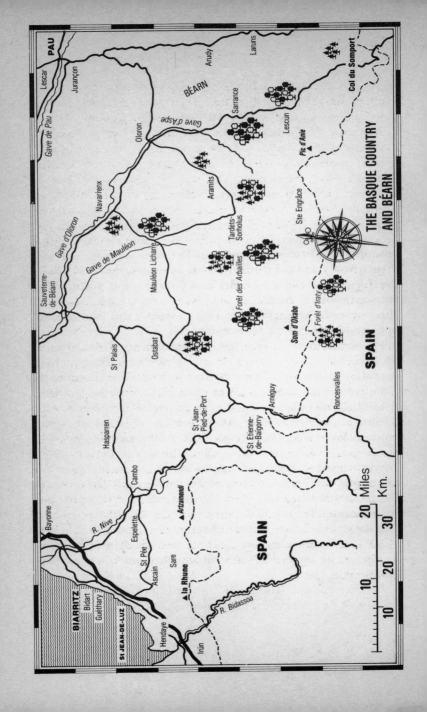

THE BASQUE COUNTRY AND BÉARN

of the great linguistic mysteries, being the only language of
Western Europe not of Indo-European stock. Scholars assume
that modern Basque derives from the original tongue of the
Celtiberians, the ancient people of Spain who were eventually
overcome by the Romans. It has never been a strong language
because it has produced little or no literature, so that it has
seemed to have more of folklore about it than utility. Nowadays, especially in Spain, Basque is being defiantly flaunted as an
alternative to the national language; but in France it is at risk,
spoken at home by Basque families but discouraged in schools,
as a lesser, marginal language likely to hold its speakers back
economically. The one concession to it you see a lot of in the
French Basque country is on the road signs which now duplicate
the French place-names with their Basque equivalents. The
strangeness and sometimes the beauty of Basque is soon
apparent in its frequent resort to the less mentionable letters of
our shared alphabet, to z, k and x.

I do not mean to stray off here into the history of the Basques;
all Pyrenean history is complicated, that of the Basques very
complicated. In the Middle Ages, when the French adjudged
them to be alien, difficult and heathen, they were held to have
descended from Scotsmen transported to Spain by Julius Caesar.
Their true ancestors were the Vascons, a people of north-
western Spain who spread very successfully into and over the
Pyrenees and occupied much of south-western France. These
more ambitious Vascons lost the use of their distinctive
language, however, and turned eventually into Gascons, the
inhabitants of Gascony, whom it takes a second or two these
days to recognize as cousins of the Basques. The Basques with a
B were those who stayed behind, closer to their ancestral lands,
either side of the mountains, and who preserved their language.
So there is a genuine and moving continuity between Basques
and the Vascons.

The Basque Coast

For a people long famous as navigators and seamen, the French Basques have a remarkably short coastline, running for not more than twenty miles from the estuary of the river Adour, three miles oceanwards from the port of Bayonne, to the Spanish frontier at Hendaye. But if it is short, it is also dynamic and various, altogether more refreshing than the endless dunes of the Landes, north of the Adour. The Basque Coast starts off flat, at the top end, with sand and pine trees, then acquires first, shapely beaches prized by athletic visitors for their peculiarly surfable Atlantic waves, and next, low but spectacular rocks and promontories, which are at their best along the curious Corniche Basque, to end in the handsome bay of Hendaye-Plage. It also has three good, markedly dissimilar towns in Bayonne, Biarritz and Saint-Jean-de-Luz; and a little inland, mercifully, a motor-way from France into northern Spain which drains off from the coast the nuisance of merely transient cars and people. This is not the most Basque part of the Basque country because it is too built-up and, in the case of Biarritz, too chic; but everyone should go at least to Saint-Jean-de-Luz, emphatically a Basque town and still in living touch with the ocean of which, as fishermen or on occasion as pirates, the Basques were for long leading citizens.

It is cheating a bit, I fear, to think of the Basque Coast as Pyrenean, because at this end of the chain, unlike at the other, the mountains fight shy of the water and make a decisive turn to the west some miles inland, to enter Spain; so you can see the most northerly or westerly Pyrenees easily enough from points along the coast, but you can't feel you are among them. You can see above all – literally above all – the somewhat flattened summit of La Rhune, the Basque mountain *par excellence*, 3,000 feet high and only seven or eight miles due south from Saint-Jean-de-Luz. That is an upstanding promise of pleasures to come, further into the range. But because it is beside rather than in the Pyrenees, the Basque Coast has a gentler climate than you might expect, with an average temperature over the whole year of nearly 14° Centigrade – almost as good as you will find in Portugal. In the coldest month, January, the average is about 8°, in the hottest, August, between 20° and 21°; so this is a very equable place, hospitable at any season. It is naturally quite wet, being an Atlantic region, even in summer and especially in the spring. There are on average some 150 days a year when rain falls, and this goes up as you move inland into the Basque country proper, whose climate gets a little more extreme as the land rises. The early autumn is the time to be in the Basque country, because it is usually drier then than in the summer, but still blessedly warm, and wonderfully 'luminous' as the French like to put it.

★　　★　　★

The logical place to begin on the Basque Coast is Bayonne, which is a port, but three and a half miles from the open sea down the navigable channel of the river Adour. It is an old and rather likeable town which, standing where it does, so near to the edge of France and commanding the coast road into Spain, has had an agitated history with numerous episodes of war. The Romans built a town and lodged their cohorts here, when what is now Bayonne was called Lapurdum; a slight corruption of that name, Labourd, is still used, to refer to the most westerly and maritime of the three distinct provinces into which the French Basque country is split, of Labourd, Basse-Navarre and Soule. The name Bayonne itself comes from the middle Middle Ages and meant 'good river' in Basque. This was a mistaken choice, because the Adour was actually a bad river, which kept on finding different ways out into the Atlantic and abandoning Bayonne altogether. Only at the end of the sixteenth century was this nomadic watercourse properly recaptured for the town and its outlet fixed by some determined engineering.

For a long time Bayonne was an English possession, having been part of the extensive territorial dowry of Eleanor of Aquitaine when she married into the Plantagenet family in the middle of the twelfth century. It was three centuries and the Hundred Years War indeed before the English lost it, in which time Bayonne did well, not least as a centre of the wine trade with England equal in·prosperity to Bordeaux. Indeed, these were, according to some local historians, Bayonne's very best years, when it became a trading centre of European stature. It was then that they scooped out for the storage of goods the extensive vaults and cellaring that still run beneath the old town today. And then too that the Bayonnais became overbearingly careful of their wealth and success, which they protected by placing chains across the river mouth to keep out marauders and by imposing stiff customs duties that enraged the local Basques. The French writer Hippolyte Taine, in the not on the whole very friendly account he published of a journey to the Pyrenees in the middle of the last century, tells, all too vividly, an unpleasant story of a fourteenth-century mayor of Bayonne who tried to extend his jurisdiction up-river as far as the tide went, so as to stop Basque smugglers from defrauding him, and who tied a number of local Basque gentry to the arches of a bridge and watched the tide come up and slowly drown them.

King Charles VII won Bayonne back from the foreigners in 1451 after a siege and, if a plaque set up in the cathedral has it right, with a little supernatural help. For at seven o'clock in the morning of 20 August in that year, the inscription has it, just as the citadel was about to fall to the besiegers, a white cross was seen in the sky 'above and to the right of the town', which then became a crucifix whose crown turned encouragingly (for the French) into a royal fleur-de-lis. Since the English and their local supporters wore red crosses, their cause could be seen, meteorologically, to be a lost one; they decided that 'God wanted that they should be French', and French they became. The portent in the sky was taken to be the outcome of a timely intercession by Joan of Arc, at that time a quite recent martyr.

In 1813–14 the English were back in Bayonne, this time as the besiegers, when the Duke of Wellington's army drove Napoleon's troops out of Spain and back within their own borders. There were a number of small battles in Labourd and eventually, in February 1814, one large one, further to the east, at Orthez, recorded as one of Wellington's deftest victories, and as an ultimate defeat for Marshal Soult and his army from Spain. The citadel of Bayonne, on the right or northern bank of the Adour, stood out against the English for three months, by which time Napoleon had abdicated and the war was over. Not far from the citadel, should you choose to cross over to that less appealing side of Bayonne, is a small English war cemetery that dates back to the siege. The passage of Wellington's soldiers through the Basque country, when they were deemed to have behaved with greater decency and correctness than their French opponents, was in some degree the origin of the considerable fashion for this part of France among the English throughout the nineteenth century. The winter weather they had fought in was atrocious but some of Wellington's veterans took kindly to the region and came back to settle there; others presumably publicized it in Britain. Its reputation for salubrity spread and drew numbers of both healthy and unhealthy emigrants from the north.

Bayonne has known many other military episodes than these; moreover, you need only to drop one of the two *n*s from its name to recognize it as the birthplace of that sinister weapon, the bayonet. But nowadays it tries hard and gracefully to live down the ferocities of its past. There are fine ramparts on the south and west of the main town, built, as so many fortifications in France seem to have been, by Louis XIV's ubiquitous and tireless fortifier, Vauban. They no longer strike you however quite as ramparts because they have been planted with grass and shrubs and are in places penetrable on foot or even by traffic; they are now a pleasance more than a deterrent. On the south of the town

I even came across one stretch of the old defence works which has had a rugby pitch squeezed into it, with a glacis for a touchline. From which peaceful act of recycling, you can tell also how extremely keen they are on rugby football in this south-western corner of France, which is where nearly all the country's most gifted players and successful teams are.

The best part of the town is on the south bank of the Adour, where it is divided into two by Bayonne's other river, the Nive, which enters from the south, from the mountains. The two rivers are very different to look at, or at least they have been whenever I have seen them. The Adour, which is much the wider, is also the clearer, approximately water-coloured, you could say; the Nive is the rich colour nearly of chocolate, which is appropriate enough given that Bayonne was long famous for the chocolate that it made and in which it traded. The part of the town on the left bank of the Nive is known as Grand or Greater Bayonne, the part on the right bank as Petit or Lesser Bayonne. Both are of quality.

Greater Bayonne has most of the town's shops, the covered market, and the cathedral. The shops fill the area between the cathedral and the point at the bottom of the town, the Place de la Liberté, where one river meets the other. In the most stylish shopping street (though Bayonne is not a *smart* place), the Rue du Port-Neuf, there are vaulted arcades which, for arcade addicts like myself, means that the shops are doubly inviting. And something I have not seen anywhere else, though it makes good sense, is that in these mainly narrow streets, the shops have their signs strung out at right-angles across the way so that you can stand at one end and read their names from there, without having to go down to look at them one by one. But as a town to shop in, Bayonne is sound, not magnetic; its covered market, beside the Adour, is a disappointment, with none of the style of good French markets.

The cathedral of Bayonne is another disappointment if, like me, you travel south in order to rest eyes sated with the Perpendicular and Pointed on the rounded splendours of the Romanesque.

This large church is northern, and Gothic. Perhaps we should blame the English for this, because it started to be built early in the thirteenth century, when Bayonne was ours, and the English royal arms of the day are apparently to be found, alongside those of France, emblazoned on some of the keystones of the very high vaulting in the nave. In the last century, the cathedral was made more northern still, when a second tower was added to the one which already existed, and two spires for good measure. The best of the decoration is certainly the stained glass in some of the side-chapels. But better still is the delightful Gothic cloister which opens on the southern side of the nave, an asylum all the more praiseworthy for opening on the far side on to the street, and with an admirable fig tree standing in one corner to remind you that, northern Gothic or no, you are in the south.

There are five bridges, no less, by which you can cross the Nive into Lesser Bayonne. The main road bridge is at the bottom of the town, facing the theatre, which has cafés outside and is an airy if also raucous place to sit and have coffee. The theatre is a more enterprising place of entertainment now than it was in the days, early in the last century, when, as a small boy, the great French writer Victor Hugo stayed in Bayonne for a month, on his way to meet his father, a general in the Napoleonic army in Spain. Young Victor, a Romantic from birth, was excited when the family was given free seats for the theatre for every night of its stay, less excited when he found out that the programme never changed, so that it meant sitting through the same melodrama every night for a month.

Lesser Bayonne is bourgeois and compact, and contains the town's two unexpectedly good museums, the Musée Bonnat and the Musée Basque, which are only a hundred yards apart. The Musée Bonnat is an art gallery and an exceedingly good one for a provincial town. It is good because Léon Bonnat, a loyal son of Bayonne, first collected these pictures and then left them to the town, which responded by building a small palace in which to show them. Bonnat (1833–1922) made his name and his money in Paris, where he was a painter of the *salon*-haunting kind and also an influential director of the École des Beaux-Arts. He knew the grandees, and sometimes painted their picture. Hence his own fine collection of oil-paintings and drawings. Indeed, if you want to find out how it was that Bonnat grew wealthy enough to buy the many works of art that he did, you need only go into the room reserved in the museum, on the ground floor, for his society portraits. Here are the famed Parisian hostesses of the age, all looking sumptuous, darkly beautiful and, I'm afraid, rather alike, the standardized objects of the artist's skilful flattery.

But Bonnat's gallery is well worth going to. It is a comfortable size, circumnavigable inside an hour, various in its contents, and pleasantly arranged. Surprisingly, he did much better as a collector of pictures from earlier centuries than of the works of his own contemporaries or friends. There are in the Musée two memorable and characteristic El Greco portraits, of a duke all in black and a cardinal; some excellent Ingres, including a full-length portrait of the depressing King Charles X, looking depressing, and an ample-backed *Baigneuse* or *Woman Bathing*; a Goya self-portrait, among other pictures by him, making him look mild and harmless; some British pictures, by Constable, Lawrence, Reynolds and Raeburn; a Géricault and an agitated Delacroix showing *Job tormented by Demons*; and some fine drawings, of which Bonnat had a most notable collection, too large to be displayed *in toto*, by artists from the early Italians onwards. One small room shows a splendid set of Rubens sketches, of scenes from the *Metamorphoses* of Ovid, done mostly for the King of Spain's hunting-lodge. Only the later nineteenth-century works are a let-down; Bonnat obviously lacked pull with the great Impressionists and bought generally insipid work.

If the Musée Bonnat is plush and metropolitan, the Musée Basque round the corner is local and very homely. I write, I have to say, as a folklorophobe, but this is an endearing and instructive collection, kept in a fine sixteenth-century Basque town house. It makes an intelligent compendium of this mysterious people's history and culture, compressed into a serpentine and bewildering suite of quite small rooms and exhibits: their furniture, their costumes, the trades they have practised, the things they have manufactured, their art and religious objects, and so on. As in all good local museums, there are some fine *trouvailles* here. Like the *makhilas* or elaborately worked sticks made of medlar, with a sharp goad concealed in the handle; these look decorative enough but they were weapons before they became art forms and Basque men always carried them when they went to markets or cattle fairs and often fought with them. Or, among much robust, dark furniture, the *zuzulu*, a wooden settle part of whose back let down to make a table. Or the little portable sundials which shepherds used to carry up into the mountains to tell the time by; or, a last reassuringly bucolic reminder that Bayonne's fighting days are over, an English bayonet from the Napoleonic wars converted for stripping corn-cobs. The Musée Basque has rooms also devoted to the game of pelota, which is a more various one in terms of the equipment its players either do use or have sometimes used than you would otherwise guess; to the centuries of Basque whaling; to witchcraft, for which and for its vicious suppression there was a vogue in the Basque country in the sixteenth and seventeenth centuries. There is a cramped, faded little room given over to the recognition of the literary achievements of the region, in homage to writers who were not themselves Basques but who settled here: the playwright Edmond Rostand, author of the extraordinary *Cyrano de Bergerac*; the exotic novelist Pierre Loti, who lived and died in Hendaye; the sentimental poet Francis Jammes, pictured here in a charming naive portrait, impossibly bearded and together with his wife and their wildly staring dog. It will be a generation or two no doubt before this determinedly old-fashioned room acknowledges one of the most remarkable of post-1945 French writers, the critic Roland Barthes, who was the complete

Parisian intellectual but was brought up in the Basque country, went to school in Bayonne and all his life kept his house along the Adour, at Urt. Barthes's was a very modern mind but he would have liked the idea of being one day accepted into this tiny pantheon of local literary notables.

Coming out of the Musée Basque, and as you turn right to recross the Nive by the Pont Marengo, you can see facing you, a little upstream, a short sequence of the best, by which I mean the most distinctive, houses in Bayonne, narrow, half-timbered, six storeys high and standing none too straight. You can see also, alas, the appalling riverside car park created on top of the covered market, which is the sort of planned ugliness one had thought only English town councils capable of.

There are various roads that you can take to get from Bayonne to Biarritz, which is about five miles south-west of Bayonne. The two roads that go by way of Anglet, a suburb which has accumulated to fill in the gap between the two towns, are no better than functional. One has the odd title of the Boulevard du B.A.B., revealing that it has taken over the line of the old tramway, the Bayonne-Anglet-Biarritz; the other, further back from the coast, is the N10, once the crowded highway along which French motorists hurtled into northern Spain but now a gentler place to drive, the motorway having supplanted it. But the more civilized route to take to Biarritz is via the mouth of the river Adour; this stretches the journey by four kilometres and makes it twice as enjoyable. The road from Bayonne leads right out past the prolonged installations of the port to the end of the estuary, at La Barre. Here, in bad weather, there are reputed to be spectacular collisions between the seawater coming in on the westerly winds and the fresh water trying to get out. And here too, you can see how sturdily the once-wandering river Adour has been walled in, to keep it in place.

Just before La Barre, the road for Biarritz bends to the left and you can drive peaceably into that still glamorous resort, with the racecourse, the pine trees and beyond them the sands on one side, and more pine trees, the little Lac de Chiberta and the best known of Biarritz's golf-courses on the other – the Basque Coast is very good for golf, with four courses all quite close to one another; this is the English influence once again, creating links out of some auspicious dunes. The last beach along here before you come to the first of the rocky headlands that are so prettily characteristic of Biarritz's coastline, is called the Chambre d'Amour or Chamber of Love, after an old depression in the sand where two lovers are said to have put themselves well and truly on the map by being surprised in their amours by the Atlantic tide.

Entering Biarritz by the coast road like this, you end by driving along the Avenue Édouard VII, which leads down into the centre of the town and sets the tone for a resort that was for a while Europe's princeliest. Fashionable Biarritz was the creation of the mid-nineteenth century. Before that the village's only successful days had occurred back in the fourteenth and fifteenth centuries, when it was a centre of the Basque whaling trade. But then, as today, the Atlantic whales were over-fished and grew scarce; the last one was caught locally in Biarritz in 1686, by when this was just one more failed fishing village. The first tourists to come to it were the townspeople of Bayonne, who traditionally made their way to Biarritz to bathe, by donkey. But it was the Empress Eugénie who remade Biarritz. As a girl in Spain she had gone there with her mother and when later she became Empress of France, as the wife of Napoleon III, she made him go there too. In 1854, three years into that very pompous and sybaritic period of French history known as the Second Empire, Emperor and Empress established Biarritz as a fashionable place to go by their own well-publicized visits there. They built a house, the Villa Eugénie, which eventually grew into the present Hôtel du Palais, a vast building close to the lush sands of the Grande Plage (formerly known as the Plage des Fous, because only the reckless, if not the insane, were thought likely to risk swimming there), very monumental and with a tricolour flying above it, as if it were some government department rather than merely a hotel.

Royalty likes to go where royalty has already been, and in the second half of the last century Biarritz became the resort of monarchs from all over. Queen Victoria went there for the first, very influential time in 1889, though even before that the surprisingly large English community in Pau had begun to colonize it, to such an extent that by the 1870s not only did the Church of England have congregations in Biarritz but they were already schismatic and the Archbishop of Canterbury had to travel out on a pastoral visit to try and stifle the factionalism. And with Anglicanism had come fox-hunting and golf. In the early 1890s, in loyal imitation of the Queen, Gladstone made the first of a number of visits. The evidence of the English occupation, apart from the golf-courses, is preserved in some of the street-names. The patrician Avenue Édouard VII on one side of the town is matched on the other by the Boulevard du Prince de Galles, this Prince of Wales I take it being Edward VII in his younger days. But although Biarritz still has a statue of Queen Victoria, that of Edward VII was blown up during the Second World War, on political rather than aesthetic or moral grounds it is said.

Biarritz remains a tremendously solid, lordly town, far wealthier than anything else in this part of France. As a resort it has changed though, having passed out of the possession of the royals and their followers and into that principally of the world's surfers, who come to this coast for technical reasons, because it has by all accounts the best waves in Europe on which to perch for the ride into town. This sea change is neatly embodied in the name of one Biarritz hotel which I noticed, the Victoria-Surf, whose owners are evidently hedging their bets, looking to the democratic future but not yet prepared to give up the blue-blooded past. Surfers are said to be as exclusive in their manners as the upper classes they have replaced, talking only among themselves and inevitably spending a good deal of their time incommunicado offshore.

Biarritz spreads amply out from its heart, at the Place Clemenceau, but its attractions lie by the sea, above all around the small, domesticated promontory that juts out into the froth and swirl of the Bay of Biscay between the Grande Plage in the centre of the town and the rather humbler Plage de la Côte des Basques to the south. You can look down on this very attractively from Biarritz's nicest small square, the Place de l'Atalaya, reachable from below up paths dense with the wispy tamarisks of which the town is so fond. Below are the linked toy basins of the old fishing port, so small they are almost lost in the rocks, and a reminder that Biarritz was not always so big and so prosperous as it is now. The Atalaya itself, or watch-tower, stands on a rock as a solitary relic of the town's whaling days. From it, the look-out man would send a smoke signal up through the chimney whenever a whale was offshore, and the fishermen would then take to their horrifyingly flimsy boats. When whales were still plentiful, the king and the clergy had the right to what was, very literally, their cut; in the case of the canons of Bayonne, to the for some reason much prized tongue. The promontory itself dissolves on the seaward side into rocks and inlets, including the delightful cove of the Plage du Port-Vieux, a sheltered bathing place recommended 'for persons who are weakly or unaccustomed to the sea' as my old *Baedeker* considerately puts it. By going down to sea level, you can walk out on to the Rocher de la Vierge, reached by a short gangway, which has a statue of the Virgin on top and the beginnings of a jetty planned by the Emperor Napoleon III but never finished because the sea kept demolishing it. Facing the Rocher de la Vierge, there is a Marine Museum, with a very presentable aquarium.

It is not always easy to find the old, late nineteenth- or early twentieth-century Biarritz amongst the new. Stone has given way to glass and concrete. But small and choice corners of the town, like the Place Sainte-Eugénie (a different Eugénie this from the empress) and the nearby Place de l'Atalaya, have kept a lot of the older, more imaginative domestic architecture, with that freakishness in the way of turrets, balconies and other appendages familiar to those of us who were raised, as I was, in seaside towns in southern England. Bits of old Torquay and bits of old Biarritz are almost interchangeable, as the inhabitants probably were too, eighty or ninety years ago. But even in Biarritz the high-fantastical style is under threat, swamped by the aggressive and severe towers of the 1960s and 70s. If you choose where to sit or loiter carefully, however, avoiding the principal seafront by the casino, it is just possible to have an illusory few minutes of the old Biarritz. As a suitable last image of the town, I offer the sky-blue onion domes of the Russian Orthodox church at one end of the promenade, an exotic remnant of old, moneyed Europe cohabiting with the brutal new culture of wetsuits and fast food.

The Basqueness that is in abeyance in Biarritz returns in full as you drive south from there towards the frontier. Royalty finally peters out in Ilbarritz, a resort that is barely distinguishable from Biarritz proper, where King Alfonso XIII of Spain apparently got engaged and where Queen Nathalie of Serbia, hardly the best-remembered of Europe's lost monarchies, had a home. Between the main road and the sea are the small, cliffside resorts, first of Bidart, which has a delightful town square, very Basque, with church, pelota wall and hotels gathered affably together, and excellent beaches to walk down to; and then of Guéthary, which is smaller, lower down and less of a village than Bidart, but has the better coastline.

Past Guéthary and fifteen kilometres in all south of Biarritz is Saint-Jean-de-Luz. This is an eminently Basque town and the one I would choose to stay in of the several alternatives along this coast; it is more intimate than Bayonne, less pompous than Biarritz and livelier than Hendaye. *Luz* being the Spanish for 'light', you might think this was a place famous for its luminosity, but Saint-Jean's Luz has a grimmer origin, in the Basque word meaning 'marsh', because the estuary of the river Nivelle on which the town stands was once a swamp.

Saint-Jean-de-Luz is a working town as well as a holiday place, for centuries past and still today a very active fishing port. It has the only real harbour you can find on the Atlantic side of France south of Bordeaux, a good sheltered anchorage that is also the entrance to the river. This is a resource for fishermen and a boon for tourists, because the port is the ideal place to sit once you have made your way down to the bottom of the town. What was long ago fished for from Saint-Jean, as from Biarritz, was whales, from as early as the eleventh century and as far away as Newfoundland. It was a skipper from here called Sopite (he has his street named after him in the old town), who made one of the great technological advances in whaling, when he found a way to render the blubber down on board the whaler instead of having to sail all the way back home with it. After whaling died out, there was cod fishing and, in the eighteenth century especially, piracy, when the Atlantic corsairs of Bayonne and Saint-Jean made mighty profits for the local burghers who put up the money to fit them out. In the 1750s, seven thousand sailors from these two small towns were living from piracy, and an exceedingly well-organized affair it sounds to have been, with the Crown, as ever, coming in for its share. Nowadays, Saint-Jean deals chiefly in the large if unappetizing tuna and the extremely appetizing but, compared with the whale, somewhat trivial catch, of anchovies; but it is a town that smells very satisfactorily of brine and can be loud with the engines of trawlers if you go down to the harbour at the right moment.

It is not, architecturally speaking, such an old town as it might have been, because there is only one house still standing built before 1558, when invading Spaniards burnt the whole place down. But there is an old part to the town, running east from the harbour, and a delight it is to walk through: Basque urbanism at its most attractive. The bigwigs of Saint-Jean were the ship-owners and they built themselves fine, ostentatious houses. One of these, which you can go round, is known now as the Maison Louis XIV, because that remarkable king lodged there in 1660 when he came to Saint-Jean to be married to Maria Theresa, the Infanta of Spain (the bride stayed across the road in a charming pink brick and stone house known ever since as the Maison de l'Infante). The marriage, which was a political one, took some time to complete, since bride and groom passed a whole month in Saint-Jean before the ceremony; but when it happened it was very splendid, with much bestowing of jewels, especially by the wealthy minister, Cardinal Mazarin, whose niece Louis had originally been most anxious to marry but who was opportunely exiled by her uncle in the interests of the nation.

Saint-Jean-de-Luz is built along a bay which makes an unusually regular, shallow curve, from a headland to the north, where the lighthouse is, to the harbour entrance to the south, facing the small, equally bright and characteristically Basque town of Ciboure, which has some really good old houses overlooking the harbour it shares with Saint-Jean, and where the composer Ravel was born. The bay of Saint-Jean is a noble, open prospect, though it has been a dangerous place too in its time. Between the admirable houses in the so-called Quartier de la Barre, which goes down to the harbour mouth, and the sandy beach, a dike has been built up, twelve or fifteen feet high, to protect the town from the waves. There is a path along the top of it to which the houses nearest the sea are joined by individual wooden gangways. The dike is there because in 1749 a particularly intrusive tidal wave swamped and destroyed some 200 houses in this otherwise favoured quarter of the town.

The alternative focus to the harbour in Saint-Jean is the church of Saint-Jean-Baptiste, which must be the largest of all the Basque churches. When I first went into it, I knew nothing about Basque churches, so this one was a great and splendid surprise. Outside it is severe, with only a few small windows and most of those grilled. But the interior is remarkable: a single aisle with a high barrel vault of painted wooden panelling looking rather like the timbers of an inverted ship's hull. On three sides are the dark oak galleries which make Basque churches both distinctive and extremely attractive and which are, in principle, reserved for the men. In Saint-Jean-Baptiste, because it is a large church, there are three tiers of galleries along the sides and five tiers, no less, at the west end, facing the altar. The effect is of a theatre, and the topmost gallery, which it makes every sense in a church to call 'the gods', is so close to the ceiling as to make you ask how comfortable it might be up there during mass. So much dark wood, quite simply carved, gives a good, plain effect in the nave, but this is garishly offset, typically again for a Basque church, by the hugely ornate altar and its baroque reredos, which is set high up, at the top of a flight of steps. Saint-Jean-Baptiste is the culmination of the Basque style, being on a larger scale than other churches in the Basque country; it shows that what, in villages such as Sare, or Itxassou, or Ainhoa, is a warmly communal style of decoration, can also be a majestic one.

From Saint-Jean-de-Luz it is only seven miles to the Spanish frontier. Should you decide to go that way, it is imperative not to take the main road, the N10 (let alone the adjacent motorway), but to turn seawards, to the right, in Ciboure, once you have crossed the Nivelle, and drive along the Corniche Basque. The road turns to follow the cliffs at the nice little village of Socoa, whose old fort once defended the entrance to the harbour of Saint-Jean. Here the strange, tilted cliffs of the Corniche begin, layers of schist or of limestone that slide off into the water at an angle of 45 degrees and there make starkly visible ridges on the seabed. From here too, you can have huge views of the coastline, northwards beyond Bayonne to the Landes and southwards past the frontier into Spain.

At the end of the Corniche is Hendaye-Plage, which is the seaside annexe to Hendaye and a resort of some substance, full of big, neo-Basque villas, apartment blocks and tamarisks; it has a luxuriously curved, soft and seductive beach too. Between Hendaye-Plage and its parent of Hendaye, there is much waterside, because Hendaye is hidden defensively away a mile from the sea, on the wide estuary of the river Bidassoa. Hendaye is not a town to dwell on, being easily outdone for charm by its partly walled Spanish equivalent of Fuenterrabía, facing it on a slight rise across the water.

The frontier between France and Spain runs along the estuary of the Bidassoa and then for some little way along the river itself, until it turns at right-angles to the east, leaving the Bidassoa exclusively to Spain. In the middle of the river, a little upstream from Hendaye, is the Île des Faisans, sometimes known also as the Île de la Conférence, famous for belonging to neither France nor Spain but to both. It is an undistinguished spit of land, barely afloat so far as one can see, but it has in its time hosted some very high-level exchanges of civilities and even persons between the two countries. In 1469, King Louis XI of France conferred with King Henry IV of Castile here; in 1526 the captive King Francis I was exchanged for his two sons, who stood in for him as hostages with his great enemy, the Emperor Charles V; in 1659, the Peace of the Pyrenees between France and Spain was negotiated on the island; and a year later, the contract of marriage was signed which consolidated that epoch-making treaty, between Louis XIV and the Infanta (it was while helping to decorate the Spanish pavilion for the occasion that the painter Velázquez is said to have caught his death of cold). And in what might have proved a momentous extension of this diplomatic sequence, it was at Hendaye that in 1940, after the fall of France, Hitler met Franco, to try and talk him into joining in the war on the German side against the British. But Franco was tougher than expected and the interview failed; after it Hitler is supposed to have said he would rather go to the dentist than meet Franco again.

Labourd

It is hard to divide up the Basque hinterland in any manageable way in order to describe it; here, I shall stick to the three provinces recognized in it by the Basques themselves, of Labourd, Basse-

Navarre and the Soule. These are ancient divisions of the territory, recognized for centuries past as distinct *pays*, but you are unlikely to find them entered on a modern map, so I should apologize for introducing what will seem like obsolete names. However, they are names freely used by the locals and they are a great convenience, because they split the Basque country into three geographically distinct regions, from the coastal and no more than foothilly Labourd, through the higher but still not fully mountainous Basse-Navarre, to the genuinely mountainous Soule, adjacent to the High Pyrenees.

There are a number of ways by which you might start inland from the Basque Coast. I would begin myself from Saint-Jean-de-Luz, from where there are at least three pleasant roads going south into the heart of Labourd. The large, cheerful village of Ascain is an excellent first taste of this lushly rural hinterland and, although still almost at sea level, a possible place to stay, because it has good hotels set where village hotels ought to be, in the main square. It also has its *frontón* or outdoor pelota wall. This particular form of the game is not that old, having come in in the middle of the last century, when changes took place in the technology of pelota. Before that, it had been a game more like tennis, played 'direct' between the players with a clumsy woollen ball which did not bounce. Then indigenous wool gave way to exotic rubber, with the result that the ball now rebounded very happily off stone walls, and new, 'indirect' varieties of pelota were invented. The *pilotari* or players took to wearing more elaborate gloves or other prosthetic aids in propelling the ball, and what had once been a lowish wall at the end of the playing area was built higher and higher to contain the far greater velocities, while the courts themselves became longer, until some of them are said to have reached 100 metres.

The smooth, high back-wall of the local *frontón*, often painted with a pink or ruddy wash, and sometimes framing the dark blocks of stone of the lower, narrower wall it has replaced, is the most striking of all evidences of Basqueness; you know you have left the real Basque country when you realize the villages no longer have a *frontón* in the middle of them. There are also indoor pelota courts, called *trinquets*, which, to the lay eye anyway, can look like royal tennis courts, and where yet other forms of pelota are played, usually professionally (I well remember, from my youth, that the then world real tennis champion was a Basque, a celebrated player who no doubt grew up democratically playing pelota and then switched easily enough to the very exclusive game of real or royal tennis). Pelota is a confusing and various game, and before going to watch it being played it is worth reading up on the technique and the scoring, if you want to follow it. Outdoor pelota you can hear long before you can see it, because the sharp crack of the ball on the end-wall carries all through or even outside the villages. This is something to bear in mind when choosing your hotel room in a Basque village: it is picturesque assuredly to have a view of the *frontón* from your window, but it might not seem such a good idea if they start playing when you want to go to sleep.

At Ascain you could turn left, or eastwards, and take the road through Saint-Pée-sur-Nivelle and Espelette, to Cambo. This is good country, with good villages in it, giving you a full exposure to the dark green or red-brown paint, on window shutters or exposed timbers, that creates such a decorative unity among Basque houses – so much so that I recall a feeling of outrage along this road, when I passed one traditionally built house whose paintwork was the vilest turquoise. Alternatively, you could carry on south out of Ascain, down a more minor road, to the village of Sare. Between Ascain and Sare you go over the Col Saint-Ignace, a very modest affair of some 500 feet. From the Col there is, in summer, a rack railway that will lift you, if you are so minded, to the conspicuous because lonely summit of La Rhune, which is far and away the most prominent mountain at this Atlantic end of the Pyrenees, even though it is no more than 3,000 feet high. To the Basque this is something of a holy, or at least legendary mountain. Today, inevitably, like all too many high places, it has far from legendary radio and television installations on top of it. But in more robust days, you would have been more likely to come upon a coven up there, since the summit of La Rhune was one of several places in the Basque lands where witches were held to convene during the very ugly years of persecution early in the seventeenth century – then it was, according to the local inquisitors, that English and Scottish travellers arriving by sea in Bordeaux saw veritable armies of devils making their way towards south-western France. It is with La Rhune that the Pyrenees make their final turn to the west, and the views from on top are immense. It is straightforward enough to climb up there on foot, if the railway is not working; the guidebooks say to allow three hours. My own ascent on foot, following the track of the railway, dwindled, I have to admit, to a halt on a warm afternoon, and to a comfortable seat on the mountain turf. You do not have to climb too high to earn yourself splendid views over the country on the French side as well as a close-up sight of raptors perched or circling amongst the rocks.

Sare, which is three kilometres beyond the Col Saint-Ignace, is another of the traditional Basque villages, with a lovely galleried church, an imposing *frontón* in the centre, and some fine old houses. A placid and leafy place indeed, except that it has also the local nickname of *Enfer des palombes* or 'The wood-pigeons' hell', because nowhere are these migrating birds more vigorously hunted on their autumn flight south than around Sare. The *chasse à la palombe* or pigeon-shooting is a custom of the Basque country which takes you by surprise, so intense is it. In October the hills around here are alive, to the sound not of music but of shotguns. Nor is shooting the only manner of the birds' destruction, because they are also trapped, by being driven into defiles and then caught in nets stretched between the trees. Their next appearance will be on the menu of the local restaurants, probably submerged in a rich *salmi*. The hunting season for the *palombe* is short but deadly, and if you go up into the hills while it is on, the local men will be crouched there in their camouflage jackets, or lined up at stands along the roads, their shotguns aimed hungrily out over the valley. It is not a very demanding version of the chase, especially on Sundays, when you may well see rows of gunmen in position only a few easy yards from the hotel where they mean to have lunch. And the shoot is for men only, you see no women with guns. In Sare itself apparently, on Sundays in October, a special mass is said in the church at 3 a.m. for those who are going out shooting, and the celebrant is later repaid for his early rising by a gift of live *palombes*.

Sare also has caves, but dolled-up, tourist ones, and since there are stupendous caves elsewhere in the Pyrenees I shall ignore those of Sare. After Sare, if you are still collecting Basque villages, the place to make for is Ainhoa, to the east, along a particularly agreeable wooded road. Ainhoa is smaller than either Sare or Ascain, and simpler. It is basically a single very wide village street, with some sturdy and impressive old houses in it, dating from the seventeenth and eighteenth centuries. Ainhoa is just the place to study the picturesque Basque tradition of inscribing the lintel stones above their doorways with the names of those who originally built the house. This is a much more significant practice than you might at first think, because the *etche* or house is the fundamental unit of Basque society, symbolizing the continuity of the family line and of the patrimony. The Basque house is an idea as much as a building. Sometimes the lintel has a brief homily, to go with the ancestral names, on the lines maybe of '*Biciac, orhoit hilciaz*', or 'You who are alive, remember death'.

Above one doorway in Ainhoa there is an inscription longer than most which is a history lesson in miniature. It reads: 'This house known as Gorritia was bought back by Marie de Gorriti mother of the late Jean Dolhagaray with the sums sent by him from the Indies which house cannot be sold nor pledged.

Written in the year 1662.' Here there is recorded an old custom that is still not extinct in the Basque country, of emigration to the Americas, and especially South America. Young Basque men emigrated because no patrimony could by custom be divided, leaving younger sons to fend for themselves. They went in great numbers; in a period of sixty years in the last century, some 80,000 French Basques are estimated to have gone from the region, out of a total population at any one time of 112,000. The birthrate could only just keep pace. But the loyalty of those who left to their 'house' and their village was such that when they were able to they sent money home, and many eventually came back in person, to die where they were born. Those who had grown rich abroad got the generic name of 'Indianoaks', on the assumption that they had gone to seek their fortune in the 'Indies'. One such Basque emigrant, who became a consul in Ecuador, even left his native village in his will one of the smaller Galapagos Islands, as an attractive if rather academic addition to its territory.

From Ainhoa the only road that will keep you on the French side of the Pyrenees runs more or less north-east, back towards Espelette. This is one of the best Basque villages, twistier than others in its layout, and the home of the red pepper, a fiery vegetable that now has an annual festival in Espelette in the autumn. As well as the pimiento, Espelette also trades in the *pottoks* or small, tough, shaggy horses which live half wild in the Basque hills and mountains. At one time *pottoks* were sold to Britain, and put to work pulling wagons in the pits; today, they are most likely to be used, if at all, for carrying tourists on safe, low-slung pony rides.

Cambo or, more fully, Cambo-les-Bains, is one of only two real towns inland in Labourd, the other being Hasparren. Cambo is on both the river Nive and the main road from Bayonne to Saint-Jean-Pied-de-Port, and you might call it a centre. It is a small but spread-out, almost incoherent town, the pleasantest part of which stands up above the river and has a row of modest hotels. Given that it is only half an hour from the coast and has charming country to both west and east, Cambo is a place to think perhaps of staying in, even if my own instincts would lead me to prefer one of the Basque villages. It is in fact the first of the great many spas you meet with in the Pyrenees, when coming from the Atlantic coast, good, so one aged guidebook has it, for 'nervous people, the neurasthenic, the scrofulous, the lymphatic, the dyspeptic, the rheumatic, the enfeebled, the asthmatic . . . '. It remains a valetudinarian place, with baths a mile out of town to the east where plenty of people still go for treatment. The first words I ever heard spoken in Cambo were 'A coffee please, not too strong,' which seemed to sum up this mild and cautious little town.

Cambo's most illustrious resident, attracted there by its salubrity, was the playwright Edmond Rostand, a florid Marseillais who built himself an extraordinary house just outside the town to the north. This is the Villa Arnaga, open for visits from April to the end of October, and curious enough to put on your visiting-list. Rostand had grown rich on the royalties from his astonishing verse drama, *Cyrano de Bergerac*, which was first performed in 1897 and so successfully that its author was reportedly made a knight of the Légion d'Honneur on the opening night in between the fourth and fifth acts. Since then *Cyrano* is estimated to have been put on more times than any other French play and to have been General de Gaulle's favourite theatrical work. The plot is the most extravagantly and sentimentally romantic it would be possible to imagine, the story of brave, generous, broken-hearted Cyrano, who loves but can never win the girl because his nose is so grotesquely large. But with his incomparable fluency, he woos her gallantly and lavishly in rhyming couplets on behalf of another. Rostand wrote other great successes also, though nothing quite on the memorable scale of *Cyrano*. Given that its hero's fatal handicap was the size of his nose, it seemed to me most tactless that there should be a 'pneumological' institute named after him in

Cambo, when the last thing he can have suffered from was breathing problems.

The Villa Arnaga is appropriately and massively theatrical: a traditional, asymmetrical Basque villa with pitched roof and balcony but inflated to several times the orthodox size for such buildings. At the back there is a long, formal garden, stretching away past ponds and flowerbeds to an ample pergola, and on the other three sides parkland, with a great many hydrangeas. The interior of the villa one can only lamely describe as southern art nouveau; there is a great deal of panelling, made out of exotic and in some cases aromatic woods, a great deal of marble, of gilt, and of inlaid flooring. There are also some, but not too many memorabilia of Rostand's life in the theatre: playbills, photographs of actors and actresses associated with his work, autograph letters. The Villa Arnaga is an eccentric, ornate memorial to the man, a rare and engaging touch of the histrionic in this otherwise sincere part of the Basque country.

To the east of Cambo there is some very pleasantly hilly country, with plenty of woodlands but some moorland too, notably above Hasparren. Were you to want to travel truly scenically from Bayonne to Cambo, or from Cambo to Bayonne for that matter, then you would take the road very magnificently known as the Route Impériale des Cimes, or 'Imperial Route of the Peaks', which lies east of the main road and is many times more beautiful. The Route Impériale was laid out by Napoleon, the First this time, for strategic rather than aesthetic purposes, but it is a delight, a quiet, curly road along a ridge with long vistas of farms and moorland to the east, and of more farms, villages and cultivation to the west. It gets its name from what you can see in the far distance, provided the weather is right, which is the first peaks of the real Pyrenees. These are to the south, which means that it is better to travel the Route Impériale starting from Bayonne, rather than enjoying the mountains only in your rear-view mirror.

It comes out on the road that joins Cambo to the small town

of Hasparren, a Roman foundation but a nondescript place today. Beyond Hasparren is the more picturesque small village of Labastide-Clairence, which has some shabby but distinguished old house fronts, deeply arcaded, in its square. This was, as you can tell from the name, a *bastide*, or one of the new towns of the thirteenth century. There are some 300 such places in south-west France, the finest of them a little north of here, in Gascony, and they were built largely to a rectangular pattern of intersecting streets with a sometimes very generous town square in the centre. Labastide-Clairence is a minor example, founded in 1314.

A little to the north of it, I was delighted to discover, is a monastery by the name of Belloc, as if in honour of the English Catholic writer and Pyrenean devotee, Hilaire Belloc (I was gratified to find later that there is at least one other Belloc or Bellocq in the Pyrenees). One misty autumn morning I drove out to the monastery for a look, crunching along lanes covered in empty chestnut husks, which are already an indication of Benedictines ahead, since Benedictines always plant chestnut trees by their buildings. Hilaire Belloc would not I think have liked his eponymous monastery; it is modern and spruce, with sacred literature in showcases and a monk sitting at a reception desk. A spiritual Holiday Inn, it seemed to me, not at all to the taste of that irascible writer, for whom the Pyrenees were so refreshingly medieval.

From Labastide-Clairence, I would strongly advise making your way eastwards, along the beautiful little road for Saint-Palais. But not to go all the way to Saint-Palais; rather, after eight miles, turn to the right, over a crest, along a very minor road that goes down to the hamlet and caves of Isturits. These are caves you should see, for the good reason that they were lived in. And here I state my prejudice over caves: I like those that have cave art or artefacts to show, I like much less those exhibited only for their concretions, their stalagmites, stalactites and other natural forms. Isturits has both art and artefacts, and is one of the most inspiring of the Pyrenean caves. There are actually two levels of cave here, one on top of the other, the upper level being called Isturits, the lower Oxocelhaya. Isturits was the residential cave, a very large chamber continuously inhabited, the prehistorians say, for many millennia in the Upper Palaeolithic period, up until 10,000 years ago. The little museum at Isturits shows some of the great many animal bones uncovered there, of bears, reindeer, mammoth and the rest; as well as examples of the flint, horn and bone weapons and tools which the generations of cave-dwellers made. But the art is the thing. In the cave itself, bas-reliefs sculpted close together on a stalagmite cone, hard to make out for the most part, except for an obvious and memorable reindeer some three feet long; in the museum, animals graphically carved or engraved on bone, many of them heads of horses, but fish too, and pieces of bone, antler and ivory carved quite elaborately into abstract patterns of diamond shapes, chevrons or spirals. No one knows what these carved objects might have been for, so perhaps they weren't for anything, but a heartening prehistoric example of art for art's sake. The chamber of Oxocelhaya, some fifty feet below Isturits, does not seem to have been occupied for long. This is the place for lovers of stalagmites and stalactites, of which there are some noble specimens and which the guides, true to their kind, will insist on likening to some human or animal shape, as if it were wrong to allow rocks to look only like rocks. There is also a third level of caves at Isturits, below the others and with much good cave art, prehistoric hearths and other attractions in it. This was first found in the 1970s but can be entered only by expert cave-divers, able to negotiate underground waters.

Strictly speaking, the caves of Isturits are in Basse-Navarre, a mile or two on the wrong side of the invisible boundary of Labourd, and so belong in my next section. I have trespassed and will retreat back to Cambo and to the country just to the south of it. Spare a diversion here for the village of Itxassou, two miles upstream from Cambo along the Nive. It is a charming place, a village with two centres, like others in the Basque country. It also has cherry trees, which are far from common in a part of France that grows less fruit than one would hope to see. The village square has a fine pink and grey *frontón*, and promising-looking hotels. From it you can walk to Itxassou's other half, which is clustered round the church, about a kilometre away and within sight of the defile known as the Pas de Roland, an opening in the rock said to have been made by the hoofs of this luckless paladin's horse (but more of Roland in the appropriate place, when we come to Roncevaux). The church is lovely, both in itself and for its bucolic setting. The graveyard especially is a good place to examine the strange and beautiful gravestones characteristic of old Basque burial grounds. These *stèles discoïdales* are formed of a roughly engraved stone disc on top of a sturdy, tapering base and you find them either buried well into the earth so that little shows above the ground except the disc or else standing clearly up above it (see Plate 1). Only since the sixteenth century have dates been carved on these stones, but many are older than that, perhaps by as much as three or four centuries. As well as in the Pyrenees, you may see them further north in the Landes, and in Spain and Portugal, which have lots of them; given which, it is possible that they are another survival, or tradition, of the Celtiberians, like the Basque language. The decoration on the discs, which seldom have names on, is usually either a variation of the Christian monogram IHS, or else the so-called 'Basque cross', which is a little like a four-leafed clover and has sometimes been argued, in an attempt to find an origin for the Basques in the East, to derive from the old Hindu symbol of the swastika.

At Itxassou there are numbers of these simple memorial stones set in a fringe along the church wall, where they make an affecting counterweight to the overblown and ugly modern gravestones and monuments all around you. These last bear looking at for one thing only, and that is the rich, exquisite Basque family names carved on them: Iharour–Lascagne, Uharretuko, Elissalde-Olaizola. Those are names it would be a pleasure to bear and that are good to hear: a minute or two spent saying them out loud should be part of any visit to the church of Itxassou.

The Basques, who took so inordinately long to be christianized in the early Middle Ages, have been conspicuously devout Roman Catholics ever since. This made things difficult for them during the aggressively secular phase of the French Revolution, when Itxassou in particular fell foul of the regime. (In common with many other local villages, it was then renamed, as Union – which is at least happier than the new name found for the village of Ustaritz downstream, which temporarily became Marat-sur-Nive.) During the Terror, forty-seven young men of Itxassou deserted from the revolutionary army. The response to which act was terrible: all the inhabitants of this and other Basque villages nearby, including Sare, Ascain, Espelette and Ainhoa, were arrested and deported into the Landes. Several thousands went and by the autumn, six months later, when they were allowed to return to their pillaged homes, almost half had died, of disease and malnutrition. Like other frontier peoples, the French Basques have not always seen eye to eye with Paris.

Basse-Navarre

South from Cambo-les-Bains, between the villages of Louhossoa and Bidarray, the province of Labourd graduates into that of Basse-Navarre. Basse-Navarre, or Lower Navarre, was originally the French end of the kingdom of Navarre, the larger part of which lay on the far side of the Pyrenees, in Spain. As a trans-Pyrenean kingdom, Navarre lasted from its foundation in the ninth century until the sixteenth century, when it got broken in two, Spanish Navarre becoming Spanish in 1512 while French or Basse-Navarre was incorporated into the French crown in 1589, when its current king became king of France as Henri IV.

In Basse-Navarre the land starts seriously to rise; there is more sense of being in the Pyrenees here than in the merely undulating Labourd. It starts to get rockier too, as you soon realize driving along the valley road past Bidarray, which has been cut through the often quite garish sandstone. Bidarray itself is a secretive village, more or less hidden from the road in the hills to the west. It is nicely ringed on three sides by colourful high hills or else low mountains, and has a delightful old humpbacked bridge. It is a quiet and comfortable village to stop in, as I know from having stopped there, with good walks up into the hills and good fishing – for trout, which begin to come into their own around here as *the* mountain fish. Indeed, it was on the road just outside Bidarray and beside the Nive that I once came close to running a fish over, a glossy trout that seemed to be flipping its way desperately to the roadside and to safety. I wondered for a moment about this strange near-miss, and what a trout might be doing crossing the road, until I saw a fisherman standing aside, who can only have dropped his slippery catch on the roadway and was waiting to recapture it. Bidarray also has an odd local cult, or did have, for I am not sure that it is still practised, in the worship of a headless and anonymous saint in a cave nearby. This particular intercessor is in fact a vaguely humanoid stalagmite, which I suppose bears out what I was saying about our common need to find resemblances between rocks and persons.

After Bidarray there is no call that I know of to stop again before the small town of Saint-Jean-Pied-de-Port. This, I suspect, is everyone's favourite town in the top half of the Pyrenees and where many of us would always choose to stay. It is both a pretty and well-organized place in its own right and one from which you can drive profitably off in every direction, up a whole sheaf of good valleys and into some ravishing high country. Saint-Jean is not a mountain town, because it is only 500 feet above sea level, but it has the feel of a mountain town, because the hills close in tightly around it, especially to the south and to the east. It is a compact place, spreading out extramurally a bit these days into the basin to the north of the river, yet basically contained on the other three sides by its fifteenth-century walls. And the river Nive, which is a good deal slimmer and perfectly limpid up here, near to its source in the watershed, flows discreetly through the middle of the town, dividing it into two quite equal parts.

Saint-Jean's history is above all that of a pilgrim halt, a celebrated resting-place along the great medieval pilgrim route to the shrine of St James in Compostela, in the far north-west corner of Spain. A little outside Saint-Jean to the north-east, in fact, near the village of Ostabat, three of the main pilgrim routes across France met up, to advance as one towards the mountain passes, so that through Saint-Jean there went the pilgrims who had travelled from Paris, from Vézelay in Burgundy, and from Le Puy and Conques further to the south; only those who had come through Provence took a different route into Spain, over the Col du Somport. Saint-Jean-Pied-de-Port they traversed from top to bottom, coming into the town through the Porte Saint-Jacques and leaving it again some four or five hundred yards lower down, through the Porte d'Espagne. This cobbled route is still a joy to follow; the top half of it, as it curves down to the church and the river, lined with sober houses built from the local cocoa-coloured stone and dating from the sixteenth and seventeenth centuries – datable precisely in some cases from the inscribed lintel stones; then the church, seventeenth-century and disappointingly dull; the old bridge over the Nive, which is the place to look up- and downstream, at the houses built along the banks with their projecting wooden galleries; and then on towards the Porte d'Espagne, past the shops and more very decent old houses.

The part of this street above the church is known as the Rue de la Citadelle, because up to the right is the large classical citadel, built in the seventeenth century and reshaped soon after, along with the town walls, by the inescapable Vauban, whose job it was to make south-west France for ever safe from incursions from across the mountains. The citadel is not open to visitors, but the hill it stands on is a good spot to zigzag your way up to, to look out over the town, the river and its basin, and the valleys that go off from it north, south, east and west. This upper part of Saint-Jean also has sections of the old ramparts, which are quite tame as these things go and now thoroughly civilian, overlooking as they do the main street or else the minute gardens of the houses of the old quarter. This main street has almost all the town's hotels, and is filled by an admirable street market on Mondays. Although I have said I do not mean to commend particular hotels or restaurants, I am compelled to break that rule here, just once, and say that Saint-Jean does have the only restaurant anywhere in the Pyrenees to which the *Guide Michelin* invariably gives two rosettes for its food. This is the Hôtel des Pyrénées. I have eaten there; it is wonderful, and not ferociously expensive. And something else I learnt in Saint-Jean is that where there is one superior restaurant there will be other good ones, not rivals so much as supporters; this in my experience is a particularly good town to dine in.

It also has one sad literary connection with England, as the place where the excellent late-Victorian novelist George Gissing died. Gissing was an unhappy man who wrote best about emotional disappointment and urban poverty, as in his splendid novel of the lower reaches of literary London, *New Grub Street*. But he had longings at the same time for the Mediterranean and travelled there. He died in the Pyrenees, quite young, of pneumonia, attended at the last by the officious H. G. Wells, who describes his mercy mission to the bedside of his friend in his autobiography. In Wells's eyes and day, Saint-Jean was 'a lonely frontier town' in which, at night, the 'deserted streets abound in howling great dogs to whom the belated wayfarer is an occasion for the fiercest demonstrations'. A sadly suitable accompaniment for the last, delirious moments of what Wells, in a chillingly unsympathetic phrase, calls 'all that flimsy inordinate stir of grey matter that was George Gissing'.

The Port in the name of Saint-Jean-Pied-de-Port relates to the passage over the mountains to the south-west of the town, the most famous in all the Pyrenees. It is one of the 'Ports de Cize', the collective name for the several cols to be found in the mountains here and once the *Summus Pyrenaeus* of the Romans, who also chose to cross them above Saint-Jean. Today it is reached by the main road, up the valley of the Petite Nive, through Arnéguy, which is the French frontier post, to the first Spanish village of Valcarlos and then Roncesvalles or, in its more familiar French form, Roncevaux. Here is one of those places, then, where the frontier does not follow the ridge of the mountains, but takes a sudden dive down on the French side. This was the route that the Compostela pilgrims took out of Saint-Jean, not because it was the easiest but because of its heroic Christian associations – though the present road, created in the 1880s, climbs a little to the west of the paths traditionally followed before then. Here, in the summer of the year 778, the rearguard of the army of the Christian King Charlemagne, on its way back into France from Spain and from warring with the paynim hordes of Islam, was set upon and routed. This was the one resounding defeat of Charlemagne's campaigns, recorded in the ninth-century life of the king by Eginhard. It became subsequently a very celebrated and gallant defeat indeed, as the subject-matter of the great Anglo-Norman epic of the *Chanson de Roland*, composed at least 300 years after the event.

In that work it is Roland and Oliver, friends and paladins, against the Saracens, or a handful of impossibly valiant Christian knights against a whole army of miscreants. But the *Song of Roland* has it wrong; all that is epic licence. In sober fact it was not the Saracens who ambushed and humiliated Charlemagne's army in the mountain pass, but the Basques, who thus confirmed for the chronicler Eginhard their already long-standing reputation for treachery. Nor was Roland in reality quite the great man and imperial favourite he is presented as in the poem, but a fairly obscure governor of Brittany. Never mind, it is a reckless, bloodthirsty tale, with Roland ultimately being punished for his hubris in refusing until it was too late to blow his oliphant, or horn, to summon back Charlemagne and the rest of the army to help his vastly outnumbered rearguard.

The historical col of Roncevaux is an essential excursion then, especially for those like myself who as undergraduates long ago wrestled bad-temperedly with the obscure medieval French of the epic. This is the first really high pass of the Pyrenees, 3,500 feet up, and a suitably stark spot once you have risen above the trees of the valley. The *Song of Roland* does not have much local colour in it, except of a perfunctory 'high are the mountains and dark the valleys' kind, so there is no particular call to read the poem before visiting the scene, in hopes of recognizing the poet's descriptions. There are reminders of it, however, on the ground. The village of Roncevaux is a short way beyond and a little way down from the col; it consists mainly of the very military-looking monastery and attendant Gothic church created there in the twelfth and thirteenth centuries for the service of pilgrims. On the col itself, there is a small modern chapel and a memorial stone, which faces back down into Spain, Roland having heroically asked that he should be buried facing not his homeland but the enemy. There is an unusual road sign here also, which must be a puzzle for those ignorant of the Roncevaux story, reading: 'Traveller stay, and harken to the oliphant . . . '

Moving clockwise on the map from the Valcarlos road, you soon come to another road leading due west from Saint-Jean. The first little place of note you pass along here is Irouléguy, a hamlet at the foot of a prominent hill by the name of Jarra. Irouléguy is unique: it has given its name to the one wine that is still produced in the whole of the Basque country. The other vineyards were all wiped out in the *phylloxera* epidemic of the last century and never replanted; but lonely though it is on the local wine lists, Irouléguy will do nicely; I have never got much beyond the stage of dividing wines into nice and nasty when it comes to describing them, so all I shall say is that Irouléguy is nice.

A short way further on is the handsome village of Saint-Étienne-de-Baïgorry, most fetchingly set amidst the hills and so long-drawn-out as to be really two villages, with the river in between them. These two half-villages were at one time in rivalry and even now, I noticed, each has its own war memorial even if the names carved on it are the same for both. It is a prosperous-looking place, either because there is wine money here, made from the vineyards of Irouléguy, or because well-off Basques have retired to this very calm and convenient valley, to renovate the old houses or build themselves shiny new ones, reminiscent but hardly imitative of the lovely old style of Basque domestic architecture. Either way, a successful village like this has a very different look from those Basque villages which have not so far been resettled. In the centre of Saint-Étienne-de-Baïgorry, crossing the torrent of the Aldudes, is a gorgeous old humpbacked bridge (a 'donkey's back' bridge the French say), that is no longer of much use to anybody except to make you ask whether modern bridges need to be quite so drably horizontal as they invariably are.

There are two roads out of Saint-Étienne, both of them leading to the Spanish frontier and both delightful to drive along. If you don't want actually to enter Spain, then the small road which follows the course of the river, the Nive des Aldudes, is the one to choose. It passes through villages that become increasingly small and simple as you get deeper into the high hills: through Banca, in the eighteenth century a centre of the local copper-mining industry, then Aldudes itself, which has a very nice small square and a Basque-style church, and finally Urepel, reached by a turning off to the left from the road that continues into Spain. Urepel is the end of the line, since here the mountains close in and the road ends. Above Urepel is what is known as the Pays Quint, a small territory of upland pastures and woods that is another of the anomalies of the Franco-Spanish frontier. Originally it was competed for, often bloodily, by the inhabitants of the valleys on either side of the watershed. Then, in 1856, the Empress Eugénie, well suited for the work of conciliation as the Spanish wife of the French Emperor, arranged a treaty whereby the territory was recognized as Spanish but was rented out perpetually to the inhabitants on the French side; so these are French citizens who farm in Spain. The lovely valley of the Aldudes is another great centre, be warned, for the *chasse aux palombes*, which means that in season, that is in late October, it is certain to be loud with trigger-happy locals and visitors, from over in nearby Spain as well as from France, blazing passionately away towards the magnificent beech woods in which the harassed wood-pigeons are presumed to be sheltering.

The valley of the Aldudes is beautiful, but the best country of all around Saint-Jean-Pied-de-Port, I think, is that which you find to the south and south-east. Here at last you are in the real mountains, with the highest peaks going up to some 5,000 feet. And you get the reality too of mountain roads, some of which are permanently rough and excitingly narrow, with fierce gradients and many blind bends. An up-to-date Michelin or other detailed road-map (number 85 is the Michelin sheet you need) is absolutely necessary, and the smaller your car the happier you may well feel, when trying, let us say, to squeeze past an opposing motorist or an unyielding sheep or cow on a track designed obviously for one. Michelin road-maps mark genuinely arduous or dangerous stretches of road with a broken red line, and though the roadways themselves quite often turn out to be less awkward than you expect from such warnings, less awkward does not mean altogether easy.

One road out of Saint-Jean-Pied-de-Port leads along the valley of the Nive, now grown quite a trifling stream, at least in the dry season. This road I recommend. You can turn off very soon to the right, and climb up to make a wonderfully airy and spectacular circuit of the very open, grassy high ground, before hairpinning down the other side on to the Valcarlos road at Arnéguy. Or, you can carry on up the narrow and beautiful Nive valley to the village of Esterençuby. This is only five miles from Saint-Jean, but it feels like fifty – a village hideaway, with nowhere beyond it. It has three plain and decent hotels, an attractive church on the hillside, with a complicated grey slate spire and spirelets, and, out of all proportion with the rest of the village, a most luxurious, roofed-over pelota court where you can even play by floodlight.

From Esterençuby you can press onwards and upwards, towards the frontier, and then either branch right, back into the complex of mountain roads to the west that would take you eventually down again to Arnéguy, or else left, along a narrow, lonely, but not totally nerve-racking road which climbs high up on the north flank of the watershed, before relapsing into the next valley to the east. On the right here is, first, the summit of Occabé or Okabe, the biggest to date, at 5,000 feet, and known for its many Iron-Age burial sites and standing stones (see Plate 2), and then the immense, noble beech forest of Iraty, which is one of Europe's largest, covering thousands of acres on either side of the frontier. Desperately remote though it seems, this forest has in its time been much worked, beechwood having been prized for making oars for ships and sent off in great quantities to the coast. But Iraty has survived gloriously, unlike other local forests, which were exploited half to death. Deforestation, whether to clear the ground for pasture or to produce timber and fuel, was a worry in these parts of the Pyrenees as long ago as the seventeenth century, when the prescient minister Colbert sent an eminent forester from Paris to report on the local resources in wood; but it is only quite recently that felling and replanting have been properly controlled. To the visitor, as opposed perhaps to the natural historian, these mountains still appear most luxuriantly and healthily treed.

But they are pastoral at the same time, as you are constantly made aware, and nowhere more so than up here on the lofty Plateau d'Iraty, where several roads meet. Large numbers of animals – a particularly aristocratic breed of sheep, with black heads and legs, and long white coats that look to have been draped over them, like wigs, rather than grown naturally; sleek, monochrome cattle; and *pottoks* as well as full-grown horses, all seem to spend an agreeable and nutritious summer on these high pastures. They are cared for by the shepherds, who would once have come up for the summer along with the animals, and slept in their traditional, bleak little cabins; nowadays, they are for the most part motorized and can commute genteelly to the livestock from their homes below.

Something else you become very aware of all over the Basque country is the bracken. In the autumn, the sweeping tracts of it on the lower, treeless hillsides are the colour of rust, and it is then that it is scythed down, to provide bedding for the animals during the winter and, once suitably impregnated, fertilizer for the fields the following spring – in a neat ecological cycle. The beehive-shaped stacks of cut bracken, sometimes held down on top with an old tyre, thrown like a successful quoit around their axial poles, are a great feature of the valleys.

At the meeting-place of roads on the Plateau d'Iraty there are four things you can do: go unadventurously back the way you came, to Esterençuby; carry on due east over the Col Bagargui along a tolerable but not always reassuring road into Larrau and the valley of Mauléon; turn sharp left along a somewhat hazardous stretch of track rather than road towards the village of Mendive (I funked this route myself, after a short trial run, but bad roads do get mended or improved in the Pyrenees, so one year's experience may be different from the next); or turn to the right along the very scenic road into the Forêt d'Iraty itself. This last choice is desirable but it only delays things so far as getting home is concerned, since the forest road stops on the frontier some three miles away, and there you can but turn round. The boldest and the best way to take is directly to the east, because there are some splendid sights to see in the valley of Larrau and beyond. But these must wait, because they are no longer in Basse-Navarre but in the third Basque province of the Soule, to which I shall be coming in a moment.

If you are still greedy for high, pastoral places to spend the day in, there is one other exhilarating excursion you can make from Saint-Jean, to the south-east, up the valley of a stream called the Laurhibar. When you get to the small conglomeration of villages called, variously, Lecumberry, Mendive and Béhorléguy, you make half-left for the Col d'Aphanize and beyond it Ahusquy. There are two roads up to the col, the more beautiful being the *corniche* road leading out of Mendive; the other starts up from Behorléguy. (The little road going off to the left here, towards Hosta, I certainly don't advise; it scared the wits out of me one afternoon, so steep, narrow and broken was it). Near Ahusquy itself the road is not good, but uneven only and never frightening. Ahusquy is, in its minuscule way, a spa, because on the hillside above it, a healthy kilometre's walk from the road and the small hotel, is a *source* you can drink from – it is held to be good for kidney and bladder sufferers. But you can also settle happily for the sublime views that you have from this generously turfed upland. To the south and south-east are the mountains on and beyond the frontier – not the major Pyrenean peaks as yet but five- or six-thousand-footers – and many dark, completely wooded valleys; on the other side, to the north, better seen by carrying a bit further on along the road for Mauléon, there is another of the wonderful Pyrenean beech forests, the Forêt des Arbailles, which masks a notoriously craggy, deeply perforated limestone plateau. There could be no grander nor more characteristic view of the mountainscapes of these Atlantic Pyrenees than the one you see from the road or the slopes around Ahusquy. This is a drive to loiter over, a spot or series of spots to invest a fine day in.

The country to the north and north-east of Saint-Jean-Pied-de-Port is much lower and for that reason more cultivated. There are some excellent villages, like Iholdy, where the church and the *frontón* are so close together they seem to be one building, and the church has an unusual, very charming wooden gallery attached to the side wall. And a short way off the main road leading from Saint-Jean to Saint-Palais, past Ostabat, where the pilgrim routes long ago converged but which today is nothing, is the hamlet – it is hardly even that – of Harambels. This was once a reputed halt for pilgrims. A tiny dilapidated chapel remains, built in the eleventh century, with a *chrisme*, or Christian monogram inscribed in a circle, sculpted over the doorway and a miniature example of the strange, three-pronged 'bell-walls' you see so many of in this region. If you can find someone with a key to let you in, the interior of the chapel is said to be interestingly decorated, but the one time I was in Harambels I could find cows but no people. Indeed, never was I anywhere so idyllically drowsy. The Compostela pilgrimage was, according to such first-hand accounts of it as there are, a robust and pretty indecorous enterprise, but there could be no more placid memento of it than Harambels. I only hope they don't spoil things here by over-restoring the chapel.

The small town of Saint-Palais, up the road from Harambels, was once the chief town of French Navarre and it still has its moments architecturally, though it is a little characterless overall. It stands (just) on the river Bidouze, or between the Bidouze and a stream called the Joyeuse. The Bidouze marks very roughly the boundary between Basse-Navarre to the west and the third Basque province of the Soule to the east, and because Saint-Palais is, additionally, very close to where the Basque country ends and the region known as Béarn begins, it is something of a transitional town, neither one thing nor the other.

Twelve kilometres to the north-east of it is somewhere better: Sauveterre-de-Béarn, an interesting old place sat up above the Gave d'Oloron. If I were pedantic I would have to exclude it from my description of the Basque country, because Sauveterre is definitely a Béarnais and not a Basque town; but it is close to the edge of Basse-Navarre, and worth a visit, so I shall rope it in here. You can tell soon enough in Sauveterre that things have changed architecturally when you look at the church. This is powerful-looking and Romanesque, and was built mainly in the twelfth century. It has a fine, strong square tower above the crossing, with a pointed roof, slender arched windows and a row of apertures at the top clearly added for defensive reasons. Inside, to right and left of the altar, are two apsidal chapels vaulted with those delectable half-domes that in French are called, and how rightly, *culs-de-four*, or literally 'oven-ends'. Outside, the apse-end of the church is tall and decorative, while at the west end there is a good three-arched portal and a simply sculpted tympanum.

The church is built close to the edge of the bluff, which falls an overgrown eighty or ninety feet down into the wide bed of the *gave* or river; and the view up or downstream is dignified further by the curtain wall of the medieval Tour Monréal, that stands at one corner of the small square in front of the church. The tower, like other of the medieval remains of Sauveterre (all of them numbered and labelled by the tourist authorities, as if they were clues in an architectural treasure hunt), is alive with pigeons and with *palombes*, wisely sitting out the shooting season in town.

It is an easy walk down from the church of Sauveterre to the riverside, where the stump of the old fortified bridge still stands, starting hopefully out from one bank but no longer reaching to the other – a *disappointed* bridge, to borrow James Joyce's perfect description of a seaside pier. This bridge has a good legend to go with it. In the year 1170, Sancie, the widow of Count Gaston V of Béarn, was sentenced to trial by water here, having given birth to a child rather too long after her husband's death. Bound hand and foot, she was thrown into the *gave* on the orders of her brother, the King of Navarre, watched, it is claimed, by a crowd of 3,000, who will not have found it easy all to fit safely into this constricted spot. Needless to say, Sancie had no trouble surviving; she was, according to the commemorative plaque you can read by the bridge, cast 'gently' ashore from the 'furious' waters at a place 'three bowshots distant' from where she had been thrown in. Had her ordeal come a century or two later than it did, the unsinkable Sancie would have had an uplifting view during her brief immersion, for the church and the tower of Sauveterre look especially well from down below here by the river.

The Soule

And so into the last, and smallest, of the three Basque provinces, La Soule, itself divisible into two parts, of the Upper and the Lower Soule, the first hard against the barrier of the high mountains to the south, the second relatively flat and bordering on Béarn. By now you are well and truly into the region of the great valleys that run off at right-angles from the watershed, the 'Pyrenees of the *gaves*', as geographers have tended to name it, to distinguish it from the configuration of the mountains further east, where the valleys are mostly more orthodox and run crossways or parallel with the frontier. The Soule has as its axis the Gave de Mauléon, which flows pretty precisely through the middle of it, though dividing into a number of tributaries south of the province's one real town, of Mauléon. In human terms, the Soule, and especially the Upper Soule, is far emptier than either of the other Basque provinces and economically, by the look of it, quite a bit more backward. But one of the unkind truths of tourism is that backward places are more appealing because they have changed much less; the Upper Soule, in its more inaccessible parts, is just what many who come to the Pyrenees want: rawly natural.

I have already mentioned two ways by which it is possible to travel eastwards out of Saint-Jean-Pied-de-Port and into the Mauléon valley, both of them remote and somewhat tortuous:

the mountain roads through Ahusquy or over the Col Bagargui
a little further south. If you are shifting your base as opposed to
just your body, these might seem demanding routes, and there is
instead a far easier but still pleasing route over the Col
d'Osquich. For this you turn sharp right off the road from
Saint-Jean to Saint-Palais, about half-way between those two
towns. The Col d'Osquich is lucky you might think to be called
·a col, because it is no more than 1,200 feet high, but from it in
fact you can see a great distance to both north and south, over
the low hills and wide, cultivated valleys in the direction of
Orthez and Pau, or into the forests and middling mountains
towards the frontier.

Mauléon-Licharre is a historical town, but without very much
history that you can actually see. It was the chief town of the
ancient viscounty of Soule, both a seat and a strongpoint, and as
such had a stormy time during the protracted wars hereabouts
with the English occupiers and during the religious wars of the
sixteenth century between Catholics and Protestants. The
inhabitants of Mauléon remained pro-English rather longer than
most, for the good reason that they found that to be governed
from England was the nearest one could then come to being
autonomous. They fell foul, on the other hand, of Simon de
Montfort, who was sent to the south-west of France by King
Henry III in 1248 to curb the unruliness there and ended up
assaulting the Viscount of Soule in his castle in Mauléon. The
suggestion has been made before now that it was among the
Basques that this future rebel against the king of England learnt
his what were, for the time, dangerously democratic principles.
The ruins of the castle in question are still there, on a small rise
to the east of the town. It is the only castle I have been to which
has a front doorbell, which you need to pull on if you want to
see round since it is not automatically open to visitors. For the
rest, Mauléon is a manufacturing town, unusually for these
parts, being the centre of a large espadrille industry. If you have
travelled this far into the mountains without espadrilles, but

49

want some, then buy them here, where the choice is incomparable. Mauléon also has a rather wonderful Renaissance château in
the centre of the town, with a roof to remember, a good thirty
feet high and pitched at an angle of 75 degrees.

South of Mauléon at some point the Gave de Mauléon turns
into the river Saison, famous for its destructive spates. It is
worth following southwards. When you do, the first notable
sight along the road is the small church of Gotein, two miles
below Mauléon, which has a particularly good *clocher-calvaire* or
saw-toothed bell-wall with, at the foot of it, a porch which is
actually wider than the nave of the church itself and a covered
wooden staircase going up the side.

On from Gotein is the little town, or alternatively the large
village, of Tardets-Sorholus. This is an old place, indeed a
Roman place, as is known from an inscription which has been
built into a chapel on top of the highest of the surrounding hills,
and which is dedicated to a local Romano-Iberic divinity of the
name of Herauscorritsehe, which cannot have tripped too easily
from the pious tongue. Tardets has a good, arcaded square but
an air of being very run-down, as if no one now loved it.

Some five miles further south, the road beside the Saison
forks, which is the same as saying that the valley of the Saison
divides. If you have time to pursue only one of the two
alternatives, then you should take the left fork, along a tributary
of the Saison called the Uhaitxa, to the Gorges de Kakouetta and
the valley of Sainte-Engrâce, two prime sites, or sights, of the
Pyrenees. The road to them is (or was, in 1985) marked on the
Michelin map with the forbidding broken red line, but do not be
put off; here Michelin's mapmakers are exaggerating, it is not
too bad at all, narrow but perfectly secure. The Gorges de
Kakouetta are five miles or so from the turning, on the right,
and a clammily spectacular experience they are, because the
micro-climate you enter once you are truly inside them is moist
to say the least. The rock here, naturally, is limestone, and
prodigiously fissured, while the walk through the Gorges is

hard-going in places, and rough, continuing for almost a mile until the prepared path, such as it is, peters out. The defile itself continues but you, unless you are hardy and ambitious, do not. The Gorges are narrow, in places improbably so, not more than ten yards across, and deep, with the walls either side rising anything from two to eight hundred feet. And though they are close to the vertical much of the way, they are thick with a stubbornly adhesive growth of trees and bushes, as well as, on the lower reaches, with the most exuberant coating of mosses you could ever hope to see.

The end-point of the walkable, or sometimes scramble-able section of the Gorges is at a waterfall, where the water shoots out from a hole in the rock on the left and falls sixty or seventy feet into the stream. Here, if you have managed to carry your food so far, there are picnic tables. The waterfall is a part of the enormously extensive and complicated subterranean water system that has been traced now through this limestone massif and which links up with the astonishingly deep fissures or *gouffres* that the speleologists have explored in the mountains to the east. The system is lucidly and interestingly displayed on the wall of the small café where you buy tickets for the Gorges.

The Gorges of Kakouetta are not the end of the road, for a little further on down this valley is the exquisite site and church of Sainte-Engrâce. Here, rather than by the splashing, sunless cascade of the Gorges, is where to have your picnic, in a greenly Arcadian valley in the heart of the mountains. Sainte-Engrâce was until very recently a remote settlement, because the road into the valley was also the only road out; as a consequence it had a fine tradition for smuggling, since the last thing Basque smugglers ever wanted was good roads along which they might be pursued by excisemen far less agile or locally knowledgeable than themselves. In 1987, however, Sainte-Engrâce got its road out, at the far, eastern end of the valley, over what suddenly became the Col de Soudet; it was inaugurated one day and used on the next by the toiling cyclists of the Tour de France, as part of one of their horribly taxing mountain climbs. Oddly enough, a few weeks before this road was opened, a fine, informative film was shown on British television describing the lives of the Basque shepherding community of the Sainte-Engrâce valley. It was a film in a series called *Vanishing Peoples*, which was discouraging. People have vanished from high valleys in the Pyrenees like this one, and continue to do so, to live different and economically more ambitious lives in the towns. One of the ways in which French governments have tried to stem this depopulation is by building new roads, as now at Sainte-Engrâce, in a process they speak of as *désenclavement* or literally 'unwedging'. The remoteness that tourists value has long been officially recognized in the mountains as an affliction.

Sainte-Engrâce, however, was also a place of pilgrimage and its glory is its mainly twelfth-century church, one of the most moving Romanesque buildings in the Pyrenees. Sainte Engrâce the saint was in fact Portuguese, and said to have been martyred in Saragossa in the fourth century. Her remains were stolen and hidden at the foot of an oak tree in this valley, to be eventually found, in the familiar manner of such discoveries, by an inquisitively rooting ox, whose horns at once lit indicatively up. The religious community that subsequently formed here was at its apogee in the twelfth century, when the present church was begun.

It is an odd building, when you look at it from the front, because it is very asymmetrical. There is a plain and severe bell-tower to the right, which is later than the main part of the building, and a projecting, half-roofed porch to the left; the nave of the church is between the two, with its tiled roof sloping steeply down unilaterally from the tower to the porch. The effect is to make you think for a second that the church is only half there, that there must once have been a second side to it, to the right of the tower. But the imbalance grows on you, even if structurally it may not be such a good idea, since some very squat buttresses on the left-hand or north wall had to be built on during a partial restoration of the building in the last century. It is now being restored again, one can only hope not *too* thoroughly, given its overpowering simplicity. There is a badly eroded sculpted tympanum and *chrisme* above the doorway, here supported by angels, and some splendid capitals in the interior, one of them showing an elephant (at a guess) with a tongue that reaches to the ground; as well as candy-striped, cruciform piers. At the back of the church is a deep, roughly worked wooden gallery, as a last reminder of the Basque style. In the graveyard outside is a crucifix of the kind known as a 'Cross of the Outrages': it is roughly hewn out of wood, with the instruments of the Passion fixed to it, a ladder, nails, pliers, hammer, a crown of thorns, all in iron.

Having walked the Gorges of Kakouetta and then rested up in the benign landscape of Sainte-Engrâce, you may feel you have the legs back to inspect another of the spectacular limestone phenomena of the Upper Soule. These are the Crevasses of Holçarté. To get to them you need to go back to the fork in the road from Tardets where before you turned left, and this time take the right fork, for the village of Larrau and the Col d'Erroymendi (yet another road into Spain, though one that is open generally for no more than five months in the year – these are snowy parts). The Crevasses are a little before you come to Larrau, on the left; and you have to park the car and walk to them. It is a reasonably steep walk up between the trees and the outcrops and takes about forty-five minutes. Your reward, which you may decide to turn down when eventually it is offered to you, is to stand on the vertiginous suspension bridge which was strung between the two sides of the gorge here in 1920. The drop is dramatic: a straight five hundred feet into the torrent below, and as the bridge sways under your weight it feels like several thousand feet more than that. I made this ascent on a lowering afternoon that turned thundery, and I stood only momentarily I will admit on the bridge, as the storms brewed noisily up in the mountains all around and the lightning began.

It was a lonely and Wagnerian moment, made no better by my noticing that a few of the wooden planks I was standing on had been replaced. Why? I couldn't help but ask myself; and made for terra firma.

Béarn

Béarn comes between the Basque country to the west and the part of the central Pyrenees known as Bigorre to the east. Like the other Pyrenean divisions, Béarn is medieval; this was once the largest of the furiously independent mountain states, a viscounty which came into existence as early as 820, was at different moments of its history the vassal of Aragon and England, became joined by marriage with the powerful viscounty of Foix and with Basse-Navarre, and finally, when Henri IV, *'le grand Béarnais'*, became king of the whole of France in 1589, was integrated with the Crown. As a tourist region, Béarn is made up of two of the classic Pyrenean valleys, of the Aspe and of the Ossau, plus, to the north, the city of Pau.

The Aspe Valley

I shall come into Béarn from the Soule by way of Tardets and through a small, thoroughly bucolic bit of country known as the Barétous. This lies between Tardets and the main road running due north and south down the Aspe valley, below its head-town of Oloron-Sainte-Marie. The maize or Indian corn is what you may well be most conscious of here, a crop introduced into the western Pyrenees in the 1600s and long a staple there, occupying now nearly half the cultivated space. When it is green, and growing, maize improves the landscape; but when, in autumn, it is tall and dried out, it is no longer so inviting, looking the more like so many thickets of brown paper. A harvest which removes the cobs but leaves the dead plants standing is not like a harvest at all.

The old capital of the Barétous was Aramits, which is eight miles due east of Tardets, and which once had an abbey but today has nothing very much. Except for a name that ought to look familiar to readers of Alexandre Dumas, because as Aramis it is that of one of the Three Musketeers. It was from round here indeed that Dumas got many of his names: Tréville, the captain of musketeers, seems to be a version of Trois-Villes, a hamlet outside Tardets, while Porthos, a second musketeer, was named after Porthau, once a prominent family in Lanne, a village between Tardets and Aramits. As for Athos, the third musketeer, there is a very small place of that name just outside Sauveterre-de-Béarn, on the river.

At the head of the Aspe valley is the town of Oloron or, in full, Oloron-Sainte-Marie. This is an attractive and historic place, and very much a river town, having formed around the point where two dynamic Pyrenean torrents, the Gave d'Aspe from high up on the Coi du Somport, and the Gave d'Ossau from even higher up on the ruggedly distinctive Pic du Midi d'Ossau, flow together. But because there are only modest hills to the north of it, and nothing too high close by on the south, Oloron is an open, not a mountain town. The greater part of it lies to the south of the confluence of the two rivers, which therefore split the town into three distinct parts. But you don't walk far in Oloron without coming to one or other river; both flow over weirs and both are well below street or house level so that there is the sound of water and a feeling of modest elevation everywhere, as well as regular riverside prospects from the various bridges as you cross from one part of town to the other. Oloron has always been a successful market town, right from the days when it traded mainly across the mountains, with Aragon. It is a good place to shop in still. I have to report, though, that it was here my own trust in the French as the most obdurately literate of all nations was dented when I went into a bookshop and asked if they had a copy of the *Song of Roland*. The girl on duty said no, she was sure not, why didn't I try the music shop.

In Roman times, Oloron was already a place of substance, by name Iluro, but after the Romans went it was much attacked, by invading Vascons from Spain, by Arabs, and by Vikings; only in the eleventh century did it recover, under the counts of Béarn. The oldest, steepest and pleasantest quarter of Oloron is that between the rivers, the Quartier Sainte-Croix. Here, finely placed, above what is left of the old ramparts, is one of the town's two quite splendid churches, the church of Sainte-Croix. This is a rough, powerful-looking building of the fortified kind, begun in the year 1080 on the site of a vanished basilica, with a ruined porch, a tall 'rustic' tower over the northern portal and a tiled tambour above the crossing – but the outside of Sainte-Croix is too complicated for an architectural amateur to describe, a beautiful jumble of roofs, slates, tiles and corbels. The inside is unified and austere, apart from an egregious baroque reredos, with a barrel vault, tremendous piers, and some excellent floral or narrative capitals. The curiosity of Sainte-Croix, however, is a small dome over the crossing (inside the tambour that is), the ribs of whose vaulting are interwoven to make an eight-pointed star pattern; this unusual work was done by Spanish stonemasons in the thirteenth century, on the model of the Great Mosque at Córdoba. As well as this lovely, uncompromising Romanesque church, the Quartier Sainte-Croix has some good old houses and is easily the pleasantest part of Oloron to walk in.

Oloron's other remarkable monument is the church of Sainte-Marie, in the quarter of that name, on the other bank of the Gave d'Aspe. This was once Oloron's cathedral, in the centuries up until 1790, when the French Revolution did away once and for all with the bishopric. The outside is the thing at

Sainte-Marie. It is gentler in appearance, and more finished than Sainte-Croix, but still military-looking, with three square, almost aperture-less towers, two at the east end and one, the largest and finest, at the west. This last would look altogether like a castle keep but for the fantasy of its roof, which has a large slate cone perched, candle-snuffer fashion, on top of an already pointed lower roof. At the bottom of this tower is the porch of Sainte-Marie, and in the porch the magnificent sculpted portal for which Oloron is chiefly visitable. It was created early in the twelfth century and in local marble, with the consequence that, far from being eroded, it has become smooth and polished, making a strong contrast with the worn stonework in which it is set. The portal was commissioned by Gaston IV, the then Count of Béarn, when he came back from the First Crusade. On his return from the east, he found Arabs in the local Pyrenees also, Saracen raids from Spain having been a regular affliction here since the eighth century. Gaston, however, disposed of the latest invaders and then commemorated his double success over the heathens by incorporating into his portal the figures of two Saracens in chains and oriental costume, to be seen still hunched submissively at the foot of the central pillar of the doorway as if having to bear all its weight. The Count himself appears on horseback on the right-hand side of the portal, above a capital, while counterbalancing him on the left is a monster devouring a man (only the bottom half of him remains to go down). In the tympanum is sculpted a fine Descent from the Cross with, below it, contrasting symbolic scenes of the Church persecuted and the Church triumphant. The figures decorating the deep-set arch above the doors are a joy. There is an outer half-circle of the twenty-four old men from the Book of the Revelation, holding long-necked jars of perfume or playing on early musical instruments: this is Heaven. Then there is an inner half-circle of local people going about their medieval business, catching and smoking the salmon of which the Gave d'Oloron was once notably full, hunting wild boar, making cheese, and so on, a different activity for each of the twelve months of the year. This is Earth, a place clearly of more varied and more mundane occupations than Heaven. An oddity of this glorious portal is that the eyes, of both men and monsters, are picked out in white with black dots for the iris. The effect is a little intimidating.

The inside of the church of Sainte-Marie is oppressively ornate, and it is hard to imagine anyone who responds to the simple exterior of the building responding to the interior as well. Pillars, walls, ceiling, all have been painted, and there are even paintings hung on the upper walls of the nave above the arches, which are a mixture of round and pointed. The Renaissance pulpit and the extremely grand organ above the west door have much to be said for them, but the overall effect of the interior is to drive you straight outside again to the restorative severity of tower, porch and portal.

There are some fine trips to be made out of Oloron, in all directions; and to start with, naturally, to the south, towards the mountains, along the valley of the Aspe. This is an ancient road, the middle one of the three Roman roads which went over the Pyrenees, though it is worth pursuing all the way to the frontier, in my view, only if you want to enter Spain (the small, walled town of Jaca, half an hour or so's drive down the other side, is extremely attractive). At one time you could have travelled up the Aspe valley by railway, and entered Spain through a tunnel five miles long under the final ridge. The track remains in position but rusty with disuse, the car having put the train almost completely out of business in the Pyrenees. This was the railway which the churlish Beachcomber, back in the 1930s, prayed might never be finished, because its only use would be 'in order that a herd of bored fools may get more quickly from one cosmopolitan cesspit to the other'. Well, now our preferred conveyance between cosmopolitan cesspits is the car, something Beachcomber reckoned to be only for 'milksops'.

There are some places to know about between Oloron and the Col du Somport, at the valley's southern end. First, after about twelve miles and just after you have driven through the limestone defile of Escot, there is Sarrance, a colourless, silent village these days but an old place of pilgrimage and of literary inspiration. Its most celebrated visitor was Marguerite de Navarre, the grandmother of the future Henri IV and a royal author. In Sarrance she is said to have written a part of her celebrated *Heptameron*, which is the French equivalent, even if frankly not the equal, of Boccaccio's *Decameron*, a collection of seventy-two intermittently salacious stories. And Sarrance is the setting in which her group of competing story-tellers gather, after they have been driven out of the spa of Cauterets, up in the mountains, by bad weather. This neglected village has not done much to draw attention to its grand literary connections, though it has quite a prepossessing seventeenth-century church with a delightful octagonal tower and a two-storey cloister.

Next, on past the villages of Bedous and of Accous, the old 'capital' of the valley, until you come to the occasion for a most desirable short digression. Go up at all costs to Lescun, three steep miles from the main road in the mountains to the right, at a height of 3,000 feet. The village as such is ordinary perhaps but its setting is sublime, in one of the most pastoral of the cirques or rings of mountains of which there are some dramatic examples in the high Pyrenees (see Plate 4). This one is gentle enough, because Lescun's valley is so green. There is a point just outside the village to the east (i.e. the direction you have come up from), from where everyone tells you the views are best. And so they are: a valley view looking across and up at a great arc of high peaks. These are still not the very highest of the Pyrenees but sufficiently massive and compacted to make a truly mountainous backdrop. The most prominent, due west of the village of Lescun as you look up the valley, is the more or less pyramidal Pic d'Anie, of 8,200 feet, the first or most westerly of the major Pyrenean summits; it is claimed by the Basques as their one high

Pyrenee, the home of wild goats and the legendary source of storms. Eastwards from the Pic d'Anie runs the half-circle of other peaks almost as high, towards the valley of the Aspe on your left. Lescun is a valley to drive up into for your picnic lunch; in winter it is shut in, and a centre for long-distance skiing; in spring, exquisitely vernal; in summer or early autumn drowsy and majestic, waiting for its famously late, September harvest.

After Lescun, the valley of the Aspe grows increasingly tight and stony, a forbidding landscape well epitomized by the man-made fortress of Le Portalet, built high up in the cliffs on the left just before you come to the final French village of Urdos. This unpleasant structure merges well with the rockscape around it and was used, during the Second World War, as a prison. To keep prisoners so near to a frontier on the far side of which they would be free, could seem a casual or risky policy, but it is hard to imagine anyone actually escaping from Le Portalet, whose grated windows you can see from the road, with a nasty drop of a good 100 feet straight on to the rocks beneath them. Rather than inciting its detainees to try and get out, Le Portalet probably taunted them with the impossibility of such a thing.

If you want a view altogether grimmer and more inhuman than the one you have just relished in the easeful valley of Lescun, then drive on up to the top of the Col du Somport. This is a high pass, above 6,000 feet, but a busy one, which is kept open by snow-ploughs all through the winter. It is a bare and also remarkably red place, much of the rock on the col being argilite and the colour almost of fresh salmon. Officially, Spain starts just over the top, but this is a Spanish landscape, dry and rough compared with most of what you see on the wetter, French side of the mountains. Even in summer there may be smudges of by now off-white snow or ice to be seen on the slopes round about. The Spaniards have managed to build a supreme ugly restaurant-cum-souvenir-shop on their side of the frontier, in a style of architecture suggesting its easy conversion, should border warfare ever one day replace tourism, into a defence post.

The Col du Somport and the upper valley of the Aspe are at the western end of the Pyrenean National Park – to be exact, a narrow tongue of this extends across on the other, western side of the valley into the ring of mountains forming the Cirque of Lescun. The Park was created in 1967 and runs along the watershed in a strip never more than twelve kilometres wide, from the Aspe valley to the massif of Néouvielle more than 100 kilometres to the east. It is a nature reserve, with not a single permanent human inhabitant. Red and white signs, showing an izard's head, are the only indication that you are entering it, the izard being a sort of chamois native to the Pyrenees which is now doing well there again after having earlier been hunted almost out of existence – its survival has been put down to the First World War, when men turned to killing one another and the animals had an armistice which enabled them to breed again. Everything in the National Park is protected: conservation here is absolute, you are not allowed even to pick any of the 400 species of wild flowers that grow in the Pyrenees. And if you are ever going to see one of the genuine though attested rarities among the local fauna, a bear, a lynx, or an eagle, the Park is the only place you might do so, though there are thought to be fewer than twenty bears still living in the Pyrenees, and only eight pairs of eagles. More common are vultures, especially in summer when they fly up from Spain to taste the carrion on the high pastures, and marmots, of which there are now more than 200 colonies after they were reintroduced here in 1948. And a final word about the National Park: it has its 'Maisons du Parc' in some of the small towns on the fringes of the Park, which are excellent places to go for information about walks, wildlife and flowers.

And now, a splendid piece of country to the west of the Aspe valley which I have been leaving out: the valleys, forests and mountains south of the village of Arette. Arette is a particularly neat, new-looking village, for the sufficient reason that it needed to be much rebuilt after an earthquake there in the summer of 1967. These days it has also a dependency in the mountains beyond, a winter-sports and high-summer annexe, called Arette-Pierre-Saint-Martin, at 5,500 feet. The road that has been made to carry visitors up to it is wide and smooth, the valley of the Arette that you start by following is beautiful, and the scene once you reach the top is by turns surprising, interesting and panoramic. Once the climb begins, the road winds steadily higher through the splendid beech trees of the Forêt d'Issaux, forever pointing you in a new direction and forever seeming to have no ultimate outlet upwards. Near the top the trees die out and the landscape which replaces them is a shock, for here the rock enters into full possession, turbulent acres of it, broken and jagged. These are the limestone *arres*, and as unwelcoming a site as you could think of for a new resort.

But turn a corner and there the resort is, one of a number which have been built in the Pyrenees since the start of the 1960s at greater altitudes than the old, so as to lengthen what would otherwise be a brief and uneconomic skiing season. When I saw it, in 1985, Arette-Pierre-Saint-Martin was far from finished and still, in part, a building site high in the mountains, which is an even stranger spectacle to come across. One does not expect, nor I trust want, to find shiny wooden chalets, let alone tall concrete apartment blocks standing arbitrarily up in this fascinating landscape, and phrases about 'cosmopolitan cesspits' can easily come to mind as you stand looking at them. On the day I came up here, there were no workmen and the deserted new village was occupied only by horses, wandering at liberty between the half-finished buildings, the machinery and the piles of materials – hardly the setting for which they had been intended when set loose for the summer to forage for themselves. The hostile rockscape in the midst and partly on top of which Arette-Pierre-Saint-Martin has been built also made me wonder whether skiers ever think about what might be underneath the snow they are skiing on. Looking back, I fancy that when I went skiing I always hoped that the snow was covering some kindly grass, certainly not something as hard and painful as the *arres* of Pierre-Saint-Martin.

The resort village is not the end of the road; indeed, it is possible to ignore it as you drive on up to the Col de la Pierre-Saint-Martin beyond. This is a high pass, and closed for seven months in the year. It is one of those informal and cheerful places to change from one country to another, unlike the lower, busier frontier posts, with bureaucrats who will more likely wave to you rather than ask to see your passport. Just across on the Spanish side of the col is the opening of the fearsome *gouffre* in the limestone that has given the name Pierre-Saint-Martin a certain resonance. This is a prodigiously deep fissure or cave system in the massif which has still not been fully explored but which by 1979 had been traced by speleologists to a depth of 4,400 feet. Its entrance was discovered in 1950 and two years later this deepest of all *gouffres* acquired a sad celebrity with the death there of Marcel Loubens, a Belgian speleologist, who was badly injured deep underground but could not be got to the surface quickly enough to save his life, a story I dimly remember reading at the time in newspapers. In the following year's explorations, the cavers came into a chamber of staggering size, 250 yards long, 200 yards wide and 500 feet high. The full extent of this system is yet to be established, but the *gouffre* Pierre-Saint-Martin is only a few miles as the Pyrenean crow flies from the Gorges de Kakouetta and forms part of the one vast hydrological network. The entrance to it is now covered over, and beside it there is a memorial inscription to Loubens and to another speleologist who has been killed there since. Higher up the col, almost indeed on the very top, there is the mouth to another *gouffre*, with a frail wooden fence around it, into which you can with difficulty peer. This one has been sounded to a depth of a mere 1,000 feet, but peer into it is as far as I would ever want to go; such crevices are no doubt thrilling to explore when they widen out into great chambers, but the thought of the narrow places I for one find exceedingly off-putting.

At the roadside on top of this col there is a boundary stone, the original Pierre-Saint-Martin itself, where a small ceremony takes place every 13 July. You will be told that it has taken place every 13 July since 1375, and perhaps it has. On that day a delegation of mayors from the Barétous, on the French side, comes up and hands over three white heifers to their counterparts from the Roncal, the valley on the Spanish side; in return they get money. This is now a symbolic exchange, but it is a relic of the numerous treaties that once were made in the Pyrenean valleys to regulate the use of the high, communal pastures and put an end to the age-old practice of trespass or holding to ransom of intrusive livestock. These treaties were often impressively strict and cunning: in some cases, for example, shepherds bound by them were obliged to walk ahead of their flocks in the mornings, so that they were unable to drive the animals to where they knew the best grass to be. On the way home to their folds, in the evening, they could of course walk which ever end they liked.

Coming down from the Col de la Pierre-Saint-Martin there is no need to drive back the way you came, through Arette, because five miles from the top you can fork off to the right and come down in sylvan splendour through the very heart of the Forêt d'Issaux, before either turning sharp left down the valley of the Lourdios and a not very good road to Issor, or carrying straight on to follow one of two better, more or less interchangeable roads back into the valley of the Aspe near Bedous.

The Ossau Valley

You can get painlessly if unimaginatively from the valley of the Aspe into the next great valley, of the Gave d'Ossau, by making straight from Oloron to Arudy and there turning south. But Arudy has little to be said for it; it is a small, mildly industrial town, best known for marking the spot where the glacier that once ground its way down the Ossau valley built a wall of debris, so causing the present-day Gave to make an abrupt swerve to westward.

Better, then, to start off down the wrong valley and take the road along the Gave d'Aspe as far as Escot; you can do this avoiding the main road, because there is a minor road out of Oloron going all the way along the eastern side of the valley as far as Escot. Here you turn left and drive up the scenically splendid road to the Col de Marie-Blanque. For more than half the road up you climb between more beech forests – the beech flourishes in these parts because it likes the moisture – and in spring or autumn you get that seasonal effect, whereby the trees that are only starting to turn brown at the foot of the pass are already losing many of their leaves at the top, or alternatively are still half-wintry at the top when already fully greened lower down. Once over the col, the beeches give way to pine trees and on the Plateau de Bénou the view opens up hugely to the south, to the Pic de Sesques and beyond that to the remarkable double hump of the Pic du Midi d'Ossau, the highest of the Pyrenees so far, and one of those forceful contours you soon learn to pick out and name, however slow you may be, as I am, at the confident identification of peaks.

From the pastoral comforts of the Plateau de Bénou, the road twists abruptly down past the villages of Bilhères and of Bielle, another valley 'capital' this, with some fine fifteenth- and sixteenth-century house fronts, but particularly commendable as a slated roofscape seen from higher up the road – this is Béarn, and grey slates are what you expect on roofs, no longer Basque tiles. Bielle is where you join the main valley road, and four miles to the south of it is Laruns, a neat and pleasing little town with a real town square which I have more than once thought might be good to stay in.

At Laruns the valley divides or, if that description is demeaning to the Gave d'Ossau, another, smaller valley joins it from the east. The main valley, and the main road with it, goes straight on, up to the Col du Pourtalet, which is actually a higher pass into Spain than its near-neighbour, the Col du Somport, though one that is closed throughout the winter and well into the spring. Hereabouts you are entering the true spa-region of the Pyrenees, the sulphurous haunts of the 'curists' who for a long time were the principal visitors to these mountains. On this road, for instance, you quickly come, after you have left Laruns, to Eaux-Chaudes, one of a pair of local resorts, which Beachcomber refers to grumpily as a 'hell-hole'. This is a little hard: Eaux-Chaudes is a gloomy place, but not hellish that I know of. Though the thermal establishment itself is quite stately, in the normal style of these amenities, the village is tightly shut in by the mountains on either side and is not much more than a ribbon of dark houses strung out along the main road. It must want for sunlight. On the other hand, like all French spas, it advertises the wonderful things it can do for your health progressively as you approach, by way of graduated signs fifty yards apart, each of which singles out an affliction or an organ that you might have treated here. In Eaux-Chaudes, as I recall, the list begins with Asthma and progresses through Bronchitis and Rheumatism to Arthritis, before, in a sudden switch of strategies, continuing with Nose, Throat and Ears. Upon which, the prognosis over, you are in the spa village.

And promptly in this case out of it again. South of Eaux-Chaudes the valley opens out somewhat and becomes more invigorating as it rises. A little way past the village of Gabas you can turn to the right off the frontier road and drive up to the lake of Bious-Artigues; the signs at the bottom may say that this is a narrow, dangerous road, but it isn't. The lake is on the edge of the National Park and, like many of the accessible Pyrenean lakes, part of the vast hydroelectric network of the region, which may mean that by late summer, if it has been dry down below, the waters have been piped off and the lake has shrunk. There is a very basic hostel here, for serious, long-range walkers, and in summer you can hire horses or ponies to ride about on the surrounding, pine-covered hillsides. You can also walk round the lake, or, more ambitiously, follow for a stretch up to the even higher Lacs d'Ayous, the red and white marked stones of the GR10, the magnificent high path that leads from one end of the Pyrenees to the other and which you keep meeting up with at these altitudes. Hard by to the south of the lower lake is the huge upstanding molar of the Pic du Midi d'Ossau, grimly handsome with, on its eastern slopes, what is by all accounts one of the Pyrenees' largest populations of izard. This is a mountain that can be climbed, but not casually.

Less than a mile from the turning for the Lac de Bious-Artigues, but on the other side of the road, is a lazier way of gaining real altitude and tremendous views, by taking the cable-car (it goes regularly only in summer and during the skiing season) up to the Pic de la Sagette, at almost 7,000 feet. On this robust eminence you can walk, climb about on the slopes or the scree, or look in amazement across at the Pic du Midi d'Ossau and down into the pale green waters of the Lac de Fabrèges in its harsh, glaciated valley directly below. You can also take the train: a mini-train, billed as Europe's highest small railway (it could just as well be smallest high railway), which coils for no less than ten very lofty, lonely kilometres around the spurs of rock to a distant terminus from which you can walk to the Lac d'Artouste, nearly 200 acres of it, in a stonily unforgiving ring of granite mountains. This is one of the Pyrenees' most Spartan panoramas, and a torrid place to be, as I know from having been there, on a day of high summer sun.

From Laruns you might also travel east, up the smaller valley of the river Valentin, which is enormously lush because it gets unusual amounts of rain. Up here is the companion spa to Eaux-Chaudes, called Eaux-Bonnes, or Good Waters as against Hot. It is a more bracing place to be than its rival, but much faded none the less from its days of greatest success in the last century, when it formed one end of the Route Thermale, a new road system, decreed by the Emperor Napoleon III, which was to link Eaux-Bonnes with Bagnères-de-Bigorre to the north-east. Eaux-Bonnes is mainly built around an oval public garden with bandstand, and of solid, four or five-storey Second Empire buildings that make a strange contrast with the thickly wooded hillsides behind them. The contrast between nature and architecture here was too much indeed for the ungenerous Hippolyte Taine, who came here on his *Journey to the Pyrenees* in the middle of the last century and wrote that 'One finds it grotesque that a bit of hot water should have brought cuisine and civilization into these declivities.' The names of Eaux-Bonnes's hotels still have the old pompous ring to them, the Hôtel d'Orient et d'Espagne, the Hôtel Richelieu, the Hôtel des Princes (the 'dearest' in a 'very wealthy little modern town' in Hilaire Belloc's day, but up for sale and miserably vandalized the last time I saw it, in the mid-1980s), but their clients are not what they once were. The curists still come, it seems, to drink, gargle or bathe in the baths at the top of the town, but since the end of the last war the *cure* has been democratized; in an age of health insurance many can afford it who before could not, and contemporary spa-goers both demand less and live less expensively than their more frivolous predecessors. Spa towns, though, are all the better for looking somewhat passé and Eaux-Bonnes is more passé than most.

Above Eaux-Bonnes is the ski resort of Gourette, which has been created in the kind of setting ski resorts ought to have, in pasture-land but at the foot of the formidable mass of the Pic de Ger to the south. From Gourette you can continue to climb, bending now sharply to the left on the way up to the Col d'Aubisque, though pausing above Gourette at a viewpoint called the Crêtes Blanches, where there is a hotel and, more to the point, a wonderful view back down over the ski village in its cirque as well as westwards to the peaks on the far side of the

Ossau valley. This beautiful high road, which passes over two superb cols before eventually going down into Arrens and the Val d'Azun, is one of the most exalting in the Pyrenees. It would be a crime not to take it when you want to go eastwards out of the Ossau valley. But that movement to the east also takes you out of Béarn and into Bigorre, so any further description of it had better wait.

Pau

Before going into Pau, there is a brief visit decidedly worth making to the north-west of Oloron. Leaving the town by the road that runs along the left bank of the Gave, you come after seven or eight miles on the left to the D25, marked for Mauléon. Three easy, rural miles down here to the west is the little church of L'Hôpital-Saint-Blaise, which is an exquisite oddity. This tiny hamlet, which has less than 100 inhabitants, was once a stopping-off point on the pilgrim route and the church, though restored from a state of picturesque dilapidation early in this century, is still rough-and-ready twelfth-century, squat in shape and only about twenty yards long from doorway to apse. The first peculiarity is over the crossing, which has a stumpy octagonal tower and pointed roof with, on the inside, a dome built in a style similar to that of Sainte-Croix in Oloron, that is, with the ribs of the vault forming an eight-pointed star (without artificial lighting you can see almost nothing of this decoration, and the artificial lighting comes expensive at L'Hôpital-Saint-Blaise; you need ten-franc coins to work it). The church has other features too that come from the Moorish Spain of the Middle Ages: above all, the queer openwork stone screens that are set into the window embrasures, hewn crudely but winningly into geometric patterns. It is also the centre of a men-only pilgrimage in February, when local farmers bring in handfuls of hair cut from the tails of their animals and burn them before the sanctuary as an offering to St Blaise, as the patron saint of stock-breeders. And as if that were not enough, the church bell is also, by ancient repute, therapeutic: place inside it if you can whatever part of your body is troubling you, get the bellringer to go about his business and you will, with luck, be cured. Be that as it may, this ancient building is a delight both inside and out, set about by old, galleried village houses (and by a small hotel bang opposite the portal), with lizards flickering over its walls and flowering plants clinging airily to the bell-tower.

And if you are already at L'Hôpital-Saint-Blaise, you could take in Navarrenx too, five miles down river. This is a small town of some character, a historic strongpoint standing up above the Gave, in which there are competitions in summer to catch the surviving salmon, no longer so abundant here as in the good medieval days. Navarrenx was refortified on Italian lines in the sixteenth century, so that its defences might be proof against the new artillery, and the ramparts and towers designed then are still largely and imposingly intact. In 1828, a plaque tells you, they were visited by the romantic Abbé Liszt, in the company of one Caroline de Saint-Cricq, who would hardly have expected to be thus immortalized for performing so brief a duet with the pianist-composer.

But now to Pau. Coming to it from below like this, from the direction of Oloron or from Laruns, it is a sound idea to leave the main road to the left and inspect the modest countryside in which the estimable wines of Jurançon are made. The turning is a little after the village of Gan, where there is a tastery and a large *cave co-opérative* where you can buy your Jurançon on trust, without troubling to check on the nearby vineyards. It is excellent wine, in either its white or its red versions, and said to travel well. The road to follow up into the low hills is marked with the sign 'Coteaux de Jurançon', though it is also quite easy to lose once you are up there; but when vineyards are so thin on the ground as it were in this part of the country, there is every reason to get briefly lost amongst them.

Together with Perpignan at the Mediterranean end, Pau is one of only two large towns in the Pyrenees: a departmental capital and a university town. It is also a historic town, after 1460 the capital of the viscounty of Béarn in succession to Lescar, Morlaas and Orthez. But its modern standing owes a surprising amount to the British, who gave Pau a great lift in the nineteenth century. The British connection dated back to the time when Jacobite refugees settled here in the eighteenth century, but it was after Wellington's victories in the region early in the 1800s that it became serious. In 1814 indeed, after his triumph over Marshal Soult at Orthez, Wellington himself was made much of by the local Royalists, who greeted him as their 'liberator' and gave a great ball in his honour. And retired soldiers from his army were among the first of the century's numerous British settlers in Pau.

These northern immigrants soon set about reinventing the climate here, which is on the damp side, and investing it with therapeutic properties it hardly possesses. Wealthy consumptives made their way down to Pau, in search of cure, a fashion set by the Earl of Selkirk, who wintered there in 1819–20. The fact that he died in the following April does not seem to have put anyone off or taken away their faith in Pau's salutoriness. Later, the vogue for the now growing town was consolidated and much expanded by Dr Alexander Taylor, who recuperated there from the typhus he had caught serving with the sottish, mutinous and incompetent 'Spanish Legion' sent from England to help the Queen of Spain in her war against the Carlists of Navarre.

Dr Taylor plugged Pau's 'curative influence' for all he was worth, and the Victorian visitors flocked there, many to become residents. With them eventually came dashing British sports, like steeplechasing, cricket, golf and fox-hunting, the last of which had runs in the nearby countryside called 'Old England', 'Leicestershire' and, best of all, as a concession to the French, 'Haut Leicestershire'. Not that Taylor had things all his own way. One must not overlook the 'crisis of 1858', when scurrilous anonymous letters appeared in the London *Times* complaining about the sewage in Pau, and the high price of lodgings, while a few years later another medical man, Dr Madden, publicly attacked the climate as pernicious for pulmonary cases. But Pau survived, and in the late 1860s was at its most popular with British and, by this time, some American winterers, with up to 1,500 of them registered yearly as staying or living there. That Anglo-Saxon connection slowly dwindled, undermined more than anything by the rise of Biarritz and the widening belief in the seaside as the better source of good health. Yet right up until the Second World War, I suspect, Pau was looked on by a certain kind of English middle-class family as a safe and congenial southern town to which one might retire, or where, if need arose, the socially disgraced might comfortably hide. Readers of Dornford Yates will not have forgotten that somewhere outside Pau was *The House that Berry Built*.

The incomparable asset of Pau is the Boulevard des Pyrénées, which runs for more than half a mile along the southern edge of the main town, between the château at one end and the casino and the Parc Beaumont at the other. It was Napoleon – the First, not the Third – who established this tremendous promenade from which, in clear or even clearish weather, you get what is prized, and rightly so, as the finest of all long-range views of the Pyrenees. The *table d'orientation* on the parapet enumerates eighty-three individual peaks to be picked out, from one extremity to the other of a sixty-mile horizon. The main summits each have a blue plaque attached to the railings at an appropriate point, so that as you walk the pavement, head turned to the south, you can put a name to your favourite mountain. This, obviously, is the place from which to inspect the western Pyrenees for a first time or, given the summary quality of the prospect, from which to take leave of them before driving north. Remember, though, that since the valetudinarian English gave Pau up the climate has reverted to what it was, so you need to be there on a day of reasonable weather, otherwise the Boulevard will not be des Pyrénées at all, but only of the closer and less pleasing scene.

For to the question: has Pau protected the magnificent view from the Boulevard des Pyrénées, the answer has to be, no it has not. There are excrescences one could do without on this side of the town. Below the boulevard is the river, the Gave de Pau, and on its northern bank, the railway station, with its attendant installations – you can get up and down on this side by free funicular. And no doubt because that is where the railway was long ago made to go, other uglinesses too have intruded between Pau and the Pyrenees, on the far bank of the Gave. Indeed, when you want to identify a particular peak from the boulevard, you are told to line up a white mark painted on the balustrade with 'the lightning-conductor on the tram factory', which is the most prominent landmark in Pau's southerly suburb. So here, if anywhere, it pays to lift up your eyes unto the hills.

The high bourgeois architecture of the apartment blocks on the town side of the Boulevard des Pyrénées is worth turning about to see. Do not miss no. 14, a rare mix of pilastered neo-classical and twiddly art nouveau, which is just the sort of building you hope to come across in Pau. But architecturally, this is a bland, rather than a distinguished provincial town, and the residential flavour, if you want it, is best to be caught on the north and east sides, where the bourgeois villas are. The Parc Beaumont, at the eastern end of the Boulevard des Pyrénées beside the casino, is a little perfunctory, hardly worthy of the names of the French poets that have been given to the roads leading through it.

The château however, at the other, western end of the boulevard, is much better. On this spur once stood the stronghold of the viscounts of Béarn from which the town of Pau got its name: from the *palisades* by which it was protected. The château of today is a successful hybrid, with the stonework and style of one century sitting happily with those of others. To the left of the entrance, at the town end, is its most military aspect: a splendid keep, built of brick in the fourteenth century by Gaston Phoebus, a vainglorious, bad-tempered (he killed his only son in an argument) but also tasteful princeling who was an early ornament of the house of Foix-Béarn. (The two towers at the north-east and south-west corners of the château are in fact older than Gaston Phoebus's noble addition, but less noteworthy.) The lower part of the *corps de logis* on the southern or river side was built at the same time as the keep, but later raised, when a northern wing was added to it. Then, in the sixteenth century, what had been a military building was converted by the Albret dynasty, who were now the rulers here, into a sophisticated civilian one, suitable as a home for courtly pursuits – there are some fine Renaissance doorways and windows dating from that conversion on the left and at the far end of the very irregular courtyard into which you first go. In the nineteenth century the château was altered further, with some hamfisted restoration and the addition by King Louis-Philippe and the Emperor Napoleon – the Third, not the First – of a sixth tower to go with the five earlier ones. A triple archway in white stone was also built across the entrance to the courtyard; this is no improvement to the château but it is not, to be fair, quite disastrous either.

The château of Pau was the birthplace of King Henry IV of France, who has been edging his way into my text all along. His is the great name in Béarn, as the local king who became king of all France. His statue stands in the delightful Place Royale, above the possessive caption of '*Lou Nouste Henric*', or 'Our Henry' in the local Gascon patois. Henry was the son of Antoine de Bourbon and, more important as it turned out, of Jeanne d'Albret, a very alarming woman who became, first, Queen of Navarre, and then, having abjured her Catholicism, a bloodthirstily militant Calvinist. The religious wars of the later sixteenth century, between Catholics and Protestants, did much damage to people and to places in the Pyrenean region, Pau included, and Jeanne d'Albret's army commander, Montgomery, who recaptured Pau from the troops of King Charles IX, achieved an especially nasty reputation for the reprisals and pillagings he carried out. Henry became King of France in 1589, having turned Catholic in order to do so. He called himself 'King of France and of Navarre' so as to demonstrate the continuing independence of the inhabitants of Béarn, an independence indeed which was not entirely removed until the French Revolution, though Béarn became part of the kingdom officially in 1620.

Of relics of 'Our Henry's' birth, the château of Pau keeps a single, peculiar example: the large turtle-shell supposed to have served him for a cradle, once his grandfather had christened him by rubbing his lips with a clove of garlic and a dab of Jurançon wine. No one will explain *why* he should have had a turtle-shell to lie in instead of some more orthodox cradle, but during the anti-monarchical excesses of the French Revolution this venerable carapace is said to have been saved from destruction by a naturalist of Pau, who was able to switch it for one without any such incriminatory associations from his own collection. There are regular guided tours of the state rooms of the château, whose contents and decoration were mostly arranged during the restorations of the nineteenth century and are not very remarkable, with the exception of the tapestries.

To either side of Pau are old places which were once the capital of Béarn. To the west is Lescar, which is close enough to the expanded, present-day Pau to count as its suburb. Lescar stands on a rise and below it, on the flat ground between it and the river, was the Roman town of Beneharnum (whence, fairly obviously, the modern form of the name Béarn), which is mentioned in a travel guide of the third century AD. It became Lescar only in the eleventh century, after having been devastated, like other sites in these desirable and prosperous pre-Pyrenean regions, first by the Moors and then by the Vikings.

The old citadel remains; a fortified entrance gate, a ruined keep, some fine slabs of wall. Inside the walls is the cathedral of Lescar, and this is splendid. It is basically a twelfth-century building, though sadly damaged later on by the iconoclastic Protestants of Jeanne d'Albret in the sixteenth century, and by the fanatical rationalists of the French Revolution who converted it into one of their Temples of Reason. It took much restoration, in the remarkably enlightened years in the middle of the last century when conservation took hold in France, to give the cathedral of Lescar its present air of authenticity. On the outside, the finest thing about it is the Romanesque triple apse, best seen by stepping into the graveyard (and turning your back on the unpleasant modern monuments). The decoration around the windows and along the string-course is delightful, the corbels especially having been sculpted into a strange and compelling variety of animals, monsters and more or less human figures.

There is some memorable decoration inside the church too. The capitals are not all genuine, but a fair number of those in the nave and side-aisles surely are. As so often, it is the monstrous ones that stick in the mind: two gross, splayed pairs of legs about to join the rest of the body they belong to in the maw of two amiable-looking man-eaters (reminiscent of Oloron); two horribly bent captives, their feet tied by a cord and their heads looking as if they are propped upright on sticks – strange motifs, yet motifs all the same, because they are not unique to Lescar. But the most beautiful things of all here are the mosaics in the floor of the choir. These were made almost certainly in the twelfth century, by Bishop Gui, founder of the cathedral, as a Latin inscription asserts, though there has been argument that they must be Gallo-Roman since the subject-matter is profane and improper for the patronage of a Christian bishop. Like almost everything else in Lescar, the mosaics have been restored, having at one time indeed been paved right over; but they are extremely decorative. The profane topic is the chase. There are three scenes. In one a huntsman, his hunting-horn swinging free from his neck, is sticking a stake into a wild boar, which also has a dog sinking its teeth into its neck; in another, two lions, one very heraldic and standoffish, are attacking a gazelle, helped by a bird of prey; in the third, which is decidedly curious, a mule leads a lolling-tongued, wolf-like animal captive while ahead of it a huntsman is tensing his bow to fire at some unseen target. But this huntsman, for all the energy and *élan* of his posture, is maimed: his crippled right leg is bent back at the knee and supported on some sort of crutch. This again is not unique to Lescar, because there are similarly maimed figures to be seen sculpted on churches in the French Pyrenees. The assumption is that these were wounded veterans, from the wars with the Saracens in Spain, rather than victims of hunting accidents, and that it was Arab, not Christian surgeons who were adept at fitting these early attempts at an artificial limb.

A short way out of Pau on the opposite side to Lescar, to the north-east, is Morlaas, a small town that tends to get left out of the local guidebooks as not somehow belonging to the Pyrenees. But between the middle of the ninth century and the end of the twelfth, when it was supplanted by Orthez, Morlaas was the capital of Béarn. The modern town is scarcely worth a detour but the church is distinguished for having a very fine and elaborate Romanesque portal; it has been heavily restored but it remains worth seeing.

Bigorre

The next of the old medieval divisions of the Pyrenees eastwards from Béarn is Bigorre, which had its own counts from the eleventh century, was nominally an English possession in the fourteenth, passed to the house of Foix-Béarn and was finally incorporated into France in 1607. The chief town of Bigorre is Tarbes, out on the plain to the north; but its chief beauty is the high mountain country to the south, for Bigorre contains many of the greatest peaks on the French side of the Pyrenees, as well as such geological splendours as the Cirque de Gavarnie. This is where the High or central Pyrenees truly begin.

The Gave de Pau

The key to Bigorre, geographically, is Lourdes, which stands at the head of the valley of the Gave de Pau, at a point where the river makes a sudden lunge to the west having long ago found its way north blocked by moraine. For this valley was scoured out by the most potent of the Pyrenean glaciers, which was fed from the big valleys to the south, of Gavarnie, Cauterets, Gèdre and Barèges, and penetrated beyond the point where Lourdes now stands, shaping the topography as it went. But it is not via Lourdes that I would choose to enter Bigorre. That would be dull. The spectacular way to leave Béarn for the east, as I have already indicated, is through Eaux-Bonnes, up along the

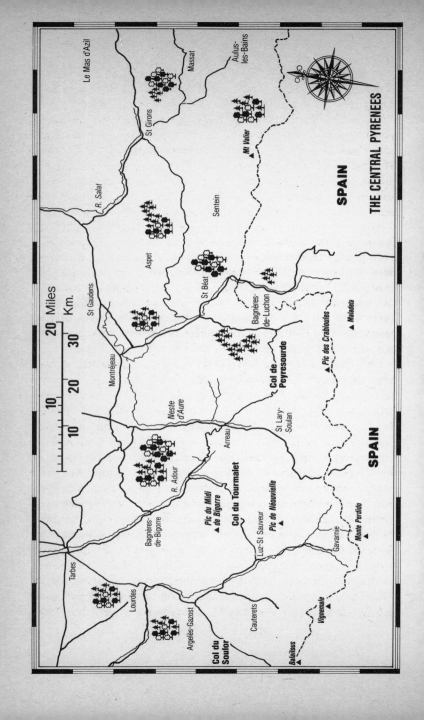

THE CENTRAL PYRENEES

'Thermal Route' to the Col d'Aubisque and then to its companion pass, a little further east, the Col du Soulor.

The Col d'Aubisque is high, at 5,600 feet, and the views that you have from it are sumptuous, both back the way you have come, and now to the east as well, across to the prominent peak of the Pic du Midi de Bigorre, once thought to be the highest in the chain because it stands rather apart and closer to the plain, and before people took to actually measuring altitudes, the nearest peaks were mistaken for the tallest. Between the Col d'Aubisque and the Col du Soulor, six miles further on, the road is a quite dramatic *corniche*, clinging hard to the southern slope of a deep valley, always close against the rock and on occasions passing through it, in brief tunnels. This is an exciting piece of road-making. Some people may find it too exciting; certainly, there is something to be said for being on the side of the road away from the steep drops into the valley, which means driving eastwards by this route and not westwards, or into Bigorre not out of it.

On both of these high cols there are bars which serve also – I hope they have not been smartened up – as ill-favoured souvenir and junk shops. Some of the goods on sale are enticing – Jurançon wines, local sausage, the ubiquitous Pyrenean *fromage de brebis* or ewe's-milk cheese, worth trying if only out of local piety though hardly one of France's great cheeses – others look likely to have a long shelf-life. The café-cum-shop up on the ravishing Col du Soulor in particular has been a wondrous mess on my two ascents there: very dark, immensely cluttered, low-ceilinged and lit as much as warmed by a large log fire. The owner fitted the place ideally, one of nature's rascals, the very model for a resourceful Pyrenean smuggler or minor desperado. Apart from toys, walking-sticks, postcards and other such tourist necessities, he was also hoping to sell *antiquités* and the old things he had gathered lay about in an indescribable miscellany. The altitude is not very good for some of them: a box of old books that I found had congealed together with the damp and had I dared to try and pull one out from the row of upturned spines, to identify it, all the others would have risen too.

One thing you hardly expect to meet with on top of a mountain pass is a choice of roads; but at the Col du Soulor there is one. Off to the north here is a road that plunges with an astonishing directness down into the valley of the Ouzon and out on to the flat, south-east of Pau. Take it, and in the space of only twenty miles you pass through a rapid summary of all the Pyrenean landscapes: high pasture first of all, nowhere richer than near the Col du Soulor, with a backing of the fearsome granite of the Cirque de Litor; then, after the village of Arbéost, dense woodland and the gorge of the river; then suddenly open, more or less flat country, well cultivated, and you are out of the mountains for good. There could be nowhere better to experience the *suddenness* of the Pyrenees here on the French side.

But then, why give them up so abruptly? Rather, carry straight on from the Col du Soulor. The road now goes down sharply into Arrens and the delectable Val d'Azun, a quite short, lateral valley, of rich grass and pleasant, grey villages. South-west from Arrens there runs another valley, with a minor road up it, to Aste and a little clutch of high lakes. Above them, and on the frontier, is the granite peak of Balaïtous, a real first-division mountain, meaning, in the Pyrenees, that it tops 3,146 metres. To be exact it is 3,146 metres or 10,480 feet high; but what is distinctive about Balaïtous, when you see it from here, is that to the left of the summit is one of the few significant glaciers still surviving in the Pyrenees. In all the chain there are less than ten square kilometres left of glacier, or about a fortieth of what there is in the Alps, though, after many years of shrinkage, the Pyrenean ice-fields are said to have spread themselves a little since 1950.

The Val d'Azun will take you down at its eastern end to the town of Argelès-Gazost, which stands in a wide basin of the Gave de Pau, some eight miles south of Lourdes. Argelès is undeniably a centre, near enough to the towns to the north and the great valleys and mountains to the south to suggest itself as a place to stay. But it is rather charmless I think, and there is at least one far more enticing place nearby if you plan to stop in this valley. Argelès is a spa town of the middling kind, neither rich nor poor: a creation, by the look of it, mainly of the later nineteenth century. Some of it, notably the spa buildings and the generous park that goes with them, is down on the floor of the valley, the rest of it up on a terrace to the west, so that from the little square in the middle of the upper town you get quite large views of the mountains.

The first direction to think of driving out of Argelès is of course to the south. But not, for the time being, very far, because two miles below Argelès, on the western slopes of the valley, is the little place where I would always choose to stay when coming to Bigorre: the village of Saint-Savin. This is small, delightful, and richly historical, perched high enough up on its fertile hillside to dominate the valley to both north and south. Saint-Savin today is small, even for a village, but at one time it was the centre of power in this valley. It began as a monastery founded here by the Benedictines in the Carolingian age, at a spot sanctified by the edifying life and death nearby of St Savin, the son of a Barcelona nobleman. The monastery may have been sacked by Vikings or it may have fallen down through neglect, but either way it needed reviving. In the 900s it was revived and became very powerful on the temporal side. In the eleventh century a particularly entrepreneurial abbot began the exploitation of the curative waters of Cauterets to the south, and the monks built roads and bridges and cleared the woods in their expanding domain.

Thus did the monastery come to run the valley and to create a classic example of a Pyrenean 'pastoral state'. But the locals did not always tolerate government by monks – perhaps suspecting what in this century has been established as a fact, that the abbey's legal title to the authority it claimed was a tenth-century

forgery. In 1317 the communes in the valley forced the Benedictines to sign an agreement to share power and for several
centuries thereafter local affairs were managed jointly by the
abbey and by the 'Republic of Saint-Savin'. The monks had the
reputation, as monks generally did, of good living more than of
holiness – a scurrilous couplet written by an early Pyrenean
traveller speaks of '*Le long dîner, la courte messe / Du bon abbé de
Saint-Savin.*' But the long story of how this valley more or less
governed itself, and in a profoundly communal spirit, is
typically Pyrenean.

The abbey church of Saint-Savin still exists, and very fine it is.
It is twelfth century and built of a pale honey-coloured stone. It
has had over the years to be much restored, having been
damaged three times by earthquakes and also outrageously
neglected by the community of monks, who seem to have had
an unnatural taste for litigation – one lawsuit between them and
the locality lasted almost throughout the eighteenth century. By
the time of the French Revolution there were in any case only
three monks left in Saint-Savin and even though the church was
spared the vindictive demolition which removed the adjacent
monastery buildings, by 1840 it was more than ready to be
rescued by the growing movement for the conservation of
ancient monuments. It was among the first buildings in France
to be listed as in need of help, even if none came for some fifteen
years.

Today the church looks robust; and it is even intended to
rebuild the long-vanished cloister on the north side. This is a
fortified church, because during the Hundred Years' War the
walls were raised and a *chemin de ronde* or covered battlement was
added all the way round the building, deducible from outside
from the row of arched apertures for the defenders set close
together under the roof-line, like large pigeon-holes. The
octagonal tower over the crossing, with its slated, candle-snuffer
spire, is Gothic and was put on when the walls were raised; after
600 years the mild incongruity of this belated infidelity to the

Romanesque style has worn off. Saint-Savin has the makings of a fine portal at the west end, but because most of the decoration is illegible for one reason or another, and not least because of the impious mutilation it suffered during the Revolution, it is nothing to dwell on. To the left of this doorway, right down on the ground, is an arched opening known as 'The Cagots' window', this having been, so one story claims, the window through which the Cagots, who were not allowed into the church, could hear the mass. While inside the church, there is a splendid holy-water basin, supported by two bent, sculpted figures, known in its turn as 'The Cagots' stoup'.

So who were the Cagots, other, similar allusions to whom you will also come across in the western Pyrenees? And why could they not worship with everyone else? They were in fact social outcasts, to whom documentary references can be found going as far back as the thirteenth century. The agreed version of their origins is that they were lepers or the descendants of lepers, whom no local community would accept as neighbours. The Cagots lived a peculiar life outside society, without rights but exempt from taxes, wearing a badge on their clothing to indicate their standing, forbidden to walk barefoot, unable to hear mass with their fellow Christians. If they married outside their own caste, they could be put to death. But, debarred from owning land as they were, they became the great craftsmen of these regions, as carpenters, builders, and weavers. Their exclusion from the normal commerce of local society was perpetuated long beyond the time when leprosy had been controlled; indeed, it was not until the nineteenth century that some Cagots finally became authentic citizens.

There are some unusually good things to see inside the church of Saint-Savin: a 'Eucharist tower' twenty feet and three storeys high, Gothic in style, and made of gilded wood; two primitive fifteenth-century panels, each containing nine scenes from the life of the church's name-saint; a Renaissance organ carried on what is left of a wooden gallery that once ran right across the

church, from transept to transept – on the front of the
instrument are three articulated mascarons, which moved their
eyes and tongues as the organ played, in representation of
wretched earthly sinners, grimacing at the intolerable sound of
joyful, heavenly music. Opposite the organ, on the north side of
the church, is the *salle capitulaire* or chapter-house, which is also
a small museum. This is a beautiful, small twelfth-century
room, used as a stable for many years after the depredations of
the Revolution but carefully restored in the 1850s. It is part
Gothic and part Romanesque, with pointed vaults but round
arches. The smooth pillars which support it in the centre have
capitals of a style that has made some art historians suppose that
they may originally have come from the Roman villa or palace
presumed to have existed on this site in the fourth century. The
double windows, divided by twin columns, are the most
pleasing thing in the room, with simply sculpted capitals, of a
demon, the head of Christ, animals, birds, stars and flowers;
these, like the door between them, once gave on to the cloister,
and it is nice to know that they will do so again, once that vital
adjunct has been rebuilt.

Saint-Savin, the village, is a particularly well-kept little place,
with much mown grass, much fresh paint and much quiet
doing-up of old houses. From it you can look across to the
well-occupied slopes on the other side of the wide river valley,
where there are numbers of small villages and some fine
agricultural land, because these glaciated valleys are celebrated
for their fertility. There is also a highly scenic road which you
can take up on to the open ski grounds and expansive prospects
of Hautacam. Beaucens, which is almost exactly facing Saint-
Savin on this eastern slope, though at a lesser altitude, has the
ideally romantic ruins of an old towered castle plus keep, where
the local chieftains, the viscounts of Lavedan, lived in the days of
their prosperity. It is still lived in, though not any more by
humans, because the castle and its grounds have been turned into
a home, and a sort of theatre, for birds of prey: vultures, falcons,

buzzards, eagles, which in the afternoons (I'm not sure why it has to be only after lunch) are allowed to fly free and which you can pay to visit. It is in its way no bad use for a building once inhabited by predatory grandees.

Cauterets

Two miles to the south of Saint-Savin is another of the double-barrelled towns in this valley: Pierrefitte-Nestalas. For the tourist, Pierrefitte is a pity, being mainly the site of a large and obtrusive works where ammonia and phosphorus are produced. So you do not feel like stopping in Pierrefitte. It is, however, the point where the valley comes apart, dividing into a western and an eastern branch. Here indeed, is the entrance to the two most celebrated high valleys of the Pyrenees. At Pierrefitte you have the choice: right for Cauterets and the Pont d'Espagne, or left for Luz, Barèges and Gavarnie. I say the choice, but since any even half-curious visitor to the High Pyrenees will want to go up both valleys, it comes down only to deciding which to visit first.

Here it will be the valley whose opening is to the west, of Cauterets. And where the road goes up, the Gave de Cauterets comes ebulliently down, first among chestnut trees and then through a much sterner landscape as the valley contracts into a defile. The spa and resort of Cauterets itself is six miles only from Pierrefitte, but at double the altitude. It is a real mountain town, though for all its remoteness one of the oldest and best patronized of the Pyrenean spas, once, as I have said, managed by the monks of Saint-Savin. Its reputation was lifted in the sixteenth century, when Marguerite de Navarre came here and (perhaps) wrote some of her *Heptameron*, as a respite from the rigours of the cure, before the atrocious weather – in the prologue she quickly complains of the rainfall in Cauterets – drove her down to Sarrance. In her wake, mud or no, came another French author, even more broad-minded, in the person of François Rabelais, while in the nineteenth century the spa's literary connections became more exalted still when the great Romantic writers, Alfred de Vigny, Chateaubriand and George Sand all visited it.

There were now reinforcements from England too, because in 1830 the young Alfred Tennyson came to Cauterets with his doomed friend Arthur Hallam, on a visit that was a cross between a vacation and a secret mission. The pair arrived with money and dispatches written in invisible ink that were to be handed over to one of the leaders of the insurrectionary party in Spain, currently conspiring to get rid of the autocratic King Ferdinand and currently enjoying the support of idealistic and poetical young Englishmen. Their small mission accomplished, Tennyson and Hallam sank back to being tourists, and Tennyson never forgot the scenery around Cauterets, which he associated for the rest of his long life with the happiness he had felt when travelling there with the beloved but now dead Hallam. He came back twice, and in 1861 wrote his poem 'In the Valley of Cauterets':

> All along the valley, stream that flashest white,
> Deepening thy voice with the deepening of the night,
> All along the valley, where thy waters flow,
> I walked with one I loved two and thirty years ago.

Actually, it was one and thirty years ago, but according to Tennyson's recent biographer, Robert Bernard Martin, the poet deliberately put euphony before mere factuality.

Cauterets claims to have a more plentiful supply of sulphurous waters than any other spa on earth, to the tune of a million and a half health-giving litres a day, and this is a claim you will not wish to dispute once you have pushed open the swing doors to the neo-Roman 'Baths of Caesar' and breathed in the warm and all too recognizably sulphur-laden air. Cauterets in fact has more healing waters than it knows what to do with, for on the roadside outside the town you pass small, steaming escapes of water as yet untapped. At one time the thermal sources on which the fortunes of Cauterets rest so securely were also claimed, as were those of other spas, as being especially radioactive, but this is, understandably, not a claim you find in the contemporary brochures, even though the radioactivity is presumably still there. But diagnostically speaking, Cauterets is not so particular: its slogan, in the local dialect, reads '*A Cautares, tout que garech*', or 'In Cauterets, we cure the lot'.

By the time Tennyson revisited Cauterets, in 1861, what he thought of as a village he now found to be, in his less poetic moods, 'an odious watering-place', and that is a transition you can readily enough trace in the architecture today. Cauterets stands on either side of its Gave, with the older, more villagey quarter on the east bank and the newer, more upstanding parts on the west. Now that it no longer seems so shocking that the town should have grown as it has, the newer half is in fact the more attractive, a fine example of what you might call the Thermal-Imperial style, imposing even in its incongruity, up here in the mountains, with its tall bourgeois hotels framed against the surrounding woods and crags. There is some excellent wrought iron to be seen in Cauterets, in the balconies of the hotels along the handsome Boulevard Latapie-Flurin.

Cauterets has a number of walks of the undemanding sort, designed for spa-goers, through woods and to viewpoints or waterfalls. It is also the launch-pad for one of the classic Pyrenean excursions, up to the Pont d'Espagne and the Lac de Gaube. And because this is a classic excursion, remember that others may be making it too; in summer I can imagine it becoming exceedingly crowded up here and the path to the Lac de Gaube an ant-trail of pedestrians bumper to bumper.

The road from Cauterets to the Pont d'Espagne, five miles away to the south, is all waterfalls – there are four or five of them, spectacular and profuse even in summer. The Pont itself is a fine place to imbibe the water effects, an old stone bridge built at a spot where three cascades come seething down to make one and create an ideal confusion of water, spray and rocks. At the Pont d'Espagne the road ends, but you can then take a reasonably comfortable path, for about three-quarters of an hour, up through the tumbled rock and ailing pine trees – they seem to be fighting a losing battle against the colonies of grey lichen – to the Lac de Gaube, at an altitude of a trifle under 6000 feet. The lake is a wild, bare place, certainly not a serene one, with scree and pine trees running down to water that is clear and dark. At the far end is the great mass of Vignemale, at 10,820 feet the highest of all the peaks on the actual frontier, though a little less high than some of those in Spain. Vignemale has the best and most photogenic of the Pyrenean glaciers, on its eastern or left-hand flank, a genuine tongue of ice, reaching downwards.

Like all mountain lakes, the Lac de Gaube used to be thought impossibly deep. Even when Victor Hugo came up here, in 1843, he was still able to declare, on no known authority but his own, that you could pile six cathedrals of Notre-Dame in Paris (the subject of one of his novels) one on top of the other 'before the balustrade on top of its towers would reach to the surface of the water'. That was a strange and beautiful exaggeration; the lake's actual depth is about 130 feet. But as a corrective to the excitable Hugo, let me quote another great French writer of the nineteenth century, a formidably astringent one this time, who likewise tramped dutifully up to the Lac de Gaube: the novelist Gustave Flaubert. He enjoyed the salmon trout he ate at the small inn there but was mighty scathing about the visitors' book (as well as about the notion that the lake might actually be beautiful): 'You will see only two kinds of exclamations in it: one about the beauty of the Lac de Gaube, the other about how good the trout are . . . which means that only fools or gluttons have picked up the pen to sign their names and their thoughts.'

The Lac de Gaube was the scene too of one of the Pyrenees' best-known accidents. In 1832, an English couple, the Pattisons, married for just one month, were drowned in it; according to the local sub-prefect's report, because Mr Pattison was amusing himself sounding the depth of the water with a pole and fell overboard, dragging his bride in after him. This drably official account of the matter was not welcomed by the media of the day, who looked for more exciting explanations, such as a double suicide brought on by the well-known English affliction of 'spleen', or a murder of Mrs Pattison by Mr following his discovery that she was pregnant by a young 'Milord'. These were the sorts of stories to be read in the pamphlets sold beside the Lac de Gaube for years after the event by the promoters of the tourist trade. Anti-English slanders they were held to be by the genteel Victorian travellers who continued to come to the Pyrenees. Monckton Milnes, a good memorialist but a forgettable poet, visited the lake in 1838 and later wrote a poem about the tragedy, taking a more honourably sentimental line towards it than had the morbid locals:

> One moment, and the gush went forth
> Of music-mingled laughter –
> The struggling splash and deathly shriek
> Were there the instant after.

Luz, Gavarnie and Barèges

The more easterly of the two valley roads which combine at Pierrefitte takes you first to the charming town of Luz-Saint-Sauveur, which may look like one place but is really two, with more than just a hyphen dividing them. For much of the distance between Pierrefitte and Luz you pass through the splendid defile of the Gorge de Luz, which then opens amply out into the brilliant, grassy basin of Luz, full of ash and poplar trees. Luz is green less from the rain – it is actually one of the drier valleys in the High Pyrenees – than from the water it gets from the mountains all around, from the lakes, the glaciers and the seasonal 'melt'. This is a peculiarly steep region, so much so in fact that the snow finds it more than usually difficult to stay where it has fallen; there have been some sadly famous avalanches near Luz, the hamlets of Chèze and Saligos which you pass as you come in from the north both having been smothered and destroyed in their time.

It is also a famously independent place, for long the capital of this little region of Barèges, and sufficiently cut off to administer itself as another of the remarkably enlightened mountain 'republics'. Luz had its *passeries* or local treaties, signed with the corresponding valleys on the Spanish side of the mountains, which guaranteed that they would continue to trade with one another even at times when the nations they were nominally part of might be at war. As a consequence, this was one of the towns that prospered in the golden age of cross-Pyrenean trade in the sixteenth and seventeenth centuries, even though at that time there was no road to Luz from the north, only a mule track through the gorge.

Let me now separate Luz from Saint-Sauveur. Luz is a small resort town, these days with its ski extension up in the mountains to the west, at Luz-Ardiden; Saint-Sauveur is a spa a mile and a half away, in a gorge. Luz I very much like; it is a bright, airy place straddling the river Bastan and unified by the pearl-grey paint you see everywhere, on doors and shutters. In the heart of Luz, touching no other building but moated about by tarmacadam, is its extraordinary fortified church (see Plate 5). This was the work originally of the military order of Hospitallers, who established themselves here, at this confluence of the two valleys of Barèges and Gavarnie, in the twelfth century and built a miniature citadel, fortifying it as a defence against raids from across the mountains by Aragonese brigands. The defensive aspects of the church of Luz are more interesting, it has to be said, than the ecclesiastical, because inside the church is a disappointment, small and scrappy. Outside, it is different. A roughly mortared, battlemented wall, some fifteen feet high, rings the church and its old graveyard completely round, with, on each of its merlons, a thin slate weighted down by a stone. The church has a rugged, rectangular tower, known as the Arsenal, where the weapons were kept, and opposite that, a tall, gabled bell-tower, formerly a look-out, that dominates the ensemble and quite unbalances it. But what you notice most of all about this astonishing arrangement are the mitre-shaped apertures high up on the walls of the nave and the apse, where, as at Saint-Savin, the old *chemin de ronde* runs.

The church has an excellent Romanesque portal, near the west end, made from some marble-like stone hard enough not to have eroded. It is a suitably simple affair, with just two sculpted capitals of indeterminate subject and only one sculpted arch or *voussure* out of the four; the tympanum is the best thing, a Christ in Majesty decisively sculpted in uncommonly high relief. There are numbers of Latin inscriptions here, from two of which, on stones set into the wall to the left of the doorway, the completion of the porch and the dedication of the church can be dated to 1200 and 1240 respectively. At the other end of this same wall of the church, beside the old graveyard, the movingly small sarcophagus of a child is set into a niche, with a heavy stone on top of it, under its own small arch and with some variously worn decoration of the stonework. The inscription crudely cut into the sarcophagus is in the old *langue d'oc* of southern France and reads 'Here lies Bena / Obat daughter of En Ramon of Barèges and of Madame Na Hera. She died in the last week of April 1236. Gile de Sere made this.'

Luz is unquestionably a town it would be pleasant to lodge in. There is in particular one very small hotel, the Hôtel des Remparts, whose rear windows look straight out on to the church and its battlements, and beyond them to the woods and escarpments rising sharply behind. Rooms with a view indeed. I'm not breaking my stated rule here and recommending this hotel, just saying that it is there and that if you could get the back bedrooms you would have a most remarkable scene to look out on.

Of Luz's other, lesser half, the spa of Saint-Sauveur, there is little to say. Like other Pyrenean spas, it is basically a single street of high hotels or 'residences' strung out between the mountainside behind and the river below. The speciality of Saint-Sauveur is gynaecological complaints, and it is known as 'the ladies' resort', having been brought to a modest celebrity by the two-month stay here in 1859 of the Imperial couple, Napoleon and Eugénie. One good thing that their patronage led to was the Pont Napoléon, which spans the torrent just outside Saint-Sauveur to the south and is a lavish piece of bridgework, a single arch some 200 feet above the water at its highest point. There is no call to go through Saint-Sauveur, because the road for Gavarnie is on the other bank of the Gave. The Cirque de Gavarnie, be it known, is even more today what it has long been, *the* place in all the Pyrenees for tourists. You should get there at all costs, because it is an absolutely astonishing place, but the nature of the spectacle is such that it can only work on you properly if the cirque is not being mobbed; it demands a certain loneliness, and on afternoons in July and August, for instance, the coaches are said to have to queue before they can get into the village of Gavarnie. But I have been to the cirque in early June and in October, and found it almost deserted, so it is not too hard to pick your moment.

The road up from Luz to Gavarnie is a pleasure in itself, tightly enclosed by rock walls in places, before it broadens out into another of those lovely high Pyrenean basins at the resort village of Gèdre. From here you can already start to see the rim of the mountains that enclose the cirque. Past Gèdre, the landscape reverts again to its harsher, more primeval mode, as you drive through what is known as the Chaos de Coumély, a wilderness of massive boulders that have rolled down from the mountain on the left. This is the point where ascending Romantic poets began to feel understandably Romantic: 'a black and hideous path' declared Victor Hugo, 'the original chaos, a hell' said George Sand. On the modern carriageway such feelings are not to be fully recaptured, but the chaos is a fit preparation of the spirit for the profoundly rugged experience of the cirque.

Gavarnie is a single-minded, ungainly village, bent on its one charge, of dispatching visitors, on foot, by donkey or on pony-back along the track to the cirque, an hour away. It has a small, not very interesting church, founded by the Knights of St John, with a cemetery in which there are the graves of a number of 'Pyreneeists', or guides and climbers killed in these mountains. For Gavarnie is the old headquarters of mountaineering in the Pyrenees, a centre not only for excursionists but for the hard men, aiming for dangerous ascents of the rocks. There is a statue in the village to the most endearing Pyreneeist of them all, Count Henry Russell, Irish on his father's side and Gascon on his mother's, who climbed obsessively and made so many ascents of Vignemale – thirty in all – that in 1889 the authorities granted him a concession to it. Russell was what you might call a social climber, inasmuch as he specialized in fitting out rock shelters for himself at various altitudes and if possible receiving his friends in them. Mountaineering in the Pyrenees began, early in the nineteenth century, with the very practical ascents made by the mappers and surveyors, but it continued, in climbers such as Russell, with something of the flair and eccentricity with which it was also evolving at much the same time in the Alps.

The track which you follow from the village of Gavarnie to the cirque is necessarily a good, well-worn one, almost a road for much of the journey, through beech woods and then across open grasslands, before the last rough and rocky stretch up into the mouth of the cirque. Rather before half-way, where the path actually goes down, instead of up, into a gentle, turfy basin, the authorities of the Parc National have made a 'botanical garden'. I put this description in quotes because it is an informal garden, discreetly signposted. It is simply an area of mountain country full of pine trees with uptilted tips to their branches, of bushes, boulders, pasture and wild flowers; and the longer you wander about there the more flowers you find, unassuming yet plentiful, in an incomparable variety, as well as exquisite fist-sized mushrooms, like polished stones. And all the time you are close enough to the mighty cirque itself to enjoy that too, with a sight of its gigantic waterfall.

Once you are wrapped around by the cirque you realize that it is not beautiful but what in the eighteenth century they knew as 'sublime'. Fearsome that is, without being dangerous. From end to end, the curve of mountain wall which faces you occupies a full 180 degrees, and measures all but nine miles along the crest; but even more than the width it is the depth that awes one at Gavarnie, because the cirque is very deep, with an average drop from crest to valley floor of 5,500 feet. The wall is not in fact vertical though it is easy to misremember it as such, because it rises in three distinct layers of limestone, to heights of 6,900, 8,500 and finally some 9,000 feet, with a filling of ice and snow on the slopes that divide one layer from the next. The cirque was made, it seems, even before the period of glaciation, by water finding its way out from the massif of the Monte Perdido behind and undermining the cliffs, though it was the glacier, shreds only of which are left, that eventually cleared this gigantic bowl of its debris. If you want, you can walk right into the cirque from the mouth, over grass first of all, but then across the stone-strewn floor; it is just about a mile to the furthest rock face. To the left is the great waterfall – the cirque has numerous supporting ones – which comes down in one huge leap of 1,400 feet when the snows are melting or in two rather more modest leaps once they are finished. This waterfall is the origin in fact of the Gave de Pau, which starts life off here through channels made in the packed snow at the foot of the sunless rock wall.

To the right of the cirque there is a large indentation or cleft in the rim known as the Brèche de Roland (see Plate 3). This is a much more imposing witness to that paladin's strength of arm than the Pas de Roland near Itxassou. It was made by the furious last sweep of his indestructible sword Durandal, when he struck it against the rock in a vain effort to break it and so stop this epic weapon from falling into the hands of the Saracens:

> He brings it down harder than I can say.
> The sword grinds, it neither bursts nor breaks.
> It rebounds heavenwards.

The cleft that Roland made is 300 feet deep, half that many long and from 130 to 190 feet wide. To climb up to it takes time – nine or ten hours to get there and back – but no special skill or nerve. Indeed in 1828, as an inscription on the Spanish side of the Brèche records, the reckless Duchesse de Berry, widow of the assassinated second son of King Charles X, ascended to it, not under her own power but under that of her hired porters, who carried her to the top in a chair. She arrived back down in Gavarnie, 'still merry and confident' according to the annalists, as well she might be for all the effort she had had to make. Juliette Drouet, the mistress of Victor Hugo and his companion on his travels, was put out that a woman other than herself should have been able to make this 'difficult ascent' and claimed that the Duchess had needed the services of thirty guides and helpers; less jaundiced reporters speak only of two. Just over the other side of the Brèche, one of the great delvers into the Pyrenees, the speleologist Norbert Casteret, discovered in 1926 an underground glacier, the highest ice-cavern known.

Gavarnie is not alone up here in having a cirque. At Gèdre, you can turn off the Gavarnie road to the east and drive up to the alternative Cirque de Troumouse. This road takes you through what I would say was the most savage landscape you are likely to see in the Pyrenees without actually setting off into the mountains on foot, a valley which has rocks where other valleys have trees. It passes first through high, increasingly thin pastures and then between tremendous rock-falls to the small settlement of Héas, the highest it is said anywhere in the Pyrenees, at 5,000 feet, swamped by an avalanche in 1915 and made up today only of a chapel and two or three houses. Past Héas, there is a toll-road, very steep, extremely tortuous and liable to be strewn with rocks, which goes way, way up, close to the centre of the cirque at an altitude of 6,600 feet. If the toll-road is not manned, that will almost certainly be because the road is closed by snow, as it normally is for a good seven months out of the twelve. In early June, I got close to the top, and to the cirque, before having to stop the car at a snow-drift; but if that happens you can simply enough walk the rest of the way or, indeed, walk directly into the cirque along the valley to the left out of Héas. As you climb by the road, you see a ring of mountains to your right which you might easily take to be the Cirque de Troumouse, but this is in fact yet a third cirque, that of Estaubé, intermediate between Gavarnie and Troumouse, imposing in its own right if too withdrawn properly to enclose you, as a good cirque should. Troumouse is magnificent, if not quite with the sublimity of Gavarnie because there is more grass here and the ring of mountain wall is more open. It is on a vast scale though: Franz Schrader, the first great cartographer of these mountains, estimated that it would hold twenty million people; modern guidebooks have cut this number churlishly, and for all I know realistically down to three million.

And so, back to Luz. The river of Luz, the Bastan, enters the town briskly from the east, along the deep lateral valley of Barèges. I shall now go some of the way up this valley, as far as the Col du Tourmalet at the end of it – what lies on the far side of the col must wait for the section of this chapter on the valley of the Adour. The Col du Tourmalet is the highest pass in the Pyrenees which you can cross by car, its altitude being almost exactly 7,000 feet; for this reason it is early to close, in November, and late to open again, in May or sometimes early June. The name Tourmalet means literally 'bad way round', but that was a billing which the col earned in more demanding times than the present, when there was no proper road over the pass but when you could hire porters to carry you from one valley to the next by chair. It was no doubt the carriers rather than the carried who gave the Tourmalet its nickname.

On the way up to the col from Luz you come first to the small resort and spa of Barèges, one street wide and squeezed tightly in in true spa style between the mountains to the south and the river to the north. But small though it is, Barèges was one of the first Pyrenean spas to make its name, mainly because Louis XIV's sick son was sent there to be treated in the 1670s. It was above all the place to which you were advised to go if you had for some reason been shot, in either war or peace. In 1742, an Englishman, Christopher Meighan, published an analysis of the waters which he described as 'A Treatise of the Nature and Powers of Barege's Baths and Waters. Wherein their Superior Effects for the cure of gun-shot wounds . . . ', but in those years it was still an uncouth place, better fitted to receive the injured soldiery than sickly, comfort-loving bourgeois. Nowadays, the spa doubles as a ski resort, having been developed along with its winter annexe, Super-Barèges, higher up the road near to the col. These slopes have the reputation of being the best you can find in the Pyrenees.

For all its great altitude, the view from the top of the Col du Tourmalet is much less open and memorable than many, blocked as it is to the south by a row of peaks and overpowered immediately to the north by the bulk of the Pic du Midi de Bigorre, which is a most assertive mountain. If it is a view you are after, then better to go to the top of the Pic du Midi than remain down on the col, for from there the prospect has for long been famous, especially to the north over the plains and, on a good day, westward to the Atlantic. So relatively accessible is it, that the Pic du Midi has become a thoroughly domesticated mountain; as Belloc noted with distaste early this century, 'No other of the great mountains of Europe have been put more thoroughly in harness,' and since Belloc was there it has been harnessed more thoroughly still. You can get to the top by cable-car from La Mongie or up a rough but bearable toll-road from the Col du Tourmalet, which is open only in July, August and September. From where you park, there is another, minor, two-minute cable-car ride to the summit, or you can zigzag up on foot in about forty minutes. Although you are here, on the summit, at 9,400 feet, well above the permanent snowline in the Pyrenees, which starts at about 8,500 feet, there is seldom any snow in the summer, because the sides of the mountain are too steep, especially on the north side, to keep it in place. The Pic du Midi has long had an observatory on top, a very substantial structure indeed and occupied since 1881, after the scientists who started it had got into the arduous habit of spending their winters up here in a small hotel. The summit also now has a television mast, which can but be one of the most visible of its kind anywhere in the world, serving at once both to identify and to pollute the poor Pic du Midi.

Lourdes

North of Argelès-Gazost, at the point where the Gave de Pau finally leaves the mountains, stands the best-known town in the Pyrenees, Lourdes. Lourdes has had two histories. For 500 years, until Bigorre was finally absorbed into the kingdom of France in 1607, it was the capital of the county of that name, and for a part of that time was in theory an English town, being recaptured by a French army, after two sieges, early in the fifteenth century. Its fallow years were between 1607 and 1858, when the second history of Lourdes began, with the eighteen appearances of the Virgin Mary there in a grotto beside the river to a miller's daughter, Bernadette Soubirous, which turned the town quite rapidly into the greatest pilgrimage centre of Roman Catholicism. That aspect of Lourdes is now of course utterly dominant: this is a place of pilgrimage and little else. More than four million people come to it every year.

But pilgrimage too is seasonal and not to be marked off too strictly from tourism any more nowadays than it could have been marked off in the great centuries of the sacred trek to

Compostela. It is possible to go to Lourdes as a tourist without being a pilgrim, and that is all I can decently do here. I would not care to go there as a tourist in the season of pilgrims, however, because then the sense of one's impertinence would surely be too strong. As it is, going to Lourdes out of season, in the late autumn or winter, brings one even more starkly face to face with what the Catholic Belloc calls this supernatural place's 'destestable earthly adjuncts'. They are the more detestable for having temporarily lost their reason for existence: that is to say, shops full of a disastrous religious trinketry no longer have any customers to sell it to, and whole street-fuls of hotels and *pensions* are all of them closed until the following spring, making parts of the town seem gloomily abandoned.

The whole point of Lourdes comes out as you walk down from the centre of the town towards the river and the Cité Religieuse on the far bank. The architecture of the Cité Religieuse is disagreeable. At the end of a long esplanade, which opens out into a concourse, there are two churches, one above the other. The lower of them is large, circular in its effect if not in its outline, and imitation Byzantine in style, shinily reliant on marble and mosaics. Inside, the circumference of the church is occupied by elaborate chapels and the marble facings are everywhere inscribed with thank-offerings. The upper church is tall and narrow, neo-Gothic in style, and in fact a little earlier than the lower church, having been finished in 1871. It too is filled with inscriptions, with banners and with a multiplicity of framed thank-offerings. To the right of the two churches, down near the water, is the grotto itself, a humbler place though naturally not spared the apparatus of the cult: a statue of the Virgin, an altar, seats, a small and poignant row of crutches that have been discarded and now hang against the rock wall. Here too are the baths where the crippled are immersed, and a line of taps providing water from the source that Bernadette was told by the Virgin to drink from. And dispensers full of candles, to be set when lit into iron trolleys – so many that even on a relatively deserted day when I was there, you could hear their crepitation. The sight later of these hundreds of flaring candles, from across the river, as the light faded on a grey evening, was as near as I was able to come in Lourdes to any sense of holiness, so oppressive otherwise is the sense of the *business* of holiness.

Architecturally, the most acceptable element of the Cité Religieuse is the enormous underground 'basilica' consecrated in the shrine's centenary year of 1958. It is scooped shallowly out on the left of the esplanade, and forms an oval more than 200 yards long; 20,000 people can be in it at any one time. Because it is so plain and built entirely of concrete, the car-park effect is instantaneous, yet once get clear of the large struts that support the roof, and this becomes a compelling structure, more stadium than church even now but reassuring to the puritanical visitor after the orgy of nineteenth-century frippery elsewhere in the Cité.

Looking back at the town of Lourdes from the esplanade, you have an excellent view of its one historical monument: the fortress, set high on a rock above the river. This was for centuries a strongpoint and later a prison; among its prisoners, during the time of the Revolutionary Wars, was Lord Elgin, he of the marbles, who was held hostage in Lourdes on his way back to England from Turkey. The military parts of the fortress have been thoroughly restored and it is possible to walk all round the battlements. But the main point of going up to it is to look at the Pyrenean Museum that has been created inside. This has some intriguing exhibits, even if they are not always quite Pyrenean. Astonishingly ornate decorations which were set on top of the yokes of working oxen, for example, in the form of painted wooden 'towers' anything up to two feet high, partly hollowed out and fitted with small bells. Or the lovely, curved local milk jugs made of some very dark wood. Or the curious *dentelle de cire* or literally 'wax lace': mourning candles resembling strings of pasta which could be wound tightly into packages or else extended and draped. There are other rooms in the

Museum showing furniture, costumes, prehistoric remains, wildlife, tools, porcelain, and so on. A good exhibit is that which commemorates the Pyrenean climbers and their notable ascents, such figures as Count Henry Russell or Ramond de Carbonnières, who was the first into the field and made thirty-five separate ascents of the Pic du Midi de Bigorre between the years 1787 and 1810. (Ramond's still very readable *Voyage dans les Pyrénées* was published in the unpropitious year of 1789, but it did well and was translated into English in 1813, so it could claim to have helped to draw English travellers to these unknown mountains.) There is a display also of various types of mountain refuge or cabin, from which you can judge how extremely uncomfortable it must have been for those invited by Count Russell to share his quarters on his favourite mountain of Vignemale, for the so-called 'Russell' is quite the most Spartan of shelters, little more than a hollow scooped out under an overhanging rock. It does not even come up to the extremely modest levels of convenience that the shepherds expected when they took to the hills for the summer with their animals; also on show in Lourdes's museum is a portable wooden cabin, with handles at either end, like a horizontal sedan chair. This has sleeping-room for one, even though it would have taken two shepherds to carry it, leaving you to wonder how the odd shepherd out spent the night.

The caves of Bétharram, a short way out of Lourdes on the main road to Pau, are not my sort of caves but I will at least mention them. They are large, covering several kilometres of galleries, and very well organized. At one point of the journey through them you can take to a boat, and to carry you back to the daylight there is a miniature railway. What you mainly see are stalactites, stalagmites and other rock formations, excellent of their kind. For myself, I would let the others go on to the caves and pass the time instead above ground in the large riverside village of Saint-Pé (the Gascon form of Pierre)-de-Bigorre, which has a nicely arcaded square and a few pleasing remains of its old abbey church, once the grandest religious building in the Pyrenees but now part in effect of the dull parish church that later replaced it, after it had been fired by Protestant arsonists in the Wars of Religion.

The Adour Valley

It is a mild puzzle at first, to come across the young river Adour flowing from south to north down its valley, when you last saw it flowing from east to west into the ocean at Bayonne. But the rivers of south-west France flow very indirectly, and the Adour makes a strange horseshoe of a tour through lower Gascony before it gets to the sea. Its Pyrenean valley is known as the most fertile of all, thanks to the kindly work of the local glacier, which laid down its moraine to a depth and at an angle that produced grasslands of great repute. When Ramond de Carbonnières came to Campan, in the later eighteenth century, he saw it as an Arcadia, both for the excellence of its pasture and for the independent spirit of its peasantry, whose self-sufficiency seemed a model to this fundamentally democratic man.

The proper way to enter the Adour valley from the west is via the Col du Tourmalet, provided it is open. The road down from the col goes through the modern, high (6,000 feet) ski resort of La Mongie, which is a neat curve of tall buildings opening to westward on to some promising-looking *pistes*. The long descent on this side of the Tourmalet ends in the village of Sainte-Marie-de-Campan, where you can either turn left up the valley of Campan, or else pursue your way east over the next high pass, the Col d'Aspin. For now, I shall turn left.

Not far up the road here is the town of Bagnères-de-Bigorre, a spa known to the Romans and envisaged by Napoleon I as the 'capital' of a Pyrenean confederation of health resorts – for a while it was given the title, which it can never have begun to merit, of 'the Athens of the Pyrenees'. Admittedly, Bagnères has captured some notable intellectual clients over the centuries: Montaigne back in the sixteenth century, and the whimsical Laurence Sterne, author of *Tristram Shandy*, in the eighteenth. Though I have also to say that English visitors have had their episodes of hooliganism in these parts, especially in the post-Napoleonic years, when, understandably, they were not always popular. In the 1830s they were being criticized for despoiling 'the crystalline beauties' of the local caves, or in other words bearing off as trophies the stalactites and stalagmites. And around this same period, an Englishman reading in the public library at Bagnères came upon an account of the battle of Toulouse in the Napoleonic wars which he thought too favourable to the French, and annotated it accordingly in the interests of accuracy. He was called out by an offended patriot of the town, but killed his opponent in the consequent duel, one of the few duels that can ever have been fought for the sake of a marginal note in a book.

Bagnères-de-Bigorre is an agreeable town, on the river; at its best on the western side, where the main spa buildings are and where the streets are older, crookeder and, over a very small area, somewhat Parisian. It has an especially fine flower market. Bagnères was and is still, seemingly, the home of the Chanteurs Montagnards, or Mountain Singers, who sang Pyrenean songs all over Europe in the 1840s, in the years when these mountains were at their most romantic.

The country to east and west of the Adour valley below Bagnères is particularly good. On the western side, below the caves of Médous – discovered only in 1948 and spared, therefore, from the loss of their 'crystalline beauties' to the English vandals of the last century – there is a lovely quiet road along the valley of the Lesponne, an ideally leafy cul-de-sac, leading to the hamlet of Chiroulet close under the northern face of the Pic du Midi; from there you can walk up to another of the more visited Pyrenean lakes, the Lac Bleu (though this is a longish, moderately gruelling climb, involving an ascent of nearly 3,000 feet).

To the east of Bagnères is a really lovely piece of country, not to be ignored. It is known as the Baronnies and fills the top half of a triangle formed by the main roads which run south from Bagnères and from La Barthe-de-Neste and which cross the mountains to the south at the Col d'Aspin. You can get into the Baronnies very easily from the north, the east or the west, but not from the south, which is closed off by forests and by mountains. It is a blissful little region through which to coast, preferably without aim, along the serpentine country lanes which link one modest cluster of grey-roofed houses to the next. And because the Baronnies are full of deep valleys, the prospect keeps changing from near to far, with enormous views to the south when you are in some of the high places.

In short, the Baronnies are beautiful. But they are also depopulated. The roads and the settlements are there all right, as you can tell from looking at the map, but many of the people are not; they have left this blessed landscape for the towns, for Tarbes or for Toulouse. Here you come up against the problem of the modern Pyrenees. Young people do not want to live in them, when as often as not work means agriculture or nothing. Town jobs are easier and make more money, so it is off to the north and let the country go hang. In the Baronnies you can see where the country is going hang, and very pretty it looks of course, with wild flowers flourishing where there were once crops or grazing animals, and the woodlands taking over cleared hillsides. But it does no harm to remember while you are there *why* this is such graceful countryside. The depopulation has been frightening: between 1856 and 1975 the population of the Baronnies dropped from just over 10,000 to just under 3,000, and those who are left are not prosperous. On the other hand, here, as in other parts of the Pyrenees, those who are left are now being joined by others who have retired or who have bought a second home in the foothills. Some of the villages on the edge of the Baronnies look all too spruce, as if the locals had by now given way completely to immigrants wealthier than themselves, who are buying up the old houses and adding new, sometimes crassly intrusive ones. This process is not going to stop, so the time to plunge into the Baronnies is surely now, before they are reclaimed for the retirement bungalow.

Tarbes

North from Bagnères and still on the Adour is Tarbes, the chief town of Bigorre. I grant it here a section on its own, though I don't know that I like Tarbes very much, or would especially recommend anyone to go there. For a southern French town, still very much in the ambience of the Pyrenees, it is graceless, with less to show than it should have for its history as a local capital, having twice been laid waste in the sixteenth century by Protestant raiders. But Tarbes does at least have what must be one of provincial France's most charming parks, the Jardin Massey, which is on the north side of the town alongside the road for Bordeaux. It was created and then given to the town in the last century by Massey – first name, and how fittingly, Placide – who had previously been the gardener in charge of the orangery of Versailles and at the Jardin des Plantes in Paris. His garden in Tarbes has its orangery too, a small one, of wrought iron and glass, as well as some superb trees, both exotic and native. It has peacocks, which like to sit on the seats when visitors are scarce, a compound with a few docile wild animals in, a small lake, a free-standing part of a Gothic cloister from the ruined abbey of Saint-Sever-de-Rustan which was removed and re-erected here, and, if you can find them among the shrubbery, busts of two French poets, one of whom was born in the town while the other went to school here: the native was the arch-Romantic Théophile Gautier, whose bust in the Jardin Massey was sculpted by his exotic daughter Judith, the outsider Jules Laforgue, the strange, consumptive young poet who so influenced T. S. Eliot and died at twenty-seven. I scoured the greenery of the Jardin Massey unsuccessfully for signs of yet another literary genius with local connections: the bizarre Isidore Ducasse, alias the Comte de Lautréamont and author of the surreal *Chants de Maldoror*, who was born, like Laforgue, in Montevideo, but went to school in Tarbes and died even younger than Laforgue, at twenty-four.

Tarbes has done well by its poets then – indeed, there is a broad avenue in the middle of town named for Laforgue; it is more discreet, and understandably, about its one serious contribution to the political history of France, in the person of the peculiarly unprincipled Revolutionary terrorist, Bertrand Barrère, who, in the judgement of Macaulay, 'approached nearer than any person mentioned in history of fiction, whether man or devil, to the idea of consummate and universal depravity'. Barrère has not been admitted to the Jardin Massey in any form, but he does get a plaque on the house where he was born, in the same street as the genial Gautier.

There is a strong military side to Tarbes also. It was the birthplace as you soon find out of Marshal Foch, supreme commander on the western front in the later stages of the First World War, who has here an equestrian statue, a main street named after him and a small museum in the house where he was born in 1851. And in the Jardin Massey there is a museum tracing the history of the regiment of Hussars over the five centuries since its first formation in Hungary. Finally, you can also visit the extremely elegant First Empire stud-farm, in the middle of the town, where the Tarbais horses, ridden in the old days by French cavalrymen and today more often by tourists, have long been bred. These horses are part-Arab, part-Basque and part-English, the English blood having been mixed in on the orders of Napoleon I, while the Arab strain has been traced, perhaps fancifully, to the horses left behind by the Saracens, who were badly defeated near here in the eighth century.

But if it is military evidences that you are pursuing, then I would leave Tarbes and go instead to the splendid castle of

Montaner, a few miles to the north-west – not quite Pyrenean I will admit, but near enough and certainly good enough to be brought in here. This was commissioned by the thrustful chatelain of Pau, Gaston Phoebus, from his distinguished military architect, Sicord de Lordat; and was built some time in the 1370s. It is cited as the very type of contemporary fortification, the last fling of the traditional style before the onset of serious and effective artillery changed the rules of defensive building; and it makes today a magnificent as well as an instructive ruin. Montaner is simple, just a huge keep and a walled enclosure; this, in fact, is a regular polygon of twenty sides, though the angles are so gentle with that many sides that the feeling you have once you are inside is that it is circular. It was built largely from bricks baked on the spot, though because it was also built in haste the kilns, designed to produce 100,000 bricks a year, could not always keep up and instead of bricks the masons settled for stones in the upper part of the walls. The keep, which is 120 feet high, has been slowly and accurately restored in recent years, but the rest of the castle is a shell, with the outlines of the rooms that ran inwards from the walls alone visible and a single stairway up one of the buttresses on to the crumbling battlements.

Montaner was built to defend Gaston Phoebus's lands from attack from the north, and not against raids from the direction of the Pyrenees; so it seems to face towards Gascony. Its time of usefulness was relatively short, though it lasted as a fortress until 1621, when some local Protestants used it as their strongpoint in an attempted uprising against the new, official Catholicism of the region. The rising was put down and so was the castle, which then became a source of building materials, a man-made quarry. From 1627 almost to the French Revolution, what was left of it belonged to the local family of Montesquiou-d'Artagnan. The village of Artagnan, indeed, lies only a few miles from Montaner, to the north-east; and it was one of the seventeenth-century counts of this Artagnan whom Alexandre Dumas, once again, took and elevated into his fictional hero.

The Aure Valley

The high road linking the valley of the Adour to that of the Aure starts from the village of Sainte-Marie-de-Campan and crosses the Col d'Aspin. This col is not enormously high, at 5,000 feet, but the view which it gives you is the vastest and most satisfying of any Pyrenean pass that I know of. The col itself is a soft, open place of pasture, with, if you are lucky, more cows than people to share it with you. The view is more stunning yet if you take the trouble to climb up a little from the road, on to the grassy hill behind, so that you can see over the top of the slightly obtrusive forested spur to the south-west; or if you follow the path through the woods to the south of the road for about half an hour you come out on a crest which dominates the country in the direction of the watershed. Immediately to the west of the col is the Pic du Midi de Bigorre, then, to the left of that, the granite massif of Néouvielle, with beyond it the rim of the Cirque de Gavarnie, and the Monte Perdido on the Spanish side; and so on round to the south-east, in a wonderfully three-dimensional arrangement of crests and hollows.

Nearer to hand, you can also see steeply down 2,500 feet from the Col d'Aspin into the broad valley of the river Aure – the Neste d'Aure as it is called, *neste* here replacing *gave* as the local designation for a river. The road drops down from the col into the valley with an exhilarating suddenness and you are then in Arreau. This is a charming small town, or perhaps overgrown village, with just the right kind of simple hotels to tempt you to stop off here. It is a place of confluence, quite noisily so I imagine in winter or during the melting season, for rivers splash down into Arreau from east, west and south, at least four of them, with the Neste d'Aure here taking on more water for the journey north.

This fertile region, hollowed out and enriched so far as the soil is concerned by glaciation, was once known as the Pays des Quatre Vallées, and Arreau was its capital, being another of the

1 A typical *stèle discoïdale* or Basque gravestone (see page 34)
   Credit: Sandra Ott

2 A stone circle on the Sommet d'Okabe (see page 43)
Credit: Jacques Blot

3 The Brèche de Roland, above the Cirque of Gavarnie (see page 96)
Credit: Richard Waite

4   The Cirque of Lescun in the Aspe valley (see page 60)
    Credit: French Government Tourist Office

5   The fortified church of Luz in the Central Pyrenees (see page 92)
    Credit: Richard Waite

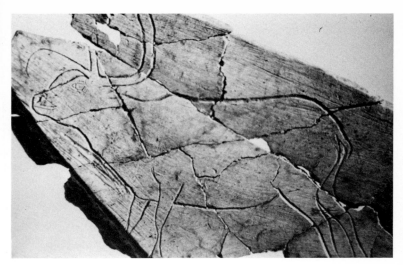

6   Reindeer engraved on bone, *c.* 15,000 BC
    Credit: Paul Bahn

7   Cave drawings at Niaux of similar age (see page 157)
    Credit: Jean Vertut

8   The 'Saracen' church of Planès in Cerdagne (see page 173)
    Credit: French Government Tourist Office

9   The cloister gallery at Serrabone in Roussillon (see page 193)
Credit: Paul Bahn

10   The fort of Salses, north of Perpignan (see page 215)
     Credit: French Government Tourist Office

11   The Cathar stronghold of Montségur (see page 164)
     Credit: SPADEM

small centres which flourished in the years when the trans-Pyrenean trade with Spain was at its height. It is not an architectural town, for it has no real monuments, bar a sixteenth-century house facing the vaulted market-building in the centre whose exposed timbers are carved all over with fleurs-de-lis. There is also a tiny eleventh-century chapel on the far bank of the Neste de Louron, the river that enters Arreau from the east and flows parallel with the main street; this chapel is admirable on the outside only, with a nice octagonal tower and a battered Romanesque portal. It is dedicated to St Exupère, a saint of Toulouse who began life in this valley as a ploughboy.

South from Arreau the main road runs along the wide valley of the Neste d'Aure to the resort town of Saint-Lary-Soulan, and then curves to the south-east as the valley narrows and the mountains get higher. There are a surprising number of villages between Arreau and Saint-Lary, but curiously, only the first of them, Cadéac, is on the river, all the others, on either side, standing somewhat back from it, towards the high ground, on terraces deposited there by the glacier. Cadéac, though you would never know to look at it, is in actuality a mini-spa, an example of the purely local spas you can find in the Pyrenees, whose reputation extends only through one valley and which attract as a consequence almost exclusively local people. The road out of the village, southwards, shrinks in a quite unforeseeable manner in order to pass under the porch of a small chapel; this could be distracting, and were something coming the other way lead perhaps to a rare collision on what is no doubt consecrated ground.

Saint-Lary-Soulan is a small resort, in summer and winter alike, an ancient Pyrenean village lost definitively to sight amidst the apartments, shops, hotels and other impositions of tourism. It is the place to go if you are staying in the valley and want a swimming-pool or a tennis-court, but hardly recommendable for anything more serious. The ski resort as such is not down in the valley at all, would that it were; rather, it is perched to devastatingly conspicuous effect on the side of a mountain to the west, up to which you can go either by car along a new road or by cable-car from the centre of Saint-Lary. By day or by night, when its lights so insolently interrupt what ought to be the dark solitude of the mountains, this extension of Saint-Lary is an offence; only when the weather closes in, and the clouds hang low, returning the high ledge on which it stands to a very satisfactory invisibility, is the valley's honour temporarily saved.

If the weather does close in in the Aure valley, and you crave sunlight, remember that Spain is close and that you can simply enough try the other side of the mountains. I have done this myself, to ideal effect, getting into the car on a sunless July morning and driving up to the road tunnel of Bielsa, some dozen miles beyond Saint-Lary. This is a lovely climb in itself, up what quite soon turns from a valley into a defile. To the left is Tramezaïgues, a hamlet said because of its position on a northern slope to get no sun at all for three months in the winter and from where a very bad road leads up through the pine forests to the Hospice de Rioumajou, and one of the numerous old mule tracks into Spain. At Fabian, three miles further on, a road turns off to the right up into the mountains: I shall come back to this in a moment. The road for the tunnel here bears off to the left and rises up along the glorious valley of Aragnouet, half pasture, half pine woods, past a road leading off to another new ski station, at Piau-Engaly. The tunnel is a novelty: three kilometres of roadway underneath the frontier ridge. It is new but it does not seem as yet to have taken on in terms of traffic. In the very middle of it you change countries and, more important, change climates. Entering on the French side still wrapped in cloud, you have a good chance of exiting on the Spanish side, as we did on the morning in question, in flawless sunshine and restorative heat. There could be no quicker way than this to appreciate how different things are climatically on the two sides of the mountains, because not only do you exchange cold cloud for sunshine but also the lush greenery of the high valleys to the north for the grassless, stony and, in summer, almost waterless river valley which leads on the Spanish side down to the small town of Bielsa (a little trippery, inevitably, but a place of some character).

At Fabian, as I have said, there is a road off to the west up into the massif of the Néouvielle, where you can get a terrific close-up view of some of the primary rocks of the Pyrenees, of the unadorned granite. There is nowhere better or, frankly, easier than this to see some of the high Pyrenean lakes, of which there are at least four that you can get to here by car, as well as a fifth reachable fairly simply on foot. The road up is a defile, steep, rugged and curvaceous, with a vast pine forest on the left hand. It brings you first to the Lac d'Orédon, which is a genial, pine-girt spot, and from which another, rather more dubious road leads off to the left up to the dam of Cap-de-Long. This is an artificial lake, the tremendous retaining wall of which you can see up above you well before you arrive there, blocking off the valley. The reservoir is a grim and comfortless place, flanked to north and west by the exceedingly severe Pic de Néouvielle and Pic Long – the Pic Long, 10,480 feet high, being the highest summit the entirety of which lies on the French side of the frontier. These giants have their permanent snows and scraps of glacier, and even by the reservoir, in late July, there are patches of grimy, left-over snow to be had. It is hard to imagine it ever turning quite summery up here. The other Néouvielle lakes are infinitely more hospitable. The Lac d'Aumar and its satellite, the Lac d'Aubert, which are on and up from the Lac d'Orédon, are somewhere to spend the day. Old guidebooks, I notice, call their site 'desolate' but that is most unfair, because although you are here at more than 7,000 feet there is a good deal of picnicable and even sleepable turf round about, a lake to fish in, and affable groups of horses browsing the summer away. You can see desolation but you are not part of it: the desolation being the rock and ice of the Pic de Néouvielle immediately at hand to the west. Indeed, clamber up through the rhododendron bushes to one of the crests beside the Lac d'Aumar and look over, and the landscape at once turns much harder and more hostile; you know then you are on the edge of the truly wild Pyrenees.

Comminges

Comminges was one of the lesser of the old Pyrenean counties, without the prestige or the influence of Bigorre or Foix-Béarn. It became French relatively early, in 1454. But long before that, the Romans dominated this region. On his way into Spain in 76 BC, Pompey annexed the valley of the river Garonne, which forms the main axis of Comminges, and four years later, on his way back from Spain, he founded at the northern end of it the city of Lugdunum Convenarum, where Saint-Bertrand-de-Comminges stands today. The name Comminges is taken to be a derivation from this name, of the Convenae, which the Romans gave to the local people whom they had brought together in their new *oppidum*.

The Luchon Valley

I shall come into Comminges, as ever, the high way, along the road which leaves Arreau in the Aure valley to the south-east and climbs up to the Col de Peyresourde. This stretch of inter-valley road was in fact the first to be created in the High Pyrenees, and was a major step forward in easing lateral communications in this difficult landscape. It was the idea of the great eighteenth-century administrator of the region, d'Étigny, an improver but even more a centralizer, who must have done more than anyone to undermine the old pattern of independence in the high mountains by thus making it easier for communities to mix. The Col de Peyresourde is relatively high, just over 5,000 feet, but the views are not so spectacular because the col is quite shut in and according to where you decide to stop, if you decide to stop at all, you can see freely in only one direction, back the way you have come, to the west, or on the way you are going, due east.

The pleasant valley which you drive down once over the top is that of the Larboust, which makes two serious demands on the tourist's attention before it reaches the flat, in the spa town of Bagnères-de-Luchon. The first of these is another of the classic lake walks of the Pyrenees, up to the Lac d'Oô. The Lac d'Oô is sometimes known by the alternative name of the Lac Seculéjo, which is not itself an easy word to say but for the nervous foreigner, horribly unsure how to achieve a recognizable pronunciation of such a short and alien word as Oô, circumflex and all, Seculéjo can seem preferable. Oô in fact is thought to be one of the numerous survivals among the place-names round here of the Ligurian influence in the Pyrenees, the Ligurians being an ancient people who either brought or sent their language in this direction from their homelands along the curve of the Mediterranean between Marseille and La Spezia.

The Lac d'Oô you get to by way of the village of the same name, along a lovely valley road, profoundly fertile because here too there is moraine from the glaciers, and lined alternately by trees and by cattle. The country grows more austere as it crosses what was once the floor of a mountain lake and the road comes to a dead end at the hamlet of the Granges d'Astau. From here it takes about an hour to climb up to the lake, gently enough for most of the time, through stone-strewn pastures, woods and then, more steeply, over rock, remarkable for the variegated lichens that colour it, black, olive-green and white. Off to the right from the path to the lake is another, up the small Val d'Esquierry, which has a reputation of being 'the botanical garden of the Pyrenees'. The lake is like nearly all its kind in the

Pyrenees, a hard, wild place rather than a beautiful one, with a tremendous waterfall at the far end, dropping 900 feet on to the rocks, and fed from a whole string of higher lakes still, to which there is a footpath. Behind the waterfall are the tough, glowering summits of the frontier, the Pic des Crabioules and the Pic Perdiguère, both of them over 10,000 feet.

The second thing to see on your way down from the Col de Peyresourde is actually beside the road, but it would still be easy enough to miss. This is the lovely village church of Saint-Aventin, about four miles before you come to Luchon. Saint-Aventin is a hillside village and no mistake, one part of it being above the road and rather more of it below. The setting, above a deep valley and looking across to the woods and grass slopes on the far side, is delectable, and because it is a most precipitous place to live Saint-Aventin is safer than most such villages from being rebuilt in a smarter, more up-to-date form by retired bourgeois.

The church is on the left of the road, up a ramp, and so hard against the side of the hill that on the north side the roof runs straight down to meet the ground, apparently because the builders decided to vault the church only once construction was under way – the eventual roof-line proved too much for the side windows of the nave, completely obscuring those on the northern side and partly covering even those on the open, valley side. But what you notice first about Saint-Aventin is its two towers, one short, one tall, and both beautiful. The short one, at the east end, is the earlier of the two and follows the ideal Romanesque pattern of having single windows lower down and then doubling them as you go up, with a slim column to divide them. The taller, western tower was built on later, as you can see if you examine the wall where it joins the main structure, which still carries the outline of an earlier gable. This tower has two storeys of windows, triple below and quadruple above.

Saint-Aventin is basically an eleventh-century building, and one of the truest of all examples of Pyrenean Romanesque. It is not large, being about eighty feet long in all, but if it seems larger

than you would expect, given the modesty of the village it
serves, that is because it houses the relics of its dedicatee saint,
Aventin. St Aventin was decapitated by the Saracens in the year
813 but then made his name by carrying his head posthumously
for 200 yards; his remains were discovered locally by a bull some
300 years later. This legend is illustrated, a little confusingly, in
the decoration of the church. On the capital to the right inside
the portal you can see the martyr being laid hold of by his infidel
enemies, one of whom is maimed – it was a popular device in
Romanesque days in south-west France to indicate moral
infirmity by means of a physical one. In the next scene Aventin
is holding his head in his hands; and finally, in a third episode of
the story, a helmeted soldier raises the same head, having just
cut it off. To the right of the portal, a rough but dramatic relief
has been cemented on to a buttress showing the bull, guided by
an angel, in the act of discovering the martyr's remains.

There are other decorations at Saint-Aventin: wall-paintings
at the east end which art historians have dated to the late twelfth
or early thirteenth century, but which were for long white-
washed over and are now barely comprehensible; a beautiful
early wrought-iron screen in front of the choir; a tympanum,
finely preserved because it is in some hard stone, showing a
Christ in Majesty, surrounded by the symbols of the evangelists;
a very powerful enthroned Virgin and Child carved from marble
and fixed to the wall to the right of the entrance to the church; a
holy-water basin engagingly sculpted with fish, birds and other
motifs; and lastly, something that you soon find out is a
commonplace in medieval churches in this region, the recycling
in a new building of bits and pieces from older ones – thus
Saint-Aventin has, built into its outside walls, several fragments
from Gallo-Roman structures: altars or funeral stones, very
simply engraved.

The town of Luchon, or Bagnères-de-Luchon to give it in
full, at the foot of the road down from the Col de Peyresourde,
is by some distance the most chic of Pyrenean spas, as well as

being the most profoundly embedded in the mountain chain itself, a few miles only from the watershed and massively overlooked by peaks to the south, not least by the highest of all the Pyrenees, the Maladeta and the Pic d'Aneto (11,165 feet). There have been those who argued that Hannibal crossed this way, *en route* for Italy, though why he should have wanted to make things so hard for himself and his army by forcing the mountains at so high a point they do not explain. Certainly, the Romans liked Luchon, which is generally taken to be the site of the Onesiorum Thermae, or baths of the Onesii, alluded to by Strabo. These were claimed to be the best baths of all after those of Naples. But they didn't survive the going of the Romans, declining into a bog, until they were rescued once and for all in the eighteenth century by the good works of the Baron d'Étigny, who gave his name to the broad and graceful avenue of lime trees, the Allées d'Étigny, that now leads from the centre of town southwards to the thermal quarter.

By the later years of the eighteenth century Luchon was already smart, even if its facilities were not always adjudged so. A visitor to it in the year 1787 was the celebrated Suffolk squire and agriculturist Arthur Young, who gives in his *Travels in France* an imposing list of the various aristocratic personages who were in Luchon taking the waters in the month of June, even if Young himself spent more time in the mountains round about, botanizing, mineralizing and admiring certain aspects of the local agriculture, such as its use of irrigation, rather than submit to the 'mortally insipid' parties given every day in the town. Modern bathing establishments were then only just being built, to replace the ones which Young describes so scathingly: 'The present baths are horrible holes; the patients lie up to their chins in hot sulphureous water, which, with the beastly dens they are placed in, one would think sufficient to cause as many distempers as they cure.' Since that time, Luchon has won itself an odd reputation for treating the respiratory system and specializing in those patients whose livelihoods depended on breathing well: this was the spa for orators, preachers, barristers, actors and singers, which suggests that it could have been an unusually vociferous place at the height of the season. The pride of the modern, grandly porticoed and very decorative bathhouse is a 'radio-vaporarium', constructed in 1932, which is a gallery of natural sauna baths hollowed out of the rock, in which the temperature varies between 38° and 48° Centigrade and where, presumably, the combination of steam and small doses of radioactivity will restore your lost eloquence.

If you are not cure-minded, then the attraction of Luchon is less in the palatial quarter, of baths, parks and great solid hotels at the far end of the Allées d'Étigny, than in the old town, which is mainly to the right of the road you come in on from Saint-Aventin. This is a plainer and more intimate setting, especially pleasant to go into on a Saturday, when the market is there, for Luchon's market is very superior. It is a fine place to buy food and a fine place to buy also the promise of good health, at a price some way below what you would pay down the luxury end of town, because it has an astonishing number of stalls selling herbal remedies. Here it was that I learnt that the dried leaves of passiflora, or the passion flower, are recommended for 'nerves and insomnia', and that hawthorn blossom is good for 'blood, anxiety, vertigo, and hot flushes'.

Out of Luchon to the south there are fine excursions you can make up into the mountains. You can follow the valley of the river Pique up what becomes a very steep road, to within a mile or so of the Hospice de France, the ancient meeting-place of no fewer than three tracks over the frontier, itself reachable now only by walking since an apparently immovable landslip has cut the road; or, by turning off to the right before the real gradient starts, you can take the alternative, thickly wooded valley of the Lys, a misnomer this as it turns out, because it is not the valley of the Lily as you might suppose but the valley of the avalanches, *lis* being the Gascon word for an avalanche. Along here there is a noble waterfall, the Cascade d'Enfer, which has an even nobler forebear half an hour's climb above it, known as the Cascade du Gouffre d'Enfer. The water comes down ultimately from the Lac du Portillon, high above the Lac d'Oô.

Off to the right of this valley road there is a turning for Superbagnères, the ski station of Luchon. Here, at 6,000 feet, is what could be the world's highest Grand Hôtel, a mighty stone palace which is, happily, entirely of the period when it was built, the early 1920s. In front of it, the ground has been cleared to provide what, when there is no snow around, looks uncomfortably like a vast parade-ground. The view *from* Superbagnères is quite magnificent, in every direction, though that is more than you might want to say for the view *of* Superbagnères should you happen to be on a different summit and hoping for the same prospect of an untenanted mountainscape. The now elderly Grand Hôtel is no longer alone, for the new *studios* and *chalets* are coming to join it. For a long time after the hotel was built there was no road to it, so you had either to walk up or take the rack-railway. But now the road is in place and well surfaced; indeed, in 1986, Superbagnères became the terminus for a day's racing in the Tour de France. A finishing-line on top of a mountain, after a ferocious six-kilometre ascent, may seem hard on the cyclists, but the awe-inspiring thing about that day's ride in the Tour was that it had already crossed three huge cols, the Tourmalet, the Aspin and the Peyresourde, before even getting to the foot of Superbagnères.

The Garonne Valley

To travel north from Luchon, there is a direct and an indirect route. The direct route, straight up the wooded valley of the Pique, is pleasant but a little functional. The indirect route is the more inspiring, and involves a short detour through Spain. At the bottom of the town of Luchon, on the east bank of the river, is a road leading up to the Col du Portillon. Just before it starts to climb, you leave France, or anyway pass through the French frontier post, though you have to wait until you have come down on the other side, in the next valley, officially to enter Spain. This is a brief and sylvan experience of extra-territoriality, for this col is all trees, showing you little or nothing by way of a view until you come out above the valley beyond.

This is the Val d'Aran, or upper valley of the river Garonne. The Garonne is one of the bigger rivers of France and takes an indecisive course from here to the sea at Bordeaux, first veering off north-east for Toulouse and then swinging around westwards, towards the Atlantic. The Val d'Aran starts over on the Spanish side of the mountains and is still Spanish at the point where you join it, coming down from the Col du Portillon. The border with France is in fact six miles to the north, at Pont-du-Roi. So this is a Spanish extension into territory you assume should be French, and far and away the most celebrated of such anomalies along the line of the Pyrenees. After having earlier belonged to the counts of Comminges, the Val d'Aran passed to the king of Aragon in the fourteenth century and has somehow never been repatriated by any of the adjustments subsequently made to the frontier. What is hard for the casual visitor to understand is how the river Garonne can apparently flow *over* the watershed at this point, from its source in the high lakes beyond. But of course it doesn't; rising where it does, the Garonne could have been tempted to flow away south, into Spain, but the lie of the land narrowly determined otherwise – so having begun by flowing more or less from east to west along its deep, glacial valley, it then turns to the north at Viella, and follows the lovely valley it has carved for itself down into France. And because their river moves in that direction, so the inhabitants of the Val d'Aran also have generally looked towards France, trading with it more than with Spain and speaking French, or at any rate a Gascon dialect, to this day. Though independence is what they have mostly been famous for; these are the archetypal Pyreneans, self-governing, jealous of their local customs and privileges, fearless smugglers.

In the sixteenth century the moral tone of the Val d'Aran had fallen to so low a point that Christian missionaries had to go in to try and improve things. But whatever their spiritual frailty, the people of the valley certainly did not lack for places of worship; for the Val d'Aran is a choice site for the Romanesque church-goer in the High Pyrenees, since you could if you wished make a slow progress towards its far end visiting a whole rosary of lovely small Romanesque or early Gothic village churches. To do that, however, is to stray into Spain. Let me make do here with what is perhaps the best and most typical of all the Val d'Aran churches, which is that in Bosost, the village that you come to immediately after joining the valley below the Col du Portillon. This is a beautifully uncomplicated basilica, with round pillars supporting the roof, and two pleasingly decorated portals, a quite elaborate one on the northern side, where a benedictory Christ in black marble in the tympanum is surrounded by the emblems of the evangelists and by a sun and moon, and a plainer one on the south, with a *chrisme* and some simple abstract motifs.

From Bosost there is no reason to stop again before re-entering France at Pont du Roi, and once into France no reason to stop before the village of Saint-Béat, 'the key to France' as it was grandly claimed to be by local strategists in the Middle Ages. Saint-Béat is well enough placed to defend its valley if not its country from attack from the south: in a defile, astride the Garonne, and squashed along a curve in the river between woods and escarpments. It is a village of austerity and some charm. The bridge which crosses the Garonne in the centre of Saint-Béat is made of marble, because marble is what this little region is famous for, and long has been – Trajan's Column in the Roman forum was made from marble quarried at Saint-Béat, in the hills to the west of the village, and many centuries after that the baths and statuary of the gardens of Versailles. My own memory of Saint-Béat for some reason is of a dramatized window display in the shop of a homoeopathic chemist, in which one marionnette was administering a narcotic draught to another presumably insomniac marionnette, who subsided instantly into rest.

In the vicinity of Saint-Béat you soon begin to notice village names ending in the ubiquitous -*ac* of south-western France – Marignac, Signac, Fronsac; evidence that this part of the Pyrenees is Gascon. Indeed, the Val d'Aran might be seen, if you were to turn it inside out, not as an extension of Spain into France, but as an extension of Gascony into the mountains. It is an extension on a very narrow front: administratively, this is the department of the Haute-Garonne, but there are points where that department is no more than a few kilometres across and where it looks to be in danger of being strangled by one or other of its neighbours to right and left, the Ariège or the Hautes-Pyrénées.

The Garonne makes its sharp turn eastwards at the small town of Montréjeau, where it also joins forces with the Neste d'Aure, arriving from the west. Montréjeau is another former *bastide*, or medieval strongpoint, though much less recognizably so today in the layout of its streets than other such creations. It has a fine situation, forward on the spur of a hill above the meeting-place of the two rivers and from the lower end of the town the view of the mountains to the south is incomparable. But Montréjeau is a very ordinary place, unable to live up architecturally to its scenery. At most, have a meal there, in clear weather and in the restaurant of the Hôtel Leclerc, on the left of the road as you enter Montréjeau from the south: the windows look out to the High Pyrenees and you may never again eat with a view like this.

Saint-Bertrand-de-Comminges and Gargas

These two remarkable sites call for a section on their own. They are utterly different from one another, but, as it chances, close together. Both are places which it would be absurd to miss if you are anywhere within reach of them.

Saint-Bertrand-de-Comminges is one of the great religious buildings of the Pyrenees, memorable both outside and in. As you come to it, in a wide valley a little to the south of Montréjeau, it makes a most beautiful and commanding sight, a tall, strongly buttressed, hilltop church which quite dominates the tiny village it is in. Beyond it rise complicated sequences of foothills, densely wooded, to make the church's setting seem almost Tuscan. Saint-Bertrand-de-Comminges's Italian connection is, as I have already mentioned, real, because this was the site of the substantial Roman town of Lugdunum Convenarum, which, in its most expansive days, has been credited with a population of some 50,000. Among these, according to the Jewish historian Josephus, were Herod Antipas, Tetrarch of Galilee, and his unpleasant wife Herodias, mother of Salome, who were exiled here by the Emperor Caligula – a suspiciously charitable sentence, you might conclude, given what a charmed spot it is.

Not all the population of Lugdunum Convenarum fitted on the small hill where the village now stands, and the Roman town spread down into the plain, where large sections of it have been excavated – its outlines you can readily follow on the ground: a forum, a temple, baths, a basilica. Early in the fifth century, the desirable residence of Lugdunum Convenarum was devastated by the Vandals, though the upper town, on the hill, survived for nearly two centuries more, until it became involved in a civil war between Frankish chieftains and was laid waste in the year 585 by Guntram, King of Burgundy. The site then dropped clean out of history.

It was revived only at the end of the eleventh century as a religious centre, by Bertrand de l'Isle, an aristocratic canon of the cathedral of Toulouse and a reformer, who was made Bishop of Comminges in 1073 and began work on the existing cathedral. Bertrand was canonized at the start of the thirteenth century, and the town then took his name, to become a place of pilgrimage. As such, its popularity meant that the original church of Bertrand was not large enough, so during the fourteenth century what had been quite a small Romanesque building became a substantial Gothic one, under the inspiration of the current Bishop of Comminges, Clément de Goth, later, as Clement V, to be the first of the Avignon popes during the Great Schism of the Church. Later still, in the sixteenth century, another enlightened bishop, Jean de Mauléon, transformed the interior of the building by commissioning the extraordinary Renaissance decoration that it contains today.

So three ages of architecture are richly and most persuasively fused in the church of Saint-Bertrand-de-Comminges. What remains of the early Romanesque church is at the west end: the narthex and lower parts of the walls; the tower (raised after it was first built and fitted with a wooden hoarding, for defensive needs); the portal, which has a fine tympanum representing the Adoration of the Magi with an unusually prominent episcopal figure shown full-face to the right of the Virgin – commonly identified as Bertrand, but as yet unhaloed because he was sculpted before his canonization was complete; and pre-eminently, the cloister on the south side of the nave. The cloister of Saint-Bertrand is perfect: nowhere could be more benignly soothing or aesthetically compelling than this. As a structure it is eccentric, and all the more beautiful, for being unlike orthodox cloisters and open to the outside world on one side, the south; this side is also the rampart of the citadel of which the cathedral is part, and through the wide embrasures of the cloister you look straight across at the hills or up and down the wooded valleys of the nascent Pyrenees. Such a prospect can have done meditative monks no harm.

The cloister is not all of the same age. The oldest of the four galleries is that on the west side, or to the right as you come into the cloister, where the capitals above the twinned columns that support the arcades have the most ambitious sculptures. On this side is the extraordinary 'Pillar of the Evangelists', where the pattern of twin columns is interrupted by a single antique pillar which has been sculpted on all four sides into standing figures of the four Evangelists, with above them a capital, barely readable alas through erosion, showing the signs of the zodiac and activities proper to the various months of the year. Others of the capitals along this western side of the cloister are better preserved, and most endearing: of an owl with its small prey underfoot, or a pair of horses being led by the bridle. The south and east galleries were made or else remade later, but are still perfectly harmonious. The fourth or northern gallery, against the nave of the church, is later still, Gothic in style, with pointed stone vaulting instead of the carpentered roof of the other three galleries, and with ancient sarcophagi set into niches in the wall.

Inside, the cathedral is far taller than you are ready for, and more crowded. The nave indeed is massively occupied by the choir, which is wholly enclosed and must fill a good third of the space between the entrance door and the chapels of the apse. It is like some inner citadel, being made entirely out of dark wood, and standing ornately out against the pale, plain stone of the walls. For this choir, commissioned by the sixteenth-century Bishop Jean de Mauléon, is one of the glories of French Renaissance woodworking. The carving is far too varied and extensive to begin to describe it, but it is at its richest on the choir-stalls themselves, sixty-six of them in all, where there are carvings above each canonical seat, carvings between the seats, carvings on the panels that divide the seats, carvings even underneath the seats, which tip up to reveal heads and other fanciful motifs. The subjects are not by any means all sacred ones, but, this being the Renaissance, mythological or profane also. The episcopal throne is astonishing: tall and fantastic, a three-storeyed pyramid with a wonderful inlaid back to the seat showing St Bertrand with St John the Baptist (the very saint whose tormentors and murderers are said by Josephus to have been exiled here). This choir is both wonderful and exhausting, if you try to itemize its splendours. Its size, relative to that part of the nave towards the entrance where the congregation had to congregate, suggests that the chapter of Saint-Bertrand was none too democratic in its forms of worship, since the space that remains is almost cramped. The screen that faces into the nave is as luxuriantly carved as the rest of the choir, with an ambo or pulpit in the centre and a triumphal arch behind it. But once you are outside here, and in the open so to speak, there is an alternative focus for the eye to the choir, which is a truly spectacular organ set at an angle across the south-west corner of the nave. Jean de Mauléon was behind the making of this mighty instrument too, whose architecture is riotous, supported on five fluted columns, bristling with small turrets, and carved with scenes of everyday life as well as with the Labours of Hercules. Musically, the organ is said to be as tremendous as it looks, and in summer, when Saint-Bertrand-de-Comminges has a music festival, a recital on it would be an event to go out of your way for – the complete audio-visual experience.

The walled village of Saint-Bertrand-de-Comminges is itself a pleasure to wander in. It has some fine old house fronts, one or two explicitly dated to the sixteenth century, two narrow fortified gateways, and a tiny terrace park looking out northwards with an old pergola and Gallo-Roman slabs and columns lying artlessly about. And – congenial thought – there is, more or less opposite the cathedral and only half a minute's walk from its inviting cloister, a single, creepered and unassuming hotel.

A mile away from Saint-Bertrand, down the valley to the east and beyond the Roman remains, there is another church of some moment, that of Saint-Just, which stands on its own amidst cypresses a little outside the village of Valcabrère. This was started some time in the eleventh century and finally consecrated in the year 1200. It is a very attractively casual building, especially in the use the builders have made in it of the old stones that were lying to hand. For there is good evidence that where the church of Saint-Just now stands there had for centuries been

a Christian burial ground, with a ready provision consequently
marble and of ancient sarcophagi waiting to be pirated by
resourceful and irreverent medieval masons. The apse of the
church seems to have been made entirely of such second-hand
materials, but it is strange for another reason too, as you can see
by looking at it from outside, where it has been given a series of
five deep, arched recesses of different heights and forms – the
general effect, of tiled roofs, windows, columns and round arches
is utterly engaging.

Inside the church there are other charming examples of
recycling, especially where the round arches over the entrance to
the little side-apses come down on to old columns, three of them
Merovingian (i.e. Frankish) in date and one Roman; or the two
holy-water stoups, hollowed out from late Roman capitals and
standing on antique columns. On the west wall of the nave there
is a Christian funeral inscription found in the ancient burial
ground, dated 347 and marking the place of burial of one Valeria
Severa and of a priest called Patroclus. The portal has a
tympanum of Christ in Majesty, and four saints sculpted on either
side of the doorway, the two outside ones being the dedicatees of
the church, St Just and St Pasteur. They were martyred in Spain
early in the fourth century and their respective punishments,
flagellation in the one case and decapitation in the other, are
recorded in the decoration of the capitals above their heads.

The caves of Gargas are in a hillside some two miles to the
north-west of Saint-Bertrand and are quite out of the ordinary –
along with those of Niaux the most out of the ordinary of all the
prehistoric sites in the Pyrenees which are actually open to
visitors. They were discovered, according to one earlier English
writer on the region, S. Baring-Gould, in a very weird fashion; I
give the gist of his lengthy and sensational account in his 1907
Book of the Pyrenees, though I have found no other sources to back
him up. Baring-Gould would have it that in the 1780s the district
was terrorized by a feral being who lay in wait to murder
milkmaids and other fragile passers-by, and who then either ate

them on the spot or bore them off to his unknown hideout. In the end this unlikely cannibal was caught, tried and executed, found guilty of an estimated eighty murders. His hideout, needless to say, was the caves of Gargas, of which, perversely, Baring-Gould has relatively little to say, finding them tame compared with the iniquities of the local 'werewolf'.

Perhaps the legend of Gargas has something to do with the contents of the caves, which were certainly inhabited 20,000 years or more before the date in question and contained, among other signs of occupation, bones both human and animal. They contained too the signs that have more recently given the caves of Gargas their celebrity among prehistorians, which is the large number of outlined hands to be found there on the walls and in some of the recesses. These prehistoric hands are not unique but at Gargas they are to be seen in quantity, more than 200 of them, 'negative' hands in the sense that the outlines were made by holding a hand up close against the surface of the rock and then going round it in red ochre or in black, colouring matters produced from the ferrous oxide and manganese to be found here. The hands themselves are curious and poignant enough, as decoration and as memorials of the human occupation of Gargas; what makes them additionally so is the fact that nearly all of them give an impression of mutilation, lacking one or even two joints from one or more fingers. Why this should be the case is uncertain. The two main theories advanced to explain it are that it might have been the effect either of a ritual amputation, performed as a token of mourning, or of some affliction such as frostbite, brought on by living through an Ice Age; but a more modern and reasonable theory is that the fingers were not amputated at all, merely 'suppressed' by being bent away from the wall so as not to show up in the outline of the hand. But why, then, should they have been bent away? The nicest answer to this further difficulty, given by the great French specialist in palaeolithic art, André Leroi-Gourhan, is that the hands so displayed might represent signs in a code used by hunters to communicate silently among themselves about their prey, since such a code is still used today by South African Bushmen. But whatever their symbolism, because these millenary impressions were made by real human hands at a particular moment in time, they are extraordinarily affecting.

Gargas also has some notable cave art from the early 'archaic' period, of animals engraved on the rock walls, sometimes solo and sometimes superimposed, in a confusion of lines for which, again, prehistorians do not quite know the reason, beyond supposing that cave artists lacked sufficient flat places on which to work or sufficient room to work in, so that they were forced to draw on top of the work of their predecessors. Nearly, though happily not quite all, the examples of cave art in Gargas, however, have to be shown only in the form of transparencies, still inside the caves but well away from the originals. For palaeolithic art cannot survive too many visitors; the light and heat generated by tourists alters the micro-climate in the caves and could, in the case of engravings, cover them in fungus, quite apart from what happens when people start longing to touch what they can see.

Saint-Gaudens

If the modern Comminges has a capital, then Saint-Gaudens is it. This is another ancient settlement which has borne its present name, that of a child martyr victimized by the Visigoths in the fifth century, only since the 1200s. It is a town set prominently up above the by now decidedly broad valley of the Garonne, which here flows due east, as if more minded to make for the warm Mediterranean rather than the chill Atlantic. Saint-Gaudens is a bigger, busier and more attractive town than nearby Montréjeau, though very similarly positioned, looking south to the high Pyrenees, and proud therefore of the boulevards that run for a mile or more on this propitious southern side. But there is a flaw in the panorama, as you soon see when you sit to have a drink in the best-placed cafés in Saint-Gaudens, which are on a terrace beside the church: on the far side of the valley, outlined against the wooded foothills, is the cellulose factory which brings jobs and money to the Saint-Gaudinois but a fair amount of sluggish malodorous smoke to those who live downwind of it, to the east.

But this is an unashamedly mercantile town, with a Thursday market that is about the most comprehensive of its kind I have ever seen, filling every open space in the centre of town and along the southern esplanades. The central townscape of Saint-Gaudens is dominated by the very powerful church, built mainly of a somewhat yellow stone though with patches of Pyrenean pink sandstone at the tower end. This is a tall, dark building, much rebuilt, having suffered as so many churches did locally at the hands of the infamous Montgomery in the Wars of Religion. It is still being rebuilt, or was on my last sight of it, in 1987, when some one and a quarter wings of a cloister had been reconstructed on the south side. The capitals high up inside the church are impressive, but they look too new to be altogether genuine, and have in fact been energetically over-restored.

While I am in Saint-Gaudens, I shall add here two other celebrated prehistoric sites to go with Gargas: Aurignac and Montmaurin. These are both to the north-east of Saint-Gaudens and therefore honorary, rather than authentic inclusions in a book on the Pyrenees.

Aurignac is a very simple, stone-built village on top of a hill which has given its name to an entire period of prehistoric culture, the Aurignacian, occupying the 10,000 years from very roughly 30,000 to 20,000 BP (Before Present). The Aurignacian was born you might say on a day in 1852, when a local workman unearthed a burial site containing human remains beneath a rock. It was thought at first to be just one more relic of the murderous religious wars of the sixteenth century, and the bones were reinterred in the local cemetery. It was another eight years before a celebrated palaeontologist of the day, Édouard Lartet, came to Aurignac and made the discoveries there of flints and carved bones which launched the whole redating and reunderstanding of Upper Palaeolithic culture. There is a little museum devoted to local prehistory at Aurignac, though you will be lucky to find it open. Indeed, this is a torpid village, resting on the laurels it earned 20,000 years ago. The church right at the top of it is intriguing, though: dull inside but possessing a most peculiar porch, with four wreathed columns, the oldest in existence it seems, which were moved here from a church demolished during the Revolution; these have capitals that are hexagonal on one side and cubic on the other.

Montmaurin is closer to being due north of Saint-Gaudens and has a historical as well as a prehistoric interest. A little way below the village is the site of an extremely luxurious Gallo-Roman villa, a marble palace of the fourth century AD, which itself replaced an earlier villa at the centre of a large Roman estate. The ground-plan of some 200 rooms has been cleared, and evidence found of patrician high living, such as numbers of ancient oyster-shells.

In the gorge of the little river Save nearby, meanwhile, several prehistoric rock shelters have been discovered and excavated. In one of them was found the tiny statuette known as the '*Vénus de Lespugue*' (Lespugue is the village near the eastern end of the gorge). This is carved out of ivory (from a mammoth-tusk) and is only fourteen centimetres high. It is a bulbous, large-breasted figurine, just the shape one would expect or want a fertility symbol to be. And in a cave near here, in 1949, a human jaw was found which is very early indeed: dated to between 300,000 and 400,000 years old.

Montmaurin, like Aurignac, has its mini-museum, of just two rooms; in one room there is a model of the palatial Gallo-Roman villa, together with some of the finds made there, in the other there are prehistoric bits and pieces, including a replica of the steatopygous Venus, the original of which is in the Musée de l'Homme in Paris.

Couserans

Couserans is no doubt the most obscure division of the Pyrenees yet, closely associated with Comminges in the old days yet claiming also, as a viscounty and a bishopric, the degree of separateness which I have accorded it here. This central Pyrenean region was in Roman times that of the people called Consorani, whence Couserans today. It has been known also as the 'land of the eighteen valleys', which is a fair indication both of what the landscape is like and also of the difficulty of describing it in any coherent fashion. But the main valley of Couserans is that of the river Salat and its main town, which is on the Salat, is Saint-Girons.

In order to get from Comminges into Couserans I shall go back to Saint-Béat, in the upper valley of the Garonne. From there a road goes due east, climbing quickly up through the grey-roofed village of Boutx to the Col de Mente, which is not far short of 5,000 feet. Twice, it so happens, I have driven over this col and twice in impenetrable cloud, so if there are views to be seen I have not seen them. I doubt, though, whether there are, because the road is almost entirely through forests on the western side of the col and still wooded at the top.

On the further side, the road drops sharply into the steep and rocky valley of the river Ger. Here it meets up with another road which you might equally well take out of the Garonne valley, a lower road but a pretty one, which passes over the Col d'Ares. Between these two roads is the large, forested hump of the Pic de Cagire (6,250 feet), another of the medium-sized peaks which stand apart from the main line of high mountains and so acquire for themselves a local pre-eminence they could not otherwise hope for. The country off to the north here, towards Saint-Gaudens and the Garonne valley, is extremely pleasant in an unobtrusive way, deeply rural right up until the moment when the ground levels out near to the river.

There is now quite a climb up to the next col, the much more open Col de Portet d'Aspet, which is the entrance to the long, lateral valley of Bellongue. This valley starts ruggedly, with some very bare country to the north as you twist down to the first village, of Saint-Lary. Not until Orgibet, a mile or two further on, does the valley open out and become more domesticated. After Orgibet, and having already been through the village of Augirein, you come successively to such village-names as Illartein, Aucazein, Argein and finally Audressein. The suffix -*ein* is not usual for place-names in France, so a whole string of -*ein*s like this needs explaining. The best and most attractive explanation is that these are names dating back to before the coming of the Romans, to the second or first millennium BC and to the Iberic language, which may or may not have been the ancestor of modern Basque. If this is right, the Bellongue valley acquires a grand air of antiquity as you pass along it, as well as of stubborn resistance to Romanization.

It is a pretty but not a prosperous valley, for here again you come up against the blatant depopulation of the High Pyrenees. The department you have just entered indeed, that of Ariège, is the poorest and most grievously depopulated of all. This loss of people began well back in the nineteenth century and the modern view among local historians is that it may have started, paradoxically, by a sudden over-population, after a strong demographic upsurge in the eighteenth century led to villages and towns having more people in them than they could well support; especially after a serious potato famine in the 1850s. The figures they give are shocking: the districts of Saint-Girons and Foix, the two principal towns of the department, had twice the number of inhabitants in 1846 that they had in 1981. And Saint-Girons is still going down, its population having declined by nearly eight per cent between 1975 and 1982.

Just past Audressein, you can turn right or left: left for Saint-Girons, right for Castillon-en-Couserans and a fair proportion of the region's 'eighteen valleys', for the landscape to the south here is deeply wrinkled. But its attractiveness goes a little too closely with human defeat, for the villages are run-down and the countryside under-used. The village of Castillon itself spreads along the road and steeply up the hill to the east. On the top of this, as a token of more lively times, is an old fortified chapel, a remnant from one of the counts of Comminges's castles, which was knocked down by Richelieu in the seventeenth century. This is an odd building in fact, strikingly defensive on the side overlooking the valley, yet with a good Romanesque portal and apse, and yet another delightful bell-wall, housing three storeys of bells.

South of Castillon there are four negotiable valleys. Three of them are cul-de-sacs, because one of the most telling things about the mountain country east of the Val d'Aran is that here there are no roads over the top into Spain. As things stand, in fact, you would need to go right across to the Ariège valley, and to Ax-les-Thermes, to find the next trans-Pyrenean road, though they are always thinking of effecting new crossings and if you look at a current map, and note the places where rough roads or forest tracks reach up close to the frontier on one or both sides, you can predict where the frontier may well next be breached. But for now Couserans is shut off on its southern side, and that has helped to empty it. It has numbers of *ports*, or the high passes that were once the crossing-points for smugglers and for legitimate traders, but otherwise it is the complete fastness.

The best of Castillon's valleys, that of Bethmale, I leave for a moment; that does lead somewhere and I shall be following it.

The most westerly of the three cul-de-sac valleys is that which
goes to Sentein and, beyond Sentein, to Eylie. Sentein has some
small charm, as a shapely village held tight in the grip of darkly
forested hills and with a once fortified small church at its heart;
but both as a village and as a would-be resort it is not doing too
well. Eylie, five kilometres beyond it, to the south, is doing
even worse, because this is a tiny ghost town. It was, you are
surprised to find, a mining community – a reminder that at one
time, and even into the present century, this part of the Pyrenees
was a mining centre. Above all, it was iron that they found and
extracted here: 'Sire, the Ariège produces men and iron,' a local
soldier is held to have told the Emperor Napoleon. But there are
other minerals too in these valleys and mountains: more than
6,000 feet up and not far from Sentein, a mine producing lead
and zinc was opened in 1850; it closed just over a century later
and with its loss the valley died too.

The Bethmale valley, which runs south-east from Castillon,
up to the considerable Col de la Core, has likewise seen a
wretched exodus of its population in the past 100 years. Long
famous for its folklore, and in particular the bold and eccentric
costume which the locals like to wear at their festivities, this is
now a half-deserted place. Bethmale is an extraordinarily
beautiful valley, one of the most beautiful anywhere in the
Pyrenees. It climbs to start with past the hillside villages of
Arrein, Samortein and Ayet, and thereafter through countryside
thick only with barns, of which these valleys have extraordinary
numbers and where families once would move up from the
villages to live during the quite short summer. To the right,
above the trees, are the peaks of the frontier, the largest and
lordliest of them Mont Valier (9,400 feet). Before you reach the
Col de la Core, there is, a few minutes' walk from the road up a
woodland path to the right, the exquisite little Lac de Bethmale,
an ideal place, of green, quite shallow water ringed only by
beech trees and a few outnumbered pines. The fishing is good,
they say, in the lake; but even if it weren't, what a matchless spot

to cast your line in vain. Beyond it is the Col de la Core, high enough for the beech trees, in late May, to be still brown with winter or only partly greened, as evidence of what we lowlanders forget, that the seasons have a vertical dimension to them, and that the spring needs time to reach the heights.

The Bethmale road descends extremely attractively from the Col de la Core into the village of Seix, on the Salat. But for the present I shall leave it, to go back to Castillon and from there to Saint-Girons, the main town of Couserans. This is not in any way a memorable town, but it is a centre, and I have stayed there happily enough in my own passages along the Pyrenees. What it has is water: the basin of Saint-Girons is where the Salat is joined by lesser streams from east and west, and Saint-Girons itself is a river town, having grown, a little shapelessly, around the confluence. In spring and early summer, when the rivers are full, the Salat in particular makes a fine noise as it splashes over its weirs. For some strange reason Saint-Girons doesn't have an entry in the invaluable green Michelin guide to the Pyrenees – which I hope is an oversight and not spite (perhaps later editions than mine have restored it).

Architecturally, Saint-Girons is overshadowed by having the glories of Saint-Lizier only a mile away down the valley. Saint-Girons first rose as a town indeed because the far older foundation of Saint-Lizier fell; the two go together, and now historic Saint-Lizier provides modern Saint-Girons with its only monuments and its chief interest. Saint-Lizier is a hillside town, originally under the Romans the Lugdunum Consoranorum, or city of the Consorani, some of whose third-century ramparts remain on the hill at the top of the town. Its history under the Visigoths and Franks who followed the Romans here is uncertain, but presumably violent. What is sure is that in 1130 the then Count of Comminges, angry at the (traditional) opposition to his authority offered by the bishop, seized and sacked Saint-Lizier and carried its inhabitants off to create what is now Saint-Girons. So Saint-Girons began as the medieval equivalent of an overspill town and Saint-Lizier entered on to a protracted decline, its temporal prestige forever lost.

Saint-Lizier can never have been a large place, but it had two cathedrals – a duplication not unheard-of elsewhere, but rare. It is not clear how or exactly when it happened in this instance. However, it is the lower of these two churches, on the hillside below the old walls, and not the much remodelled, relatively modest upper one, within the Roman precinct, which is the glory of Saint-Lizier and one of the finest of Pyrenean Romanesque buildings. (Ecclesiastically speaking, the two cathedrals were merged into one in the 1650s, though the bishopric itself was not abolished until the Revolution.) It was begun in the eleventh century and if you look at the very shapely east end from the square in front of the church you can soon see that it was built providently, in the true fashion of the time, by re-using where possible older stones that already lay to hand in this well-established site – not least two pieces from a very elegant frieze which have been built in high up the walls. The church went on being added to, both before and after its consecration in 1117. The single nave, as you can't help noticing, is distinctly bent rather than being at right-angles to the transept. The vaulting came later, between the twelfth and fifteenth centuries, while the extremely handsome octagonal brick tower, in the style established by the great church of Saint-Sernin in Toulouse, was an addition of the early thirteenth century. The sculptures of the capitals are somewhat primitive and worn, but quite recent restoration of the church has uncovered extensive wall-paintings in the apse and the choir, as well as in the left-hand side-apse. The subjects of them are hard indeed to make out because they are in a poor state. But there were two rows of paintings one above the other: in an upper row between the arches are the Apostles, two by two, with, beneath them, a frieze and scenes of, on the left, the Magi, and on the right the Annunciation and the Visitation. These decorations have now been dated to the first years of the twelth century, just before the church's consecration. On the ceiling of the apse and the choir is a painting of Christ in Majesty, done late in the same century when the vaulting was added.

Saint-Lizier also has a magnificent cloister, on the south side, a two-storey one, though the upper level was added only much later, in the sixteenth century, to the original Romanesque structure. The marble columns supporting the arches alternate between single and double, with a bundle of four no less in the centre of the gallery on the western side. The capitals are pleasing without being spectacular, the best of them to be seen on the northern side nearest to the church. These date to the later part of the twelfth century and contain only one religious subject among the floral and animal motifs, that of Adam and Eve. The other galleries seem to have been imitated, none too gracefully, from the earliest, northern one – a disappointing process of degeneration which you get used to in studying the decoration of these Romanesque cloisters in the eastern half of the Pyrenees. Just when the artistry of the sculptors ought, you would think, to be getting more assured and inventive, by building on the past, it fails, and has eventually to give way to a later, Gothic style.

What is left of the old town of Saint-Lizier, between the lower church and the citadel above, is a complex of good, decorative house fronts, alleyways or vaulted passageways, and one or two deep arcades beneath the houses. The upper cathedral and the pompous, seventeenth-century bishop's palace that swamps it – this was used as a lunatic asylum up until 1969 – are not open to visitors, nor by all accounts very interesting. When you leave Saint-Lizier, you can, instead of simply going back down the hill to the river and the valley road into Saint-Girons, take a small road due east, to the curious little village of Montjoie, two miles away. This is an old walled village of the fourteenth century, no longer quite contained within its original limits but not greatly expanded beyond them either. The ring wall has two small towers on the side you arrive at and two entrance gates. And the fortified church in the centre of Montjoie has a façade to treasure, with twin turrets and twin layers of crenellations, as well as a fine bell-wall. A building which was long ago intended to look martial now looks engagingly fantastic.

North of Saint-Girons as we temporarily are, I shall here signal the one other remarkable site that lies in this general direction: the caves of Le Mas d'Azil, to the north-east. This is one of the greatest of prehistoric sites in the Pyrenees, a cave system hollowed out in the limestone of the Plantaurel. The Plantaurel themselves form a very distinct ridge of high hills, going up to 2,000 feet, which is a true horizontal 'fold' in the terrain, parallel, as such folds ought to be, to the main ridge of the Pyrenees further south. The 'Little Pyrenees' the Plantaurel are sometimes called, and they are usually taken as marking the northern limit of the real mountains.

At Le Mas d'Azil you do not have actually to enter the caves or even to go underground to be vastly impressed. For before you come to the caves as such there is the tunnel; and what a tunnel – a giant passage created by aeons of persistence on the part of the river Arize, which here burrows clean through the hillside. The entrance to this opening is awesome, being some 200 feet high. Into it flows the river that first created it, to emerge a full quarter of a mile further on, on the northern side of this dorsal ridge of the Plantaurel. Its passage is the more dramatic for being curved, so that you can see into the tunnel from either end, but not through it. On the right bank of the river, if you come to Le Mas d'Azil from the south, there runs the road, for which a separate opening has had to be cut in the rock wall but which then curves off also into this astonishing cavern. Towards half-way, the space widens hugely out and there is a great rock pillar, thirty feet across, to support the roof (and the 500 feet of rock and earth above it); then the passage contracts again, to a width of no more than thirty or forty feet. And where you come out, at the foot of a sheer cliff, the roof is only twenty-five feet above your head.

After this, an actual visit to the caves, or 'cavities' as they are advertised, may seem a let-down. The entrance to them is half-way through the tunnel, at a point wide enough for a car park to have been made. The guided tour, however, is superficial or even silly, in so far as these caves have been fitted with, of all monstrosities, Muzak. The engravings and paintings which Le Mas d'Azil contains cannot be shown for the usual sad reason, that to show them would in the end ruin them. But the finest items found at Le Mas d'Azil in any case have been examples of 'mobiliary art' from the Magdalenian or subsequent 'Azilian' period (after 15,000 BP); that is, art of the movable kind as opposed to wall art: engraved or carved fragments of bone and antler, and a speciality of this site, flat pebbles from the river-bed decorated with dabs of red colouring. Many of these finds are now in museums elsewhere but some are shown in glass cases in the caves themselves, including a reproduction of one of the most esteemed of all discoveries at Le Mas d'Azil, a sculpture of the head of a neighing horse. There is also a small museum in the village of Le Mas d'Azil, which has more prehistoric tools and artefacts, and is well worth visiting to see the 'spear-thrower', an antler carved wittily into the shape of a fawn which is looking over its shoulder at a large emergent turd with a pair of birds perched on it.

Although there is one rather touching moment in the tour of the caves where you can look down on an ossuary of cave-bear bones, the bears having perished there in numbers as the consequence of a flood, these are in fact abnormally dry caves, because the water from above cannot penetrate the thickness of the clay. Being so dry, and so accessible, they have served in their time as a popular refuge for those with reason to hide themselves away. They may have been used by early Christians, in the still Roman third century AD; and they were certainly used by French Protestants, both during the religious wars of the sixteenth century and during the persecution of Protestantism in the century following. Then, a vindictive Cardinal Richelieu altered their internal layout radically, with explosives, after Huguenots had been found hiding there. The village of Le Mas d'Azil, indeed, just north of the caves, was always a staunchly Protestant place and its name, respelt with an *s* instead of a *z*, as Mas d'Asile, reveals it as a place commemorated for offering asylum to the persecuted.

There are other great prehistoric caves in this area, but none that you can visit. I mention just one, that of Les Trois-Frères, near the hamlet of Montesquieu-Avantès, so called for the good reason that it was found by three brothers. This has some of the finest cave art in Europe, but it remains private, for scholars alone. Its celebrity is the 'sorcerer', one of several such presences in Les Trois-Frères: a horned figure 75 centimetres long, both engraved and painted, with a human body and legs, but also with a tail, antlers and wearing a bearded mask. The presumption is that a part of these caves was set aside as the scene for some unknown ritual.

To the south and south-east of Saint-Girons, the land is all valleys once again, pretty, remote and – the sorry motif of this region – economically unsound. The road into this very Pyrenean country leaves Saint-Girons along the river, through the gorges of Ribaouto – though if you should drive back again into the town by this route note that there is a one-way road on the opposite, right bank of the Salat which passes through a series of rock tunnels. Up to the left, or to the east, just here is an especially fine valley, that of the Nert. So intensely pastoral is it today, it is hard to credit that this valley was once the focus of the local mining industry and astonishingly rich in raw materials: copper, iron, manganese, three shades of marble and other things besides have been extracted here. No doubt there are traces if you know where to look of the abandoned workings, but these certainly aren't obvious and you can travel unknowing up an uninterruptedly rural valley. At the eastern end there is a big climb, up to the Col de Rille, where you find out how thoroughly forested this massif is. At the crossroads near the col is a memorial to some of those, including Spaniards, who fought and died up here for the Resistance during the German occupation. The vegetation is not that of the much bushier *maquis* of the Mediterranean coasts from which the Resistance derived its early name, but it is propitious enough all the same for the actions of guerrillas with the thickness of its cover.

At the southern end of the Gorges de Ribaouto, the road divides. To the left is Massat, the ancient capital of Couserans, and the road I shall shortly follow eastwards, into the valley of the Ariège. To the right are the villages of Seix and Oust, where again you have a choice of valleys. Beyond Seix you can go on towards the frontier, down the tight valley of the seething, though by now diminished, river Salat to Couflens. This is a shut-in and cheerless place with, beyond it, France's one and only tungsten mine, at Salau, opened in the 1960s and very productive; and for once an agency for the partial revival of what would otherwise have been a typically neglected valley. It is a cul-de-sac, because the little road which goes out of Couflens up to the Col de Pause and the frontier stops there (there is a sort of road which comes up almost to meet it on the Spanish side; so this could well be the point where the next trans-Pyrenean road is made, even if it would join nowhere very much to nowhere very much). As yet, the way up to the Col de Pause is both very rough and extremely steep; it is also, one is assured, and I say 'assured' because I did not myself have the stomach for it, very scenic.

At Pont de la Taule, a little north of Couflens, a road starts up the exceedingly pleasant valley of Ustou, which is wider and more pastoral than that of the Salat: a place of sheep. In the eighteenth century this valley had its own local aristocracy and was famous for the intensity of the class war – the class war has been a strong speciality of this part of France, whose traditions have ever been radical: Ariège was the one department in all France whose representatives voted unanimously for the guillotining of King Louis XVI in 1793.

The valley of Oust ends majestically on the Col de Latrape, where almost without expecting it you are elevated to abundant views of the mountains to the south. On the far side of the col is the small and struggling spa of Aulus-les-Bains, where the Romans, as usual, seem to have been the first to take the waters. Aulus became a spa for a second time in the heyday of the cure, in the 1850s, but it barely functions as one today, even though the installations are still in place. The most picturesque fact about this forgotten small resort, however, is that it, together with the nearby communities of Ustou and Ercé, was at one time known as the place where the trainers and exhibitors of bears came from. Whether the unfortunate bears were ones caught locally – the bear population of the mountains being then much greater than the tiny rump now thought to have survived – I do not know; but the people of Aulus were scorned by their enemies as being of a level of culture no higher than that of the animals they specialized in. And when they emigrated, they specialized again, by working mainly in New York hotels, which is an oddly metropolitan connection to bring to mind in this bucolic spot.

From Aulus you can turn back towards Saint-Girons, along the Garbet valley to Ercé and then Oust again, or continue eastwards, over the Col d'Agnès and down to the Étang de Lers, a smallish, moderately comely lake at the foot of the Pic de Montbéas. This for tourists is the single most visited spot in the department of Ariège, its trout and its pedalos clearly appealing to the Ariégeois. At the Étang there is a small road northwards, for Massat, or you can carry on over the very scenic Port de Lers. Beyond that is Vicdessos and the Ariège valley; but they belong to Foix, not to Couserans, so at the Port de Lers I shall for the present stop.

Foix

Foix is the name both of a town and of a *pays* or region. The town of Foix is the capital of the modern department of Ariège, named from the river which flows through the middle of it; the *pays de Foix* is the region once covered by the ancient medieval fief of this name (except that old Foix extended also into Spain). Foix was one of the more splendid and aggressive of the feudal counties of the south-west, and its counts were constantly in action, mainly in war. Early in the thirteenth century, they were vassals of the greatest power in southern France, the counts of Toulouse, and became much caught up in the politico-religious wars of the Albigensian heretics (of which more in due course). In 1229, Count Roger-Bernard, who had supported the heretics, submitted, as haughtily as he was able, to the King of France and thereafter the power of the Foix counts was reduced. At the end of that century, in 1290, they inherited the counties of Béarn and Bigorre, and chose thereafter to have their capital in the west, at Pau. Foix became part of France, along with Béarn, in 1607.

The town of Foix

But first to get there. The main road from Saint-Girons is very ordinary; you can do better than that. The mountain route, through Aulus and Vicdessos, is as spectacular as it is tortuous, but it takes time. Here, I shall compromise, and take the middle

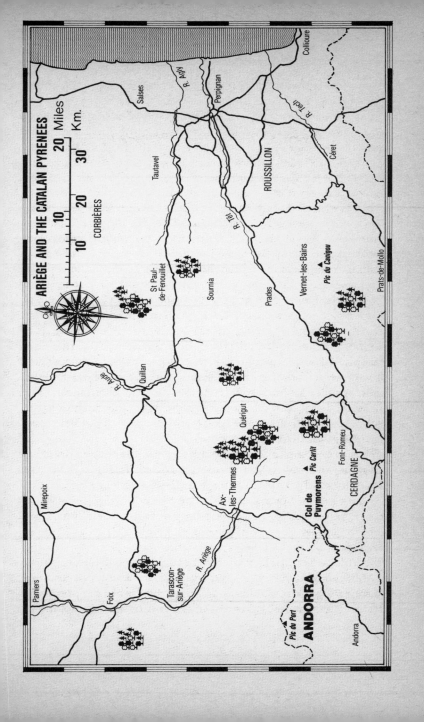

route, via Massat and over the Col de Port, which is quicker but almost as commendable for its scenery as the higher roads to the south. To start with, it is nearly all thickly wooded gorges, first those of the Salat and then, once you have turned off for Massat, those of the river Arac. Eventually, at the village of Biert, the Arac valley broadens out. Massat itself is old, but unremarkable. The road beyond it is quite a twister, up first to the Col des Caougnous and then to the higher and exhilarating Col de Port (4,150 feet). At the Col des Caougnous a road goes off to the north which takes you a particularly beautiful way to Foix: this is the Route Verte and has huge views to both north and south. But the snow hangs around on these crests and this road may well be closed until early June. Should it be so, the Col de Port is good enough in all conscience, with magnificent views back towards the massif of Mont Valier to the south-west. This col is frequently declared to be the cardinal point of the Pyrenees, where an Atlantic regime gives way to a Mediterranean one. It is a smooth, grazable spot (in the spring, at any rate) and for that reason alone you would say that this was still an Atlantic climate. But looking down from the col to the east, the landscape does indeed seem barer and more Mediterranean. Yet as the road descends, the same healthy vegetation takes charge again, so that all you have so far got is a hint of the drier and much warmer places to come.

This road comes out in the Ariège valley just above Tarascon, but rather than dwell there I shall pass downstream to Foix – by the minor road on the left bank of the river, incidentally, and not the crowded and unpleasant N20 opposite. Foix is the place to stay in in this valley, a romantic and rewarding town in its own right and easily got out of when you want to tour. It stands in the valley of the Ariège a little above the point where the powerful glacier that shaped this landscape came to a halt. North of Foix the land very quickly becomes flat, as you can find out by travelling the few miles to Pamiers. South of Foix you enter instantly into the real Pyrenees and from your hotel room, if you have chosen it carefully, you may well be able to look south to the high peaks of the frontier, where now, on the far side, you have not Spain but Andorra (a half-share in which, together with the bishops of Urgel in Spain, was once part of the counts of Foix's fiefdom, before it passed to the French crown). You don't have to be a strategist to understand why Foix is where it is, at the entrance to, or exit from the mountains; and the advantages once prized by its warrior counts and traders are advantages now to the tourist.

The castle of Foix is what you are sure to remember of the town, whether you have stayed in Foix or not. It stands high on a rock in the north-west corner, above the point where the small river Arget joins the Ariège. This is a stronghold all right, though it appears that Foix castle was never in fact called upon to defend itself. Some guidebooks speak of a siege in 1272, when the King of France, Philip the Bold, conceived a scheme, bold even by his lights, to reduce the place by the elementary method of chipping away at the rock it stands on with pickaxes, but this, one is not surprised to learn from the guide who shows you round the castle, is a historical fantasy, because that particular tiff between the king and the count was settled diplomatically downstream at Pamiers, without a single pickaxe being swung in anger.

To call the castle of Foix a castle is perhaps to exaggerate, because all it really is is three splendid and conspicuous towers. The long building which joins two of the towers together dates only from the 1820s. These towers are all three of them different, in architectural terms: the most northerly is the oldest, built in the twelfth century, square in shape, with a steep slate roof and a small openwork belfry above the crenellations; the middle tower is also square, a bit taller than that to the north, and with a single corner turret; the third tower, or keep, is round and handsome, and is attributed, inevitably, to Gaston Phoebus, a resident in Pau but still the count of Foix, who may indeed have planned it though it was quite certainly built some time after his death.

Partly in this tower, and partly in the building between the other two, Foix has its small museum. The best I can say of it is that it is mildly interesting. It has a prehistoric section, dominated necessarily by pieces from the skeleton of a mammoth found near Foix when the railway was being constructed in the last century; furniture – in the form of one of those demented room-settings which have been made to contain an example of everything ever made in the local style; weapons; and metalwork, in tribute to the industrial history of the Ariège valley. There are relics too of the long period when the castle acted as a prison, handily placed as it is straight above the departmental courts of justice. The convicts it was who built the arduous stone path you need to follow up on to the castle rock from the street below, and who also, cruelly, may have been made to build the law courts themselves.

If the firmly geometrical layout of the old *bastides* be taken as some kind of local norm for medieval town planning, then Foix must go down as an *anti-bastide*, because the old town is a most heart-warming confusion of narrow streets which go to great pains not to meet at right-angles. It forms a triangle, between the two rivers and the broad Cours Gabriel Fauré to the south – Fauré is fortunate to be so generously commemorated here, for he was a native son not of Foix but of Pamiers. Properly sequestered on the far side of the Cours are the pompous administrative buildings put up in the last century, including the most formidably comfortless *lycée* I have ever seen. This new part of Foix may be ignored, but the old part is a pleasure to walk and to shop in, especially such streets as the Rue de la Faurie, near the start of which there is a wonderful Renaissance doorway in wood that now makes an irresistible entrance to a furniture shop.

The church of Foix is large and for the most part Gothic of the fourteenth century, though there are red brick portions of the earlier Romanesque building still to be seen on the south side below the Gothic stone, as well as evidence of defence-mindedness in this traditionally heretical town in the powerful tower that rises above the porch at the west end and the walkway created below the roof-line around the strongly buttressed and arcaded apse. Facing the church at the tower end there is a remarkable seventeenth-century neo-classical house front, with two storeys of paired columns of different orders and then a third storey of caryatids. This is delightfully out of place in medieval Foix.

Immediately to the west of Foix is a very pleasant country region known as the Barguillère. Geologically it is unusual, a more or less circular granite basin that has been formed between the ridge of the Plantaurel to the north and the high mountains and forests of the Arize massif to the south. For all its evident fertility, it is not much cultivated. But towards the end of the nineteenth century, the Barguillère had a certain celebrity as a centre of the nail-making industry, with more than 700 nailsmiths at work in what one imagines to have been the very noisy setting of such small villages as Ganac, only three miles from Foix. That industry slowly went but nowadays, understandably, the Barguillère is being colonized from Foix and from towns further away, such as Toulouse, as a gentle and accessible rural landscape. Here is yet another place in the Pyrenees to apply the test: count how many houses have all their shutters closed. Those that have are sure to be holiday homes, the retreat of an absentee bourgeois. Nail-making may have been a noisy business, but it will have brought more life to the Barguillère than its new colonists.

Leaving Foix to the north, there are, as so often in France, two roads, one either side of the river. It is not hard to see from the map which to prefer: the small road on the left bank, as against the juggernaut-infested N20 on the right. The first village you come to along here is Vernajoul, which has a tiny, rather nice, and certainly very simple Romanesque church (though with one or two crass later additions), a church so small as to be almost dwarfed by the admittedly monstrous family tombs in its graveyard. Out of Vernajoul to the west a country road leads to the underground river of Labouiche, where you can go subterranean boating along two and a half kilometres of waterway, through galleries and chambers, and past stalagmites and stalactites. In the cave-rich Ariège this is too much like frivolity; I have not been to Labouiche.

A short way north of Vernajoul and astride the river is the village of Saint-Jean-de-Verges, which marks the spot where the Foix glacier finally stopped. It has a very good church, where the local Romanesque is at its most straightforward and appealing. It was in this church, in 1229, that the rebellious and heretical Count Roger-Bernard made his submission to the Crown. The fact that he had been allowed to make it on his own lands was a concession, but when he later travelled to Paris to ratify it he found himself handing over his castle in Foix for the next five years to the formidable Queen-Regent, Blanche of Castile, in return for a royal pension.

It is stretching things to call Pamiers a Pyrenean town, but it is close enough to Foix to demand admittance here. In Pamiers you feel you have come out on to the plain; from here all the way to Toulouse, you are on the flat. This a bigger town than Foix, memorable architecturally chiefly for the astounding brick façade of the church of Notre-Dame-du-Camp. The church behind it is nondescript, mainly seventeenth and eighteenth century; but the façade is overpowering, immensely tall and with powerful buttresses at the sides, as well as turrets and crenellations. If there were only a good church to go with it, Pamiers might have a building to equal the cathedral of Albi. The town suffered heavily in the Wars of Religion and the one really good feature of the cathedral is its fine octagonal tower and the fortified porch beneath it, which are survivors from an earlier structure destroyed by Calvinists.

Pamiers is scarcely worth going out of your way for. But a little to the east of it, *en route* for Mirepoix, is something you should see: the rock-church of Vals. This is a beautiful oddity, a church built into as well as on top of a massive hump of rock. The way into it is by a flight of twenty-three steps which curve off in semi-darkness up a quite narrow fissure in the pudding-stone. These lead into an obscure nave of rough masonry; a nave that is referred to as the crypt, though it isn't one. It has been carved out of the rock and has small chapels running off either side of it whose effect is of cellars; this is the oldest part of the building and some of it must have formed part, the church's most recent historians argue, of a pre-Romanesque church so constructed as barely to rise above the surface of the rock. At the far end of this almost underground nave, up a few steps, is the second level of this extraordinary church: the apse, where it is suddenly light and where the vaulting is covered with damaged but in parts fairly legible murals (they were found only in 1956). Turn about, go up some more steps, and you are in another, higher nave, restored and raised in the last century. Beyond this, and higher still, this small building has yet a fourth storey, in the form of a delightful little Romanesque chapel of the twelfth century set at right-angles to the nave below. Above this chapel is a tower, added later as a part of the fortifications which the church needed during the wars and raids of the fourteenth century. Originally, this upper chapel stood alone, unconnected with the church, and it may have been for defensive reasons again that the two were made into one, since in the wall that was added to unify them there is a door leading on to a tiny terrace outside. As a whole, the church of Vals is irresistible, much more than quaint, and layered like an archaeological site.

Mirepoix, to the east of Vals, is another medieval *bastide* and good to see if only for its central square, which is a delight, surrounded as it still is by its fourteenth- and fifteenth-century *couverts* or projecting first floors, on their robust sustaining timbers. The nearby Gothic cathedral is rather fine, and its single nave has the abnormality, although it takes a moment or two to realize it once you are inside, of being wider than it is high. To return from Mirepoix to Foix, it would be a crime not to rely on some of the small, leisurely country roads that take you up into the admirable landscapes of the Plantaurel.

The Ariège Valley

South of Foix, the valley of the Ariège is a jagged place, whose pale limestone has been famously hollowed out into caves and used in times of persecution as a centre of refuge. Past the isolated and distinctive 'sugar-loaf' peak of Montgaillard, the valley contracts, before spreading out again at Tarascon, where other waters from the mountains round about have combined with those of the Ariège to create a basin. Tarascon's full name, which will distinguish it from the better known Tarascon in Provence, is Tarascon-sur-Ariège. It is a beautifully placed town, in its rocky depression, and a fine centre from which to go off visiting caves; but as a town it has far less to offer than Foix. The old part of Tarascon is on the hill to the east, where there is a good but dilapidated old square in front of the (featureless) church, which you might have expected them to make more of. And on top of a rock is an old medieval tower, which is all that is left of the castle of Tarascon, demolished as so many of them were in the seventeenth century on the orders of that prime scourge of provincial strongholds, Cardinal Richelieu. But vitality in Tarascon has migrated down from the original hill and on to the flat, by the river, where there are several factories, producing such things as aluminium. In fact, this was once a more industrialized town than it is today, because up until the early 1930s it had blast furnaces – the last to survive from the once considerable Pyrenean iron industry.

The caves, however, are the thing here. A little way to the west of Tarascon, on the road down from the Col de Port which I have already described, is Bédeilhac, a cave so vast that during the Second World War the occupying Germans equipped it as an aircraft factory. And inside there is a stalagmite of suitably generous proportions: 400 feet round, it has been measured to be. Bédeilhac also has paintings and engravings of animals (some done on the floor of the cave) from the Magdalenian period.

Just outside Tarascon on the other side, to the south-east, is another cave system of great size, that of Lombrives. This has a central chamber 300 feet high known as 'the Cathedral', for Lombrives's interest is not prehistoric but historical; some of the human remains that have been found here, in a place evidently used – there are many inscriptions and graffiti to prove it – over many centuries as a refuge, were said to have been those of a large number of Albigensian or Catharist heretics who were immured here along with their bishop by the Inquisition in 1328 and starved themselves to death rather than give up their faith. This, if true, would have been a very late act of defiance and self-sacrifice on the part of the Cathars, who by that time had been persecuted almost out of existence. The story is given its plausibility, however, by the proximity of the caves of Lombrives to Montségur, the supreme and legendary Catharist stronghold – to which I shall be coming in a moment.

Bédeilhac and Lombrives, however, are as nothing compared with the caves of Niaux, the entrance to which is in the hillside some two and a half miles south-east of Tarascon off the road to Vicdessos – this is in fact a modern way into the caves, punched through recently from a vast rock-shelter and replacing the original modest opening in the hillside. The cave art which you can see at Niaux is, for me, the single most remarkable experience you can have as a visitor to the Pyrenees. Indeed, now that the cave of Lascaux in the Dordogne has been closed to public view, as a victim of its own popularity, nowhere else in France, nor I dare say in Europe, can you look directly on prehistoric art of such tremendous accomplishment as at Niaux.

This is a place for tourists but it is not touristy. It has kept, praise be, its dignity and even its loneliness; Niaux is a serious spectacle, and not like rather too many underground sites in the

Pyrenees, a jaunt. Indeed, you cannot just turn up at Niaux and hope to be immediately taken round; you need to book ahead (either by telephone or by going to the caves and putting your name down). For the reason these caves are still open to visitors, when Lascaux for example has had to be closed, is that the numbers of people allowed into them at any one time or on any one day have been kept carefully down, so that the art will not suffer the pollution of heat and of light. Thus, in parties of never more than twenty at once, and lit only by the hand-lamps issued to you at the start, you are guided directly to the great Salon Noir of Niaux, where the finest paintings are.

The Salon Noir is some 800 relatively easy if at times slithery yards from the entrance to the caves, a distance that prehistorians have puzzled over, since this was a long way for palaeolithic artists to go in order to paint pictures on walls. At Niaux, however, the artists could and did go even deeper than this into the hillside, since engravings, footprints and painted signs have been found at points in the system of galleries beyond the Salon Noir. But it is reasonable to suppose that a chamber like this was a place apart, decorated for some deep religious or ritual purpose, far away from the profanities of the open air. This supposition is made the more real when, at Niaux, you are made to turn off your lamp before being shown the pictures by the light of a single hand-held torch, not so very different in its effect perhaps from the illumination the artists themselves must have got from their grease-lamps (examples of which have been found in other decorated caves).

The paintings which are shown are on four distinct panels of smooth rock, polished by glaciation; so inviting a surface does this rock offer that it brought back to my mind the delightful fancy of the French writer Georges Bataille, who proposed that palaeolithic draughtsmen were actually the first graffito-artists, who could not find a flat, vacant surface in their caves without feeling the urge to violate it. The animals portrayed at Niaux are mainly bison and horses, with just a few ibex and a single deer.

Some of the drawings, especially the smaller ones, are simply black outlines, others have broader outlines and thick shading or hatching to show the hair (see Plate 7). As so often, there is a certain amount of superimposition, with one drawing done on top of others. It is the horses above all that stand out, for their stunning naturalism. They have been claimed to belong to a breed, now extinct, of Przewalski's Horse, and associated, whether fancifully or not, with a well-known breed of small horses raised and still to be found at the village of Mérens, higher up the valley of the Ariège. Something like a quarter of the seventy-one animal figures to be found at Niaux (not all of them are shown) bear a V-sign in their flanks to indicate a wound, and so support the old idea that this art had to do with sympathetic magic, that its subjects were the familiar prey of the palaeolithic hunters and that the higher the degree of realism the artists could achieve in their depiction the greater the hunters' chances of future successes would be. On the other hand, this unusual prevalence of animals with wounds seems to have been a speciality local to the Pyrenees, so one could just as well conclude that it has to do with aesthetics, or with a local style of cave art, rather than with the propitiation of nature. In any case, the mysteriousness and beauty of this underground wall art are absolute, and exceed all the arguments, however seductive, advanced to explain what it is doing there.

Beyond the village of Niaux the road presses on into the splendid mountain country of Vicdessos, where numerous side roads serve the small villages perched high on the northern shoulder of the valley – the sunny side that is, always the better populated and cultivated in the mountains. On the southern, shady side is the best known of all the old iron-mines of Ariège, that of Rancié, which was producing up to 30,000 tons of ore a year early in the nineteenth century and was famous also for being run by the miners themselves, as a workers' co-operative as we would now want to call it, owned indivisibly by the eight communes of the valley rather as if it were not a mineral deposit but a pasture. The valley which runs off south from Rancié towards the Port de Siguer on the frontier is another of the ancient trading and smuggling routes which, because of its relative ease, was frequently taken during the Second World War by some of the 50,000 French people and others estimated to have escaped by way of the Pyrenees into the Iberian peninsula. Such made-up roads as lead south from Vicdessos, towards the bulky Pic Montcalm (10,150 feet) and other peaks along the frontier, do not lead south for very long, because all of them are cul-de-sacs. But if you want to lose yourself for the day on some remote height, then they are just the thing.

I shall turn back now to the Ariège valley, and to Tarascon. From Tarascon the valley and the main road run south-east, towards Ax-les-Thermes. However, if you are not pressed for time, there is a far more secluded and spectacular way of travelling in this same direction. It starts two miles to the north of Tarascon, at the village of Bompas, where you can turn off up the valley of the Arnive and go through the village of the same name on to the splendid Route des Corniches. This runs at altitude along the western flank of the massif of Saint-Barthélemy, in a valley created by quite minor glaciers, 1,200 feet higher but more or less parallel with the major valley of the Ariège. This is the slow but sensible way to get to Ax-les-Thermes.

Some of the small villages through which you pass have fine attractions in them too. Axiat has a charming Romanesque church, while Lordat, just beyond it, has the ruins of its late medieval castle dramatically upraised on a rock – this was the native village of Sicord de Lordat, military architect to Gaston Phoebus and designer of the glorious brick keeps of Pau and of Montaner. At Vernaux there is another delightful little church, and at Unac – by now you are almost down in the Ariège valley – a third, good enough this time to stop and look. This is an eleventh-century building of stature, standing against a ledged hillside to the north and open to the west and to the valley of the Ariège. The tower is tall, bare and imposing, with four levels of apertures; and the apse has some lovely decoration around the windows. Inside, there are two unusually good capitals on either side of the entrance to the choir, sculpted with rosettes and with leaves, though the nave is tall here and they are not so easy to admire. There are signs of restoration having gone on at Unac, not all of it well-judged; the decoration of the choir is horrid.

In the mountains to the north of Unac is the enormous talc quarry of Trimouns, which is the largest and most successful industrial enterprise in the whole of Ariège, sending 300,000 tons of stone a year down the mountainside to Luzenac in the valley to be crushed. But being at the remarkable altitude that it is, of 6,200 feet, this is a quarry that has to close in the winter; in summer, however, you can visit it and see above all the bright seam of talc, produced at the crucial geological meeting-place of the schist and the granite. It is odd to think of something as soft as talc, destined maybe for application to the tender parts of babies, being torn or blasted originally from these relentless escarpments.

It is possible to remain on this lovely high road, and make your way down into Ax through Caussou and Tignac, or even from the Col de Marmare (where you could also turn directly away from Ax, and travel north). But Ax it shall now be. This is another spa known, it is claimed, to the Romans – the old spelling of its name, Acqs, makes it look much more like somewhere reputed for its A(c)quae or waters. Armies favoured it: Hannibal may or may not have sent wounded men here to be cured, but certainly in the Middle Ages French soldiers who had caught leprosy crusading in Palestine were sent here by King Louis IX – St Louis, that is – to be treated. Ax still functions as a spa, as the third most frequented spa in the Pyrenees indeed, after Luchon and Amélie-les-Bains. Like other small spas all over France, it recovered its clientele largely when it became possible for *curistes* to take the waters paid for by their health insurance. Ax is a modest town, neat without being smart, filled with hotels and 'residences' and possessing a florid casino as well as its neo-classical baths. On the hills round about are a few architectural reminders, in the shape of ambitious villas, of the late nineteenth and early twentieth centuries, when the *cure* really was the *cure*. Ax today is less restful than a spa town ought to be, placed as it is astride the main road from France into Andorra. In the summer especially, it has more of a throughput of visitors than a lasting input.

Two roads lead eastwards out of Ax, one of which goes somewhere and the other of which doesn't. The one which goes somewhere is that for the very high Port de Pailhères (6,600 feet), or else its neighbour to the north, the Col du Pradel, and then the Pays de Sault – magnificently rugged, forested high country that I shall save for my next section. The other road is much gentler, rising hardly at all as it follows the valley of Orlu beside the river Oriège. This is a lush but in human terms mainly empty valley, with high, steep sides and plenty of water running down into it – a good place to fish, by repute, either in the small lake of Orgeix near the start or in the Oriège itself. At the old Forge d'Orlu, at the far end, there is a magnificent waterfall, which drops 1,000 feet in three stages and is fed from the Lac de Naguilles up above. The waters of this lake have inevitably been tapped for power: they are brought by pipeline 3,000 precipitous feet down into the valley at Orlu – and that was once a world record in the hydroelectricity business. Up above the Lac de Naguilles is a higher and larger lake still, the Étang de Lanous, which is the most extensive in the Pyrenees. It is at a height of 7,000 feet and covers 220 acres; it is frozen over for anything up to eight months in the year but even more lavishly productive of kilowatts than the Lac de Naguilles.

Due south from Ax-les-Thermes the main road goes straight for Andorra, steadily up through the villages of Mérens, where the small black horses – now liable to be renamed '*poneys*' in the

English style, but an ancient breed none the less – come from, and of L'Hospitalet. By this time the gradients are getting stiff, and the country wild. But as well as a main road there is also a railway up here: the trans-Pyrenean line joining Toulouse to Barcelona, which goes higher than any other regular railway line in France, and is, as you can appreciate from following its escalade of these mountains, a noble work of engineering. Near L'Hospitalet it vanishes into a last tunnel beneath the Col de Puymorens, to reappear two or three miles further on, still in France but now in the valley of the river Carol, on the way to Puigcerdà and the Spanish frontier.

It would be a beautiful ride assuredly, to take the train from Ax, say as far as Puigcerdà; but very few people do take it and this bit of railway looks likely to follow other mountain lines into early retirement. And driving from Ax up to the Col de Puymorens, you soon learn why: everyone who wants to go up this way goes up by car. This is a busy road, and in summer or at weekends, a very busy road: high, steep near the top and through grand mountain landscapes, yet used with an awful urgency. The reason is Andorra, because there is only one way into Andorra from France and this is it. It is an extremely high way in, for you have to cross the Port d'Envalira and that is 8,000 feet up – an altitude that used to do for the radiators of cars, numbers of which you would see stopped, steaming with exhaustion, beside the road. But nowadays cars don't suffer as they once did and the visitors race easily up and over the Port, along a road so necessary to them that it is kept open all through the winter.

Nor I am afraid is it the natural beauties of Andorra that draw these people so; what they are on their way to is some duty-free shopping. For to many today Andorra is not its lonely pastures, peaks and Romanesque churches, but the entrepôts of cut-price goods and spreading holiday complexes along its axial valley, of Gran Valira. I do not propose to describe it in this guide. This is not to be dismissive of Andorra; rather, I don't see it as truly a part of the French Pyrenees. It is an independent 'principality' and as such a touching reminder of how the Pyrenees were once divided up and of how they ruled themselves in small, communally minded populations. But that must do; as far as I am concerned, Andorra is over the border.

So instead of joining in the rush up to the Port d'Envalira, I shall bear austerely left at the point beyond L'Hospitalet where the road divides and make instead for the lofty Col de Puymorens (6,300 feet). This is a very open spot with enormous winter snowfields. From here the road goes down the rocky valley of the river Carol to the south-east and out on to the remarkable plain of Cerdagne, a historic area which will get a chapter of its own.

Montségur and the Pays de Sault

'Nature, Prehistory, the Cathars', those are the three entice-ments the department of Ariège offers you as a tourist on its road signs. The Cathars means, mainly, Montségur, their celebrated mountain-top citadel, which is another place reached easily enough from Foix.

But something about the Cathars first, as southern heretics who are not much known about in Britain even though they made a few converts in England in the latter part of the twelfth century and a crusade was preached there against them. Even in France, it has to be said, they are a relatively modern interest, rediscovered after 600 years of neglect by the nineteenth-century Romantics. (Even so, my 1907 *Baedeker* guide to southern France makes no mention of Montségur whatsoever.) But radical as ever, Ariège is happy to be able to claim Catharism as a heroic episode of dissidence and independence of thought in the Middle Ages, though its main centres, with the remarkable exception of Montségur, were further to the north, in the Corbières, around Toulouse and across southern France into Italy.

Catharism was not originally French. It spread to southern France, as to other parts of Europe, from Bulgaria, and the Gnostic heresy of the Bogomils. The name 'cathars' meant 'the pure ones' and although no proper documentary record of Cathar doctrine has survived it is clear that it attracted converts or adherents through the rigour and seriousness of its beliefs in an age of slackness and decadence in the Catholic Church. Briefly, Cathars were dualists: they believed that the material world was the creation exclusively of the Devil and that Evil competed with Good in the world on equal terms. As material beings, men and women were evil; but though fallen and trapped in matter, they could be saved because they still had spiritual, God-provided souls. After 1150, in the southern part of France, the Cathars amounted to an alternative Church and a far more conspicuously devout one than official Catholicism; but their religious opposition to papal institutions became confused also with the political ambitions and warring of the late feudal overlords in Languedoc, in these years when the French crown in the north had as yet not extended its authority over such aristocrats as the counts of Toulouse. The Catharists were bloodily put down or hunted out, by a papal crusade declared by Pope Innocent III in 1208 and then by the apparatus of the Inquisition. Their story is a most depressing one.

The siege and 'massacre' of Montségur may have been its most dramatic moment, but it was not the most lethal nor was it absolutely conclusive, since so stubborn and widespread a heresy could not be suddenly silenced. There had been worse episodes of killing before Montségur, as at the sack of the town of Béziers by the Crusader army in 1209, or the siege and capture of the small town of Lavaur near Toulouse in 1211, when 400 Cathars were burnt alive. The villain of this campaign was the vicious and appalling Simon de Montfort, whose consequent violent death at the siege of Toulouse led his enemies to write a simple, joyful lyric to celebrate the fact that

Montfort
Es mort
Es mort
Es mort!

(This was not of course *our* Simon de Montfort, who led the barons of England against King Henry III, but his father.)

But to Montségur. It is the amazing setting of this fortress more than anything which has raised it to its symbolic place in the modern history of Catharism. To get to it most pleasantly from Foix take, not the main road to Lavelanet, which runs along the bottom of the Baure valley, but a smaller road, the D9, which stays high up on the northern slopes of the same valley. The views to the south are splendid and, by way of a trailer for Montségur, which is the ultimate in perched castles, you have the ruins of the castle of Roquefixade, high above the village of that name to the left – this is in fact the highest point (3,300 feet) along the forty-mile ridge of the Plantaurel. For Montségur you stay on this same road, the D9, which eventually crosses both the valley and the main road and moves off into the mountains to the south.

Looking at this castle, you cannot credit that it was once captured, for it is the most self-evidently impregnable site you have ever looked on; starved out, yes, but surely not capturable by force of arms. It stands on the narrow summit of an exceedingly steep, unfriendly mountain, at an altitude of almost exactly 4,000 feet. The climb up to it is a stiff and, once you have left the grass at the bottom for the stones of the mountainside, a rough one, a good half-hour long. A nice touch is that you don't have to pay until you are a third of the way up and already engaged on the hard part, by when you may be feeling like staying down below. But it is richly worth keeping going, to find out from close to what sort of place it was that the Cathars defended right through a harsh winter.

The castle itself is a shell (see Plate 11), much the same now as immediately after it was demolished by the successful besiegers of 1244, in accordance with the contemporary rules of warfare whereby the walls were reduced by half their height. Its position could not be more dominant, occupying a natural platform of rock on an isolated peak, and yet, as has been observed by historians of Montségur, it dominates nothing in particular: no trade or invasion route from over the Pyrenees, no river, no pass. Montségur appears a spectacular rather than a useful stronghold, almost as if it were intended as a landmark. So its erection here is a little mysterious and has given rise to ideas that it was perhaps more of a sacred than a defensive place. There are peculiarities in the architecture of the castle too: it is orientated by reference to the rising sun and has, or had, two gateways, one to the south and another to the north; and the main gateway, on the southern side, was unusual, far wider than is to be found in other medieval castles and without any defence works to protect it.

Inevitably then, Montségur has been seen as the centre of some ancient cult and its temporary occupation by the Cathars in the thirteenth century as simply perpetuating a much older tradition into medieval and Christian times; all of which has helped the case of those who would like Catharism to be some kind of mystery religion rather than a Christian heresy. The castle was in fact restored at the request of the Cathars in 1204, and that request was itself an indication presumably that to them this was already a propitious spot and a centre of pilgrimage. By the late 1230s it had become the headquarters of the heresy as a whole: its arsenal and also its treasury, since the Cathars, for all their unworldliness, were not a sect only of the under-privileged. Catharism had wealthy followers too, whose bequests to the Cathar 'Church' gave it a respectable income. To the Cathars' enemies, Montségur was known as 'the synagogue of Satan'.

The great siege, conducted by an army of those foreigners from the north, the 'French', began in May 1243. There were, at different times, anything up to 10,000 besiegers, but they were not able to stop all commerce with the castle from below; supplies and a few men got through to the garrison. Of troops and Cathars in the castle there were between 450 and 500: up to 150 soldiers, together with their families, and some 200 heretics. The soldiers were not all of them Cathars by conviction though some it seems were converted during the siege, impressed as so many outsiders commonly were by the extraordinary conviction and integrity of the sect. Once you are inside the ruins of the castle, such numbers seem impossible: how could so many people survive in so small a space for so long? Not all of them fitted inside the castle walls as it happens, because many of the Cathars lived in exposed wooden huts on the small patches of inhabitable terrain outside, where they survived through a whole autumn and a hard mountain winter.

In the end it was Basque mercenaries in the French service, famed and fearless climbers as they were, who made the breakthrough on to the platform of the summit that led to the castle being stormed and taken, though not until March 1244, after a siege of ten months. The terms of the surrender were generous, to the garrison, but the Cathars refused to recant and all 200 of them were led down the mountainside to the field at the bottom from where you start the climb up, which acquired on that day its sinister name of the Camp des Crémats, or 'Field of the Burnt Ones'. The 200 heretics were there burnt on what may well have been a single giant pyre. The only ones to avoid the massacre were three Cathars who, together with a guide, stayed hidden in a cave on the mountainside and, on the same day as their co-religionists were burnt, carried the sect's treasure to safety down below. There, according to contemporary evidence, it was successfully 'hidden in the forest'. It has never been found, and that has given birth to wild legends as to the wealth and 'secret' nature of the Cathar Church which do what was, by any reading of it, a selfless and idealistic sect no service at all. The Cathars survived the destruction of Montségur, but symbolically its capture was the end of their real hopes of defeating the official Church.

When at Montségur carry on through the village and on towards Bélesta. Off to the right, or east, is the Pays de Sault, an extensive, isolated and beautiful tract of high country divided into two on the south-eastern side by the deep canyon formed by the river Rébenty. The main road through this remote region runs from Quillan to Ax-les-Thermes, but you can get up into the Pays de Sault along minor roads from just about every direction. This is very much where the pine trees take over from the beeches: you are no longer in the department of Ariège now, but in that of Aude, and Aude is proud of its pines. Bélesta, should you come to it, has splendid pine forests, owned by the Rothschilds, though most local forests are, true to Pyrenean tradition, owned communally. Between Bélesta and Quillan stretches the ample and agreeable valley of Puivert, which ends with the descent, far steeper than you expect, into the dullish small town of Quillan.

The Pays de Sault is remote, but not as remote as it seemed to me when I first crossed it, early in the 1960s. Then, driving up out of Quillan towards Ax late one evening I was sure it was the loneliest and most elemental corner of France I had ever come to. It has been opened up since then, but not too much; it still has rather few people, tremendous pine forests, deep gorges and fine grasslands. On the northern side of the main road, there is a system of forest tracks and some grand places to go walking. The country is especially good at the south-western end of the plateau, near the festively named village of Comus, up from which you can walk to an astonishing viewpoint known as the Pas de l'Ours. There, from a tiny terrace built on the hillside, you can gaze 2,000 feet straight down into the stony Gorges de la Frau, wondering as always at the adhesiveness of trees and bushes on what look like vertical mountainsides. And a short way off to the north-west is Montségur.

On the other, southern side of the road, the country is equally fine, rising higher and becoming more mountainous beyond the Gorges du Rébenty. The equivalent of Comus on this side is certainly the most celebrated village in the Pyrenees and, one might even think, in the whole of France: Montaillou, about whose early fourteenth-century inhabitants the French historian Emmanuel Le Roy Ladurie published in 1975 an extraordinary book. In it he re-creates with wonderful fullness the way of life, the beliefs and the daily practices of a mountain community 650 years ago. Ladurie's book is based on the meticulous records of the searching and intimate inquiries made into Montaillou's affairs by the Bishop of Pamiers. This man, later pope in Avignon during the Great Schism, was a zealous searcher-out of heretics and Montaillou in the 1320s, eighty years after the fall of Montségur, was a remote mountain village where Catharism could still be practised. It was not only the religious lives of the villagers that the inquisitor probed, however, but their lives as a whole and it is their lives as a whole that Ladurie has reconstructed, most memorably.

Montaillou today is a sorry, half-deserted place. According to Ladurie, in the first half of the fourteenth century it and the neighbouring village of Prades would have had between them up to 300 inhabitants. Now Montaillou itself is down to twenty and is very visibly a dead community. It has not tried to make anything out of its literary celebrity, but then it is I fear better to read of the dynamism of fourteenth-century Montaillou than to see first-hand its inertia now. What I took away from its landscape was the sight of massed dandelions, of which this patchily cultivated plateau has the most luxuriant crops, brilliant, yellow acres of them.

Cerdagne and the Aude Valley

Modern Cerdagne is the region anciently lived in by the Ceretani, and already famous in Strabo's day for the excellence of its *charcuterie*. Given its high and handsome isolation, locked in by mountains, it became inevitably a place of asylum and of political independence during the disorderly centuries after the Arabs had been pushed back deeper into Spain. In the middle of the ninth century there were already eighty-four parishes in Cerdagne. By the tenth century it had its own counts, who ruled the valleys to the north and east, as well as part of Roussillon; but theirs was a brief dynasty and their county soon passed to the kings of Aragon. It has been French, all bar a bit of it, since the definitive Treaty of the Pyrenees, in 1659.

From whichever direction you come upon Cerdagne, it is a shock: a great boat-shaped depression, the French part of which, to the north-east, is twelve miles from end to end and about four miles across at the widest point – this is hardly something you expect to find at 4,000 feet. It is in fact the bed of an ancient lake, though by no means dead flat, as you soon learn if you take one of the little roads that cross it from one side to the other in its eastern half. There are high mountains both to the north, where the dominant presence is that of the Pic Carlit, and to the south, where the summit of Puigmal (*puig* is the Catalan word for 'peak') on the Spanish frontier matches the Pic Carlit almost foot for foot, both being close on 10,000 feet. Thus, shut in as it is, the plateau or basin of Cerdagne even *looks* like a refuge, and its medieval reputation for security has in this century been easily supplanted by a reputation for salubrity. Cerdagne has good air, and a great deal of sunshine.

Its river is the Segre, but the Segre takes its waters off not into France but into Spain; even the French portion of Cerdagne, you find, is on the southern side of the Pyrenean watershed. For a part of France this of course is wrong, but the fate of Cerdagne became tied in historically with that of Roussillon, as two Catalan territories that passed to and fro as bargaining counters between France and Spain. Even today, Cerdagne is not quite all French, because a small area around and including the old town of Llivia – once the Roman capital of the region – at the western end belongs to Spain. This is a real curiosity, for it is wholly enclosed in French territory. It is joined to the rest of Spain at the frontier post of Puigcerdà by a road which declares itself to be 'neutral' and which you are asked not to take unless you have genuine business in Llivia; whether sightseeing counts as genuine business I'm not sure, but Llivia is a characterful old town and worthy of a short visit. The oddity of its status goes back to the treaty of 1659. By this, Spain gave up to France thirty-three Cerdagne villages, but because Llivia was considered to be not a village but a town, it was excluded and has stayed Spanish ever since.

If you come into Cerdagne from the west, from the Col de Puymorens, it is at Latour-de-Carol that the mountains on either side start to withdraw and a couple of miles further on, at the village of Ur, the road divides. Here you need to decide whether to go along the north or the south side of the oval formed by French Cerdagne – though you can if you want drive all the way round it in under the hour. The northern side is known as the Soulane – that is, the sunny side – the southern, or shady side, as the Ombrée (in other parts of the Pyrenees the *ombrée* becomes the *ubac*). Cerdagne on its northern side has a great reputation for sunshine, claiming as many clear days in a year as Algiers. This record, together with the famed dryness of the mountain air, has led to the building-up of the resort town of Font-Romeu here, hard against the pine-covered slopes of the huge Forêt de Barres.

Font-Romeu is almost entirely a new town, and a high one, its altitude of 6,000 feet making it the highest resort in Europe at so southerly a latitude. Before it became a resort, it was a principal centre of pilgrimage for Catalans from Spain and France alike, the name Font-Romeu indeed meaning 'The Fountain of the Pilgrim'. What the pilgrims came for was a wooden statue of the Virgin, lost during the Arab invasions in the early Middle Ages and then miraculously rediscovered near the fountain by a persistent bull. The statue, which is not quite old enough to authenticate its legend, is kept on display in the Hermitage of Font-Romeu, except when it is carried solemnly and colourfully below, to the church in Odeillo, between 8 September and Trinity Sunday.

If, before 1914, you had wanted to stay in Font-Romeu, the hermitage was your one resource: 'Cheap accommodation may be obtained from the hermit,' reads the entry in my Edwardian edition of *Baedeker*. But that was before the hotels came to Font-Romeu, as they have now done in great numbers; in 1987, there were forty-one, no less, listed on the tourist map in the middle of town. Modern Font-Romeu began in fact as a hotel, when the Compagnie des Chemins de Fer du Midi built its enormous Grand Hôtel on a hillside site above the modern town where previously there had been nothing. This was finished building in 1914 but, understandably, it was not until after 1918 that it attracted to itself customers and eventually led to the making of a resort. The Grand Hôtel stands there still, happily, the most prominent building in all Cerdagne, visible the moment you enter the basin. It is perfectly of its kind and period, massive, ornate, wasteful. A drink on the terrace, with Cerdagne stretched freshly out before you, would be an agreeably lordly experience in this otherwise modest setting.

The rest of Font-Romeu, which is mostly very new indeed, is

not of the same quality as the Grand Hôtel, though its architecture is enterprising and various. This is not just a holiday resort because it is the place also to which French and other athletes are sent for high-altitude training, a sports complex having been specially built to acclimatize French runners before the Olympics of Mexico City in 1968. Font-Romeu is famous too for its 'solar oven', which is a modern, high-tech tribute to the virtues of the *soulane*. This large and rather beautiful piece of apparatus you can see, standing on the slope outside Odeillo, to the south-west of Font-Romeu. It is a glittering concave surface, made up of 9,500 little mirrors, on to which the rays of the sun are concentrated by an arrangement of sixty-three movable reflectors; the temperature so raised at the centre of the mirror is of the order of 3,500° Centigrade. The 'oven' began working in 1969, but in 1986 it was all of a sudden stopped. There is a new plan now to convert this solar centre into the world's most ingenious detector of gamma rays, coming from the far reaches of the universe – this too, it seems, you can do with mirrors.

The northern side of Cerdagne has a number of villages, one of them, Angoustrine, with a granite church of a delightfully rudimentary kind. And between Angoustrine and Font-Romeu, at Targassonne, there is a fine *chaos*, where blocks of granite have been piled and scattered by the glacier into a sublime disorder.

So far as countryside goes, I would say that the Ombrée, or southern side of Cerdagne, is more congenial than the other. Bourg-Madame, the frontier post on the French side, facing its Spanish equivalent at Puigcerdà, is not worth notice; it has a glamorous name but nothing to back it up with. Before 1815, this was in fact Les Guinguettes d'Hix, meaning roughly Hix Cottages, which as a name was obviously *infra dig.* for a frontier post. In 1815, when royalty was returning to France after the Napoleonic interlude, Hix Cottages was renamed at the prompting of the Duc d'Angoulême, nephew of the guillotined King Louis XVI, who came back into France by this mountain route and whose wife bore the title of Madame Royale – hence Bourg-Madame. Puigcerdà, on the Spanish side of the frontier, is the more charming town, a new capital for Cerdagne when it was first created, on the site of an ancient market, back in 1177. (The stress in its name should really fall on the final *a*, to show that this is Puig-cerda(ña).) Hix, once one of the more important settlements in Cerdagne, is now a barely noticeable hamlet just outside Bourg-Madame to the east. It has a nice little Romanesque church, one of eight or nine such in French Cerdagne as a whole.

Another of these is in the village of Llo, off in the mountains east of Saillagouse. Here, for me, is quite the finest country you can find in Cerdagne. The small road which leads from Llo to Eyne, for example, is a delight, a mini-corniche where the earth is ruddy, the pastures are mild and the two villages themselves merge splendidly, for geometry and for colour, into their bold mountain settings.

At the eastern end of the plain, down in a valley to the east from the Col de la Perche, is the peculiar little church of Planès – Cerdagne's most interesting monument (see Plate 8). (It is easy to find, but not so easy to get into, because first you have to find the keyholder.) This is a church built to an odd plan, a domed, circular structure inscribed inside an equilateral triangle, with three semi-circular, half-domed apses built on to the triangle's three sides. This fascinating geometry has given rise to some reckless speculation as to the origins of the church. The nineteenth-century Romantics favoured the idea, based on an early chronicle, that this somewhat Arabic structure, known locally as 'the Mosque', went all the way back to the eighth century, when it was built by the Christian wife of the Berber ruler of Cerdagne as a memorial to her husband, who had rebelled against his overlord, the Arab governor of Spain, and been put to death. His widow's punishment was to be packed off to the harems of Damascus, so it is unclear how she could have had the chance of erecting this monument to him. Later, credit for the building was given instead to the Templars, said to have established themselves clandestinely in what is certainly a remote site and to have built the church as a centre for the initiation of new members. Sober architectural historians meanwhile have no great difficulty in assimilating the plan of the church to that used not far away, at the great monastery of Saint-Michel-de-Cuxa. The same symbolism is to be traced there, of a circle, standing for the Virgin, being set inside an equilateral triangle, standing for the Trinity. But the short side-trip to Planès I recommend.

At the eastern entrance to Cerdagne stands the fortified townlet of Mont-Louis, a most strategic place in its day, commanding the roads into Cerdagne, into the valley of the Aude to the north, and into the Têt valley down into Roussillon, the principal highway of French Catalonia. So Mont-Louis had every reason to be fortified. The present town is the creation of the later seventeenth century, after Roussillon and Cerdagne had passed definitively to France but still needed to be made safe against possible incursions from Spain. Vauban, who else, came up here to plan the defences and they are still in place today, the strong but elegant gateway into the town, the ramparts and, at the top, the citadel. Their stoniness has been muted by the planting of grass and of trees, but Mont-Louis remains a sombre little place. Thirty years ago, it was still being described as a resort but it is hardly that today, with only one small hotel. At this altitude, and with some tremendous scenery to hand, it should be doing better. The one evidence of modernity is a small solar oven, a junior version of the one to be seen at Font-Romeu; so if there is enough sunshine to run a successful solar oven, there is enough to restore Mont-Louis to something of its past as a tourist place. Meanwhile its only visitors seem to be French commandos, who occupy Vauban's citadel and train in the harsh uplands round about.

From Mont-Louis then, there is a choice of valleys: you can follow the river Aude or the river Têt. The Aude or Capcir valley runs due north, to Axat, Quillan and eventually Carcassonne; the Têt valley, also called the Conflent, goes east, down on to the plain of Roussillon. Here, I mean to go by the Aude valley, but before abandoning Cerdagne, I should mention a lazy way of visiting it which is also a fine, even an exciting way of visiting the upper valley of the Têt; by the narrow-gauge railway, or 'little yellow train', which starts out from Villefranche-de-Conflent some twenty miles and 4,000 feet below Mont-Louis and climbs this steep and desolate valley with the necessary help of some very distinguished engineering and railway architecture, by way of viaducts, tunnels and cuttings; after Mont-Louis, the line meanders across the plain all the way to Bourg-Madame and a short way up the valley of the Carol.

The Capcir would itself come as a surprise, geologically, if you had not just left Cerdagne; this is another glacial plateau but considerably higher overall than Cerdagne and with a much grimmer climate, because there is nothing here to stand in the way of the north wind. The true entrance to the Capcir is at the Col de la Quillane, about three miles from Mont-Louis. You are high here, almost 6,000 feet, but with no real sense of altitude because of the lack of declivities: everywhere is high on this plateau. On the north side of the col the plateau widens out until it is a good five miles across. To the left, beyond the artificial lake of Matemale, is the new ski resort of Les Angles, built in the 1960s and on a generous if also conspicuous scale. It is cited as one of the greater successes in the creation of high-altitude ski stations in the Pyrenees, both in itself and because it has led, as you can soon see, to the building nearby of a good many holiday homes, in a bleak country which has the reputation of being one of the coldest inhabited places in France.

The scenery of the Capcir is imposing but hardly comfortable, especially if you prefer the intimacy of valleys to the openness of plateaux. However, after Puyvalador, the plateau ends and the sides start to close in again. This is a first taste of the gorges through which the river Aude makes a good deal of its way between here and Quillan. Rather than follow the main road however, take the lesser road to the left, for Quérigut, a small

place but once the capital of its own little region, of the
Donézan. This was nominally a fief of the kings of Aragon, but
in practice came under the sway of the counts of Foix, for the
Catalan connection has already been broken by now, only a few
miles from Cerdagne. Quérigut is in touch with Foix and the
department of Ariège to the west, over the demanding Port de
Pailhères (6,600 feet).

It makes a lovely short detour off the road down the Aude
valley, through beech forest at first, and then into the open,
across fertile countryside. But fertile or not, the granite basin of
Quérigut is now more of a tourist than a truly agricultural
region, with almost as many second homes as first ones and a
holiday village at Le Pla, very close to Quérigut itself, some of
whose architecture you may see sticking up above the trees as an
earnest of the modernization of these somnolent parts. Quérigut
has other extrusions too: heaped outcrops of granite which, I
was startled to learn, have the local name of *tors*, as in south-west
England.

The Quérigut road rejoins the main valley road at the minute
ex-spa of Usson and soon bears off to the east, through the long
Gorges de l'Aude and then the very narrow and spectacular
Gorges de Saint-Georges. At Axat you come out on the main
road leading east from Quillan to Perpignan and the Roussillon
plain. But if you want more gorges still, turn to the left, for
Quillan, before which road and river pass through the magnificent Défilé de Pierre-Lys, where there is much overhanging
rock and a number of brief tunnels. It was the Church,
surprisingly, which first got a road made through this obdurate
rockscape; a verse inscription by the road tells you that to the
abbé Félix Armand (1742–1823), priest of the nearby parish of
Saint-Martin-Lys, goes the credit for the first of the rock
tunnels, which has been known ever since as the 'Priest's Hole'.

Roussillon

To end a guidebook to the mountains with a chapter on Roussillon could seem unsuitable, for Roussillon in the main is an exceedingly flat piece of south-western France: the hugely fertile plain built up over the ages by debris from the three mountain rivers, the Agly, the Têt and the Tech, which all enter the Mediterranean independently but within a few miles of each other.

The name of Roussillon derives from that of Ruscino, the Roman settlement established after the second century BC along the river Têt but a little nearer to the sea than modern Perpignan. Before the Romans, this had been the site chosen for their capital by the local people whom the Romans called Sordes. Ruscino was created as a stronghold along the Domitian Way, which led from northern Italy into the Roman province of Spain, via the low pass over the Pyrenees at what is now Le Perthus.

As a region, Roussillon extends over the plain of Perpignan and up into the various ranges of mountains, along the valleys of the Têt and the Tech, as well as into the Albères mountains to the south, along the frontier with Spain. For at this southern end of the chain, unlike in the Pays Basque, the Pyrenees go right on to the end, finally plunging into the waters of the Mediterranean. Roussillon is thus the Catalan region of south-western France and for that reason, above all a linguistic entity. If the local people speak Catalan you can be sure you are in Roussillon (or else in Cerdagne, which is also Catalan-speaking). Unlike

Basque, Catalan is an Indo-European language, a sort of cross between French and Spanish and reasonably easy to get the hang of, at least when written. It has a fine literature and a nobler history than Basque.

It binds together the Catalans on either side of the frontier and makes French Catalans seem more Spanish than French. The Spanish Catalans, like the Spanish Basques, have campaigned and, during the Civil War, fought for autonomy; the French Catalans have been more quiescent. But these days you will see plenty of red and yellow Catalan flags flying on official buildings in Roussillon and the old sense of a Catalan identity is still strongly alive there. But rather than join up with Spanish Catalans, the ambition of such autonomists as there are in Roussillon seems just as much to become part of an independent Occitan-speaking region – Occitan being the *langue d'oc* spoken long ago across the southern part of France, for the re-establishment of which political campaigns have been mounted in recent years.

The Fenouillèdes and the Têt Valley

The way into Roussillon which I shall follow here is by the road running from Quillan to Perpignan, whose keenest pleasure for some of us is that quite abruptly, once you have left behind the forests and defiles of the Aude, you find yourself driving between vineyards. At last and unequivocally you are in a Mediterranean landscape, drier, barer and hotter. This, on the French side of the Pyrenees, is the western limit of the olive tree, which expires no more than forty miles from the sea – on the Spanish side it travels further inland. To the left of the road are the mountains of the Corbières, which on this southern side are remarkably wall-like, but belong, geologists say, with the Massif Central rather than with the Pyrenees and so would be gatecrashing were I to admit them here. To the right is the

craggy, unfamiliar, but profoundly attractive region of the
Fenouillèdes; and *fenouil* being the French word for fennel, such
a name sets you looking forward to those aromatic southern
hillscapes covered in wild herbs. Which is just what you will
find up in the Fenouillèdes.

So it would be a sad mistake to go all the way along the main
road into Perpignan when to the south here there is a lovely
drive across into the valley of the Têt. The Fenouillèdes is not
many miles wide but it is seductive: the roads are winding and
the temptation is to go extremely slowly. There would be
no harm in taking the whole day over these twenty-odd miles.
The point I would pick to turn off the main road is at
Saint-Paul-de-Fenouillet, which is getting on for halfway
between Quillan and Perpignan. By then, you have absorbed
enough vineyards to convince you you are in the far south, and
although the vintages of Roussillon become rather more
distinguished the further east you go, at Maury or Estagel, as a
spectator it is the vines themselves and not their product that one
enjoys – and never more so than in early summer, when the
plants are still young enough to have kept their independence of
one another. So, at the attractive small town of Saint-Paul-de-
Fenouillet, turn south, for Prades.

To begin with, this road keeps close to the river Agly, which
for all its modest size is a doughty cutter-out of defiles, since
before crossing the valley it has already created, on the southern
edge of the Corbières, the astonishing gorges of Galamus. And
now here, in the limestone ridge that faces the Corbières, it does
the same again, though on a lesser scale, at the Pont or Clue de la
Fou. The Agly remains more or less in sight, flowing
southwards, as far as the village of Ansignan, which is in a valley
where every possible scrap of land seems to have been made into
a vineyard, to the point where there are grapes growing in the
very centre of the village itself. Below Ansignan, to the left, is a
fine aqueduct, claimed by the locals as a Roman one but ascribed
by the guidebooks to the thirteenth century.

At Ansignan the river turns off, to the east, and the country starts to get higher. The next place to make for, along roads lined with flowering acacias, is Sournia, which has two very early churches, one or two small hotels and a glorious mountain situation. This could be an ideal asylum in spring or early summer, before it gets too arid, with vast tracts of flowery and generally hospitable hillside to walk on and massive views both north to the Corbières, south to the great bulk of the Canigou, and east towards the sea. After Sournia the road climbs through a deserted, growingly wild country strewn with blocks of granite, up to the Col de Roque-Jalère, and then goes down quickly enough into the by comparison decidedly crowded landscape of the Têt valley, just to the north of Prades.

The Têt valley is the one which I abandoned previously at Mont-Louis. Prades in fact is no more than twenty miles downstream from Mont-Louis, although the word downstream may give a rather weak idea of the river Têt, which is rightly famous in its upper reaches for dropping more than 2,000 feet in only four miles. Thus the twenty miles from Mont-Louis to Prades will carry you down from 5,200 feet to only 1,150. In Mont-Louis you are absolutely in the mountains; in Prades there is every promise of the plain and of the sea.

This is the valley of the monasteries, the great buildings of Roussillon that are among the best things anywhere in the Pyrenees. To see them slowly, you need a centre. My own centre would be Vernet-les-Bains, or anyway its environs. Vernet is a small spa town but of the sunny, bracing sort, quite different from many of the gloomier spas deeper into the mountains. It is a spa also which displays a certain anglophilia, I'm not sure why, symbolized in its little Anglican church, a waterfall called the Cascade des Anglais, and a war memorial dedicated unusually to the *Entente Cordiale* (and listing all the countries which joined in on the Allied side in 1914–18 – a list that makes surprising reading, containing as it does such names as Japan, China, Cuba and Siam). Rudyard Kipling helped to make Vernet pro-English, because he came here regularly and used it as his base in southern France, writing in his little book called *Souvenirs of France* of how, once seized of the pleasures of motoring in this country, he would unfold his maps in a 'meadow' at the foot of the Canigou and plan his summer trips.

Vernet is mainly a modern town but with an old core, on a hill on the right bank of the river Cady, which comes down from the mountains to the south. On one terrible occasion, this innocent-looking torrent came down with much violence, during the historic storms which struck this region in October 1940. In Vernet, floodwater demolished a number of houses and hotels and removed more than half the gardens belonging to the spa. But the best of Vernet is up from the river, where the decorative streets and alleys of the old town make a congenial small quarter to walk in, with good wrought-iron and flower-festooned balconies. On top of the hill is the unremarkable twelfth-century church of Vernet and next to that the castle, which is not the real thing but a ruin restored ninety years ago as a private house.

Vernet is right at the foot of the Pic du Canigou, the most prominent and revered mountain in the eastern Pyrenees. The Canigou is 9,200 feet high, deeply ravined and a proper mountain shape, that is, a pyramid. It is, disappointingly, quite simple to climb. Indeed, according to one of the chronicles, it was first climbed in the year 1285, by King Pedro III of Aragon. In the present century, it has been attacked by bicycle, by car and on horseback – though none of these could get right to the top. Now, in summer, jeeps go up and down the worn, narrow but in good weather manageable road that leads to the Chalet-Hôtel des Cortalets. From there, you can walk up to the summit and back in three and a half hours; or so they tell you. I have not tried it because I do not remember having seen the Canigou entirely free of cloud, though in high summer it no doubt commonly is so. To climb to the top and see nothing, however, would be deeply frustrating, since the view is by all accounts prodigious.

If you can see *from* the Canigou all those places from which the Canigou is said to be visible, then prodigious is the word: for the summit-cone is reportedly to be picked out against the westering sun from as far away as Marseille.

The woods and crags on the western side of the massif of the Canigou make an incomparable décor for one of the most exquisite of Pyrenean monuments, the monastery of Saint-Martin-du-Canigou, which can be reached only on foot from the village of Casteil, a mile and a half upstream of Vernet (a jeep can, by arrangement, be hired to take disabled people up). This is a steady climb of twenty-five to thirty minutes, mainly through oak and chestnut trees, whose shade would be a blessing in summer, and to the sound of a torrent below. The site is extraordinary, but the approach to it restrained: the monastery buildings come into view piecemeal, the tower and apse of the church first and then the rest. To grasp it as a whole and the glory of its position, you need to see it from above, from the viewpoint on the hillside from where it is traditionally photographed. Looking slightly down on it, you can take in the harmony of the conjoined buildings and the precipitousness of the spur on which they stand, buttressed strongly on the southern side, above the drop.

This is a very old foundation, though a great deal of what you see at Saint-Martin today is there because of restoration work carried faithfully and slowly out in the course of the present century. The first mention of a church in this high, isolated spot comes in 997, and ten years later, at the very beginning of our own millennium, a Benedictine monastery was endowed here by Count Wilfred of Cerdagne and his wife; it was consecrated in 1009. In 1035 the count himself withdrew from the world to become a monk of Saint-Martin. But the monastery did not flourish. At the time of its founding, this part of south-western France had a population swollen by Christian refugees from Muslim Spain, but as the Reconquest proceeded and the Muslims were driven further from the Pyrenees, that population declined so that, for demographic reasons if for no other, Saint-Martin-du-Canigou languished. It was badly damaged in an earthquake in 1428, from which it never properly recovered, though it was not until 1781 that it was finally suppressed by papal decree and the few remaining brothers returned to secular life. The old buildings then fell into ruin and became a quarry for local villagers in search of building stone. Throughout the nineteenth century, it was a well-known, romantic and neglected ruin. In 1902 it was bought by the Bishop of Perpignan, who set about gradually rebuilding it – after 1916 with the help of the State. Some pieces from the original dismantled structure – columns and capitals – were discovered at a house in Vernet and bought back, to be reincorporated in the new building work. Since the Second World War, the complex of buildings has been added to, to allow room for monastic retreats to be held up here, in a quite remarkably tranquil and propitious site for them.

There are in fact two churches at Saint-Martin, one above the other, the upper one dedicated to the foundation's patron saint, the lower one to the Virgin. The Virgin's church is half-underground, and both dark and primitive, and it is built in two strikingly distinct styles of architecture; the older, eastern part has groined vaulting, supported by squat granite columns with rudimentary capitals, while the western part, built a little later, has cruciform pillars holding up the vault. The upper church, though naturally for the most part later than the lower, has only one pair of pillars and is supported for the rest by the less sophisticated method of columns, in this instance monolithic, almost cigar-shaped columns whose lower parts are buried in the floor. In this church too, the capitals are movingly simple, floral motifs mostly and sculpted in low, flat relief.

The existing cloister of Saint-Martin is a token, not an accurate reconstruction of the old cloister, which could not be rebuilt because of the many changes there had been over time in the disposition of the monastic buildings. The cloister is thus a single gallery built so as to display some of the capitals and columns recovered earlier in the present century from their long diaspora. The gallery is open to the mountain view, which the ancient cloister was not, since the contemplative mind was not intended to be stirred or seduced by the changing spectacle of nature outside. But as a cloister walk for tourists, Saint-Martin is perfect, and some of the later capitals, sculpted from a stone you soon become familiar with in these parts, the pinkish marble found at Villefranche-de-Conflent, are delightful. There are, too, some fine early mortuary bas-reliefs set into the facing wall. On the north side of the church are two body-shaped graves scooped laboriously out of the granite, the larger of them having been hollowed out by the founder of the monastery, Count Wilfred, for himself.

You can walk down from Saint-Martin-du-Canigou by a different path from the one you go up by: leading sharply down through the woods to the torrent at the bottom. And if you follow the little road through Casteil further, to the south-west, it climbs rapidly up to the inviting Col de Jou, from where forest roads or tracks fan out in three directions. The road down from here to the villages of Sahorre and Fuilla is charming, and both these villages have good Romanesque churches of the early, simple kind. That at Sahorre is in prominent isolation on a hillside to the left of the village and has suffered somewhat from the instability of its foundations; the decoration of the apse is extremely pretty. The church of Fuilla is notable for having a nave conspicuously higher than its side-aisles, but is spoilt by having been partly invaded by village houses at the east end.

This road down from the col comes out in the Têt valley at the remarkable fortified town of Villefranche-de-Conflent. Villefranche dates back as a stronghold to the end of the eleventh century, having been established by the counts of Cerdagne in the geographical centre of their domains as a 'free' town with market rights extending for 100 kilometres. Later, it became for a long time a part of the northern defences of the kingdom of Aragon, against trouble arriving from Languedoc or from

France. With the Treaty of the Pyrenees, in 1659, it passed with the rest of Roussillon to France and turned, as it were, to face in the opposite direction, commanding the road down from Cerdagne rather than the road up. The fortifications engineered by the Spaniards were taken over and improved by Vauban, and it is the Vaubanized town that you see today, more or less untouched in its essentials.

Unlike orthodox defence posts, Villefranche does not over-look the land round about, but is overlooked from it, because it is tightly hemmed in by hills on three sides. To cover it against this dangerous exposure, it has a citadel high up on a hill to the north, reachable by an underground staircase from the town, of 999 steps. During the First World War this perched castle was turned into a secure lodging for German prisoners, having much earlier served as a prison for four women incriminated in a celebrated and scandalous poisoning case in Paris in the 1670s – one of the four survived up there for forty years. The town of Villefranche remains wholly enclosed within its tall defensive walls. These you can walk round on the south and west sides, at two different levels, first up above by the roofed-over *chemin de ronde*, which has wide apertures and gives you pleasant prospects of the countryside; and then by a gloomy, uneven passage down below, which has slits only in the walls and is much more the secretive walkway you would expect to find in ramparts such as these. It makes a curious but also somewhat monotonous short excursion.

Better perhaps to walk round the town below, which consists of two parallel streets, with the handsome, classical Porte de France at one end and the Porte d'Espagne at the other. There are some fine old Catalan town houses, tall and serious-looking, two towers from the late Middle Ages and a twelfth-century church, later enlarged, which has a nice crenellated tower and two conspicuous portals on the north side, made from the local pink marble. The smaller of these doorways was in fact moved here from the west wall some time after 1700; it is less richly decorated than its larger companion, which has fine capitals attributed to the masons of the monastery of Saint-Michel- de-Cuxa and a splendid curly-maned lion with a human head between its paws sculpted above. The best things inside the church are the fifteenth-century Gothic choir-stalls displayed at the west end, with, in the centre of them, a large recumbent Christ carved in wood in the cruel Catalan style which tells you that, aesthetically, the Catalans are Spanish, not French.

Midway between Villefranche and Vernet is the village of Corneilla-de-Conflent, which is today a nondescript place but was once a residence of the counts of Cerdagne and has a splendid church to prove it. If Villefranche was the counts' commercial foundation, then Corneilla was the ecclesiastical one. Remnants of the palace which they built for themselves here can still be made out, on the other side of the road from the church. When this royal palace passed into the hands of the canons of Corneilla, and was turned into the residence of the prior, it was joined to the church by a stone viaduct, but during the French Revolution the local peasants demolished this, against the objections of the prior, on the grounds that it hindered their hay-carts on the way up the road.

The church of Corneilla-de-Conflent is finer on the outside than on the inside. It has a lovely eleventh-century tower, with pilasters at the corners and decorative bands, and apertures which grow larger at each successive storey. To the left of the tower, the façade is of granite and crenellated, with an ornate window of pink marble and a deep, finely decorated portal of the same stone. This is admirable above all for its tympanum, which is one of the few in Roussillon to have been sculpted: its subject, of the Virgin in Majesty, is also a rarity. The entrance doors to the church are decorated with some of the beautiful, convoluted ironwork which has survived on several of the Romanesque churches in Roussillon, though the expert opinion is that at Corneilla the style is in decline, and the effect of the ironwork indeed is stiff compared with other, more energetic examples. The other delight of Corneilla is the apse, whose stonework is quite extraordinarily regular and which is delicately decorated with arches, dentellations and deep-set windows arranged like tiny portals, with two pairs of slim, capitalled columns to each. Inside, the church is dark and takes time to become visible. It has some splendid marble altar-tables and three wooden statues of the Virgin, dating from the twelfth to the fourteenth centuries – the most compelling of these by far is the oldest, to the left of the altar: a Virgin who is very stiffly draped, and holding an equally rigid Christ on her left knee, his hand raised in blessing.

The second great monastic site of Conflent is that of Saint-Michel-de-Cuxa, outside Prades. Rather than approach it from Prades, try to come on it from the other side, from the south that is, by way of the village of Fillols and a charming road that skirts the underpinnings of the Pic du Canigou. Here the road runs straight at the old abbey buildings, between orchards, and you get a particularly inspiring view of tiled roofs and the lovely, crenellated tower of Saint-Michel, with its four storeys of windows.

Saint-Michel was a Benedictine foundation of the late ninth century, built in this kindly spot for a struggling community of monks who had been driven out of their monastery higher up the Têt valley by a catastrophic spate. In the second half of the tenth century and the first half of the eleventh, Saint-Michel-de-Cuxa was an influential place, ecclesiastically, and in the century following it became an influential place architecturally too, as the first great centre in Roussillon of Romanesque church sculpture. But then, like Saint-Martin-du-Canigou, the monastery went into a slow, mournful decline. In the sixteenth century it was refashioned somewhat though hardly revived. By the time of the French Revolution, there were still monks in residence, but their piety was doubtful and in 1790 the monastery was secularized, to be laid waste three years later by anti-clerical vandals. In the nineteenth century, as private property, Saint-Michel had a most unhappy history, with portions of the cloister being removed and sold or dispersed, while the roof of the church was allowed to fall in and one of the two towers collapsed during a storm.

But the most extraordinary episode in the story of Saint-Michel and its dispersion came in the first years of the present century – an episode of what French art historians tend to call, embarrassingly for ourselves, '*elginisme*', after the predatory Lord Elgin of the Athens Marbles. In 1906–7, an American sculptor called George Grey Barnard began buying up bits and pieces of Romanesque architecture in southern France and offering to sell them to American museums. In February 1907, he offered the director of the Metropolitan Museum in New York 'half a rare treasure', on the other half of which he already held an option. The rare treasure was the cloister of Saint-Michel-de-Cuxa, which he suggested would be like 'a poem for Americans unable to see Europe'. He attempted to buy up the scattered elements of it piecemeal, a few capitals, arches or columns at a time, from whoever now owned them – quite a number had travelled no further than the nearby town of Prades, where they ornamented such buildings as the public bathhouse. The eventual result of George Grey Barnard's 'elginism', among the relics of Saint-Michel and other vanished masterpieces, was the celebrated Cloisters Museum in New York, opened by Barnard himself on his own lands there in 1914 and sold in 1925 to John D. Rockefeller, who gave it to the Metropolitan Museum. Rockefeller paid 600,000 dollars for what Barnard was estimated to have paid in all less than 3,000 dollars for.

So Saint-Michel-de-Cuxa is another incomplete, much restored site, but a very beautiful one all the same. The oldest part of the church is actually pre-Romanesque, the building having been consecrated in 975. The most noticeable thing about it is the great thickness of the masonry and the large number of horseshoe arches, which give it a Moorish look, though suggestions that the number and proportions of these arches at

Cuxa imply the presence there during the building of architects from Muslim Spain have not been generally accepted, since the horseshoes can equally well be taken as deriving from Visigothic or Carolingian models. Something else which is unexpected, and attractive, in Saint-Michel, is the narrow passage that opens on either side of the choir, the entrances to which also have horseshoe arches opening above the lintel of the doorway. This is a splendid, plain church.

Beyond the west end, in the eleventh century, a second, much smaller church was created, underground, in the area of the crypt. This is known now as the Chapel of the Crèche and is dedicated to the Virgin, though the wooden statue of the Virgin once worshipped here is that now to be seen in the nearby church of Corneilla, where it was carried at the time of the Revolution. The chapel is dim and circular, with an annular vault supported on a large central pillar; in the vaulting you can clearly see the rectangular patterns made by the original coffering.

The cloister of Saint-Michel was a construction of the twelfth century and survived intact up until 1789. It is on the northern side of the church, though several steps down from it in level. Its arcaded galleries contained sixty-three columns in all, set singly or in pairs, with sculpted capitals. Engravings from the first part of the nineteenth century record the cloister's rapid break-up, leading in the end to the irrevocable export of significant sections of it to the United States.

Its partial reconstruction dates from 1952, and what you see there now is a mixture of the authentic and the imitation. Some of the original arches, columns and capitals were recovered from various parts of the country, notably eleven arches which had been re-erected at the Prades baths, and narrowly escaped joining so many of the others in New York; these now form the major part of the southern gallery next to the church, the only one of the four that is complete. The north-east corner has been rebuilt from new materials, though using ancient capitals, to establish the limits of the original cloister, but all the remaining capitals that were recovered were built into the new western gallery, to the left that is, as you come out of the church. The capitals best worth looking at are those in the southern gallery next to the church. These are sculpted from pink Villefranche marble and all of them bear either floral or zoological motifs – religious subjects turn out to be quite a rarity on Roussillon's Romanesque capitals. At Saint-Michel it is all leaves and lions. Many of the lions are wonderfully bold and vital in their posture, safely heraldic in side-view but monstrous when shown face on, with hanging tongues or else with the tail-end of their prey disappearing into their mouths.

Nor are the capitals the only sculptures of unusual quality to be seen on this side of the cloister; for the entrance door to the church itself has been set into an archway made from slabs of marble most exquisitely decorated, though in a low, unemphatic relief, except for the more deeply sculpted figures of two seraphim and of a lion and a bull, the second of which finds it hard to fit its head into the arched space allotted to it. Look closely and you can see the small round holes made everywhere by the process, new at the time when this work was being created, known as trepanning and used to emphasize outlines or to mark the centres of flowers and the pupils of eyes. This archway does not belong where it now stands even though it looks so well there, for it was once the front of a tribune or raised choir inside the church, like the magnificent one which is still in place at the nearby monastery church of Serrabone. On either side of the arch of Saint-Michel are two pillars bearing similar sculptures in very low relief of St Peter and St Paul, the first identifiable by his key, the second by his baldness – his distinguishing sign, seemingly, but is there something in the New Testament to say that he was bald?

In summer, the monastery of Saint-Michel-de-Cuxa is the setting – and what a setting – for the concerts given at the Prades music festival, which is certainly the most distinguished of the growing number of such events in south-west France. It is the most distinguished because it was started back in the 1950s by the great Spanish – or, more to the point, Catalan – cellist, Pablo Casals, who settled in Prades after he came out of Spain at the time of the Spanish Civil War. Prades itself, the principal town of the Têt valley, is a busy, not very historic place, though it is curious walking around it to see how casually the local pink marble has been used in houses or pavements, and even for the runnels that carry the rainwater away down the middle of the streets.

To the north, some four miles away, Prades has its spa, of Molitg-les-Bains, which stands in a deep, wooded ravine; and beyond Molitg is the old fortified village of Mosset, sitting up above a narrow road that would carry you back into the Pays de Sault to the west. But rather than head up this particular valley, it is more rewarding to turn to the right, or east, at the village of Catllar, and go first to Eus and then up to Marcevol in the mountains above. Eus makes the grand claim for itself that it is 'one of the most beautiful villages in France'; but it is quaint rather than beautiful, piled up any old how on a hillside and with its houses built in amongst the stone, so that you may find yourself passing through a rock tunnel to get from one part of the village to another. The effect is picturesque but shapeless, in that Eus has no obvious centre to it and all villages should have that.

The little road up to Marcevol takes you out of the Têt valley, into the dry, terraced country around Arboussols, where the vineyards have been squeezed into every cultivable piece of land, however cramped. Marcevol has a ruined monastery, on a glorious, turfy site just below the old village. This is a very simple, partly derelict complex of buildings, which passed long ago from being a monastery to serving as a wine store and then as a barn; now, it is being restored and used as a centre for retreats and other religious assemblies. The church has a charming Romanesque doorway, with a window dressed in

pink marble above it in the façade; and best of all it has some
superb whorls of twelfth-century ironwork on the door,
furniture that is incomplete but still one of the most captivating
examples you will find of this local art. When leaving Marcevol,
it is pleasanter to carry on eastwards, towards Tarerach, and go
back down into the Têt valley by the Vinça road, which comes
out above the elongated reservoir that has been made from the
river at this point.

From Vinça, the same minor road by which you have just
come down on the other side of the valley, the D13, would take
you on a most desirable round trip up into the mountains on this
southern side. It passes first through a wooded defile, up to the
villages of Baillestavy and then Valmanya, by when the road is
climbing and from where you get close views of the rutted
eastern flank of the Canigou. At the top is the open, pastoral
country round the Col Palomère. From there you can descend to
the east, into the rocky valley of the Boulès and on to the road
which leaves the Têt valley at Bouleternère and after a
dauntingly sinuous passage through the mountains emerges into
the valley of the Tech at Amélie-les-Bains. I say 'dauntingly
sinuous' advisedly, because it was just outside Bouleternère, as I
began to drive south along this road, that I passed a road sign
promising me forty-three kilometres, no less, of *virages* ahead.
Since the full distance from valley to valley is only forty-five
kilometres, one can say that this road is bends all the way.

A main object in taking it would be to see Serrabone, the third
of the trinity of celebrated monasteries in Roussillon. This is off
to the right, and very steeply off to the right, between
Bouleternère and Boule d'Amont, in a site which is as penitential
in its ruggedness as it is soothing in its isolation. Serrabone, or
serra bona, means 'good mountain', but the mountains here are
known as the Aspres, and in that name you are intended to hear
what you cannot help but notice at Serrabone, their asperity.
This was never a favoured region where the land could be easily
worked or profited from. The first monastic community came

to Serrabone at the end of the eleventh century, but the monastery did not flourish for very long. Within two centuries it was in decline and by the end of the sixteenth had vanished completely. The buildings belonged thereafter to the cathedral of Solsona, in Spanish Catalonia, and were used more for the sheltering of sheep than for the cure of human souls. In the 1830s, Prosper Mérimée, the French writer who for seven years was a most enlightened and successful Inspector of Ancient Monuments in France, visited Serrabone, but he did not think too highly of the quality of its ruins. They remained as ruins for a good while longer until, right at the end of the century, they were finally bought back from the cathedral of Solsona and a measure of restoration began.

On the outside, Serrabone is finely suited architecturally to its unyielding landscape, with much strength and rather few graces to show. The stone from which it is built is very obviously the local schist and the impression is ascetic – with the tower especially so, because it has no openings in it worthy of the name before you get almost to the top, at the level of the bells, where there are some strictly rectangular apertures. But this dour exterior harbours what are agreed to be the best of all the Romanesque sculptures in Roussillon, of a delicacy and elaboration out of the ordinary. You get a hint of this from the delightful gallery or cloister that opens on the south side of the church, overlooking a very narrow garden and then a terraced drop into the torrent below (see Plate 9). The contrast is striking in this tiny cloister between the horizontal, slaty appearance of the walls, and the pairs of marble columns that subdivide the arcades. The columns are all the more attractive for having long lapsed from the vertical to form gently divergent couples, in sympathy with the south wall of the church facing them, which is also bowed outwards. There are some lovely capitals in this gallery, the best of them on the inside and showing the same motifs as at Cuxa, of leaves, eagles and lions, some of these reduced once again merely to enormous heads and jaws from which protrude the feet of their prey.

The glory of Serrabone, however, is inside the church: the tribune, which cuts the central nave in two half-way down and on top of which the canons would once have had their choir. But it is the underneath of the tribune which is important, for the superlative quality of its decoration. It rests on vaulting peculiar for having ribs that are more or less independent of the stones above them. The columns that support the vault are of marble, arranged in ones or twos, and have splendid capitals. The triple-arched marble façade of the tribune is on the west side, facing the congregation, and this is the best thing of all, with its mass of decoration in low relief surmounting the glorious capitals of the pillars and columns that support it. The façade has a religious subject, though set in the midst of much mainly floral decoration: a theophany, unorthodox in this case for showing the Lamb of God instead of the usual human figure of Christ, together with the symbols of the four Evangelists, a lion, an eagle, a bull and a man. The capitals to either side of this arcade are especially memorable: on one a centaur with the body of a lion is shooting an arrow at a deer, though a deer with a gorgeous ornamental mane – this is the satanic huntsman in pursuit of the gently pious soul. Facing this scene is another capital, on which a powerful human figure is sculpted upright between a lion and a centaur, holding the first by its tongue and the second by an ear; the two animals each have a paw on the man's shoulders as a sign of submission. The symbolism here is assumed to be the victory of piety over bestiality. Others of the capitals at Serrabone are the equal of these two, in their vitality and certainty of form, and are all the easier to appreciate because here at least they are at eye level, unlike those you have to peer up at in the dimness of churches. They are also, by the same token, at hand level, and on the most admired of them the marble has become unnaturally smooth and glossy; erosion by human touch is under way at Serrabone.

Should you leave Serrabone in the southerly direction, for Amélie-les-Bains, there is another, minor but attractive,

Romanesque monument right beside the road, a little before the Col Xatard. This is the very early Chapel of La Trinité, which has two naves, the original eleventh-century nave having been duplicated in the twelfth century – a sign that this now depopulated region was then experiencing a demographic growth. The chapel is worth a moment or two because it has on its entrance doors some of the very best of the decorative ironwork of Roussillon, as well as, inside, a celebrated Romanesque crucifix, on which the Christ-figure is clothed and serene, not at all like the naked, suffering figures of the Catalan style.

The Tech Valley

It is confusing that the two major valleys of Roussillon should have names which are so alike: it is easy to get the Têt muddled with the Tech, especially when both pursue a parallel course down from the Pyrenees and on to the plain. More confusing still is that both these valleys go under two different names: just as the Têt valley is known alternatively as the Conflent, you will also find the Tech valley being referred to as the Vallespir – upstream from Amélie-les-Bains as the High Vallespir, down-stream as the Low Vallespir (I will not be tempted, for obvious reasons, to refer to the High-Tech and the Low-Tech valleys). The climate of this extreme south-eastern corner of the country is always said to be the most 'African' in France, because it gets a great deal of hot sun, but 'African' suggests something more arid and treeless certainly than the High Vallespir, which is above all wooded. Certainly, there is far less rain here than at the other end of the Pyrenees: forty-five wet days a year is the average for Roussillon, though that total rises as the ground rises, and the mountain climate is significantly wetter than that of Perpignan and the Mediterranean coast, where ten inches of rain at most in the year is normal.

Amélie, to start there, is a bright, modern spa and resort, named in 1840 for the wife of King Louis-Philippe. Previous to the French Revolution, the baths here had belonged to the abbey of Arles-sur-Tech a mile or two up-river, which had received them as a gift from the Emperor Charlemagne. At Amélie the Tech has a wide bed with more stones and bushes in it than water, as if to reassure you as to the dryness of a town which boasts of having 210 cloudless days a year. (Amélie and the Tech valley suffered too, however, in the great floods of October 1940, when the local railway station, among other things, was swept off.) As with so many spas, Amélie-les-Bains is a long town rather than a deep one, stretched out along the banks of the river – and increasingly on the northern bank, where large numbers of heliotropic hotels and apartment blocks have been put up, overlooking that other necessary amenity of a French resort, the *boulodrome*, or gritty arena for the playing of the salubrious game of *pétanque*. Amélie is a modest spa which is doing nicely, the second most favoured in the Pyrenees, after Luchon.

The principal and most historic town of the High Vallespir is Arles, an old place and the site of a distinguished abbey. The first monastic foundation here goes back to the end of the eighth century, but some time in the middle of the ninth century that first building was destroyed by Viking pirates. The surviving abbey church is deeply embedded in the narrow alleys of the medieval town and was consecrated in 1046. But the original structure was much altered in the twelfth century, when it was vaulted over – as you can see for yourself, from the way the pillars of the tall nave have had to be buttressed to support the extra weight of the stone – and when, strangely, the orientation of the church was reversed, in that the apse was removed from the east end and added to the west. Arles also has a plain, quite small but delectable cloister, built at the end of the thirteenth century and thus one of the earlier examples of the southern Gothic style. The façade of the church has some good

Romanesque lions on it and an excellent tympanum, with a Christ inscribed in a Greek cross and surrounded by the symbols of the Evangelists. Above the doorway inside the church, remarkably, a chapel was discovered only quite recently painted with some badly damaged murals, done perhaps at the time of the church's second consecration in 1157. What can be enjoyed of them, principally, is two fine angels on either side of the central window, which are good enough to make the destruction of the rest seem a deplorable loss.

Advancing upstream from Arles, towards Prats-de-Mollo, you come almost at once to the Gorges de la Fou, off the road to the right. These are indeed extraordinary, the world's narrowest gorges according to the local publicity, and I for one will believe it, for there are places along the journey of some three-quarters of a mile up this mighty fissure where the rock walls are only eight or nine feet apart. This can be a wet walk and, towards the far end, a tiring one, when you need to climb a whole series of damp wooden staircases. And to make the whole thing seem more adventurous you are made to wear a safety helmet, even though it is dripping water rather than falling rocks that it is likely to save you from. There are one or two points along the way, admittedly, where giant boulders have become wedged in the crevice overhead, but securely enough to stay up there for a good many million years to come. At other places, the walkway turns subterranean, passing through rock caverns whose walls have been seductively polished by the torrent. At the far end, the vegetation, barely able to keep any rootholds at all in the more vertical parts of the gorges, resumes, and the passage widens out into the sunlight. Along with Kakouetta, in the Basque country, the Gorges de la Fou are the most spectacular of their kind in the Pyrenees.

There is no other particular cause to stop, on the way up the Tech valley, before the little fortified town of Prats-de-Mollo at the western end. Prats is not in fact at the terminus of the valley, even though, with its fine seventeenth-century ramparts, it looks as if it should be. But beyond Prats in one direction is the little spa and resort of La Preste and beyond it in another a fairly new main road into Spain. This crosses the frontier at the Col d'Ares (5,000 feet), the point where, the orologists would have it, the lowish Mediterranean range of the Albères merges seamlessly with the High Pyrenees.

Prats-de-Mollo is a pretty place, though not all of it is still contained within the old, charmingly turreted walls. It has coherence, though. On the north side the town scales the hillside, up as far as the church, which is large, but an uninspired seventeenth-century replacement for an earlier building – of which a nice crenellated tower and some fine traditional ironwork on the doors alone remain. Inside the church is a towering example of the baroque reredoses so fashionable in Roussillon; this one must be a good forty feet high. There are some handsome buildings in Prats, both in the upper town on the far side of the stream that divides it in two, and in the lower town, where the shops are: the town hall here, dated on the façade to 1614, is especially likeable.

There are grand trips up into the mountains to be had on either side of this upper valley. To the south you can follow a lovely circuitous course through pasture and woodlands, mainly chestnut trees and oaks, to villages such as Serralongue (where there is a good, plain Romanesque church, with more early ironwork on the doors, signed, on the bolt, with the name of the craftsman), Lamanère, which is the most southerly human settlement in the territory of France, and Coustouges. The one village to shut your eyes to is the largest, Saint-Laurent-de-Cerdans, which is a featureless place given over to the manufacture of espadrilles and the local cloth. Coustouges has an unexpectedly grand church, though from here it is an easy passage on foot into Spain and consequently the village was for long somewhere of local importance. Today it is far from flourishing and the church, with its ample, crenellated tower, seems disproportionate. Inside, where it is exceedingly dark alas, it has two small chapels on either side of the choir which contain the first known examples of genuine rib vaulting in Roussillon, as opposed to the merely decorative kind you can see in the tribune at Serrabone. But it is the portal more than anything else that one comes to Coustouges for. This is not in good condition because it was sculpted from some softer and less enduring stone than the local marble, but the decoration is, in its simple way, imposing, formed of the traditional Romanesque pine cones, foliage and human and animal figures. What is most surprising here is that even the tympanum, where you would expect to see a Christ in Majesty, is purely decorative, being filled with three rows of linked circles containing foliage.

On the other, northern side of the High Vallespir, the country is more ravishing still. The road to follow here is that which leaves the valley at the village of Le Tech and climbs up to Montferrer and Corsavy, before rejoining the valley road again at Arles. By the time you reach the little village of Montferrer, in its pastoral setting amidst the crags, the views to the east are wonderful, sweeping round through a good 180 degrees. So thickly treed are these mountains that from up here you can see nothing but forest, as if there were no inhabited valleys like the Tech within miles. Between Montferrer and Corsavy, at the grassy viewpoint of the Col de Casteill, you get a different sense of the country again, because now it is easy to grasp the way in which the mountains run down towards the plain of Roussillon, which opens visibly out beyond Amélie-les-Bains and Céret. To the north-west the omnipresent upper slopes of the Canigou are quite close, looking deeply and forbiddingly scoured from this angle.

Corsavy is a pleasant village, out of which a road goes high up into the Canigou massif, to one of the most famous of the old iron-workings in these mountains, at Batère – the iron deposits of the Canigou were being worked as early as the twelfth century, and at different times there were at least twenty Catalan 'forges' or wood-fired 'iron-mills' operating in the two valleys of the Têt and the Tech. A little outside Corsavy, on a hillside to the left of the road, is the shell of a twelfth-century church, quite isolated and now being peacefully restored. It is an Arcadian site, with one or two picnic tables, the smartened-up graves of four medieval *gent de Cortsavi* to serve as a *memento mori*, and, if you have the patience and the nose for it, a chance of digging up your own supply of lunchtime truffles from fields said to be especially rich in them.

Moving down-river now from Amélie-les-Bains, it is only a short way before the hills on either side start to draw back, especially to the south. At the point where the plain of Roussillon begins is the market town of Céret, which is the most lively and civilized of the smaller towns in Roussillon. It is a commercial place, the centre of a famous fruit-growing district – Céret has the earliest cherries in France, picked before the end of April. It is also in a small way an arty town, because before the First World War it became a favourite resort of the Cubists, who worked on some of their more revolutionary pictorial ideas here and later attracted other painters to the town. There are echoes of those artistically formative years in some of the place-names in Céret: the Place Pablo Picasso most notably (whose alternative Catalan name, on the other hand, is the Placeta d'En Duran), or the Bar El Pablo that faces it. Another consequence of this patronage by Picasso, Braque, Juan Gris and other painters is the town's excellent Museum of Modern Art, which occupies a delightful, rambling building just off the main shopping street. You can find it, appropriately enough, given Picasso's well-known political affiliations, by reference to the local headquarters of the French Communist Party, of which he was long a member and which in Céret has premises bang opposite the art gallery.

What you can see in the gallery may not be outstanding but it is good, and quite different in its resolute modernity from anything you would normally expect to find in a small local gallery. There are some charming Chagall lithographs, one or two fine Mirós, a crucified skeleton by another Catalan artist, Salvador Dali, and some beautifully austere paintings by the contemporary Spanish Catalan painter, Tapiés. Of Picasso there are lithographs, drawings, one or two paintings and a bronze, but best of all, a series of ceramic bowls with bullfight scenes painted on them, together with a splendid *pichet* or wine-jug similarly decorated.

As a town, Céret has largely outgrown its old quarter, which is partly walled and a pleasure to walk in, with an occasional fine Catalan house front to enjoy and one or two small, irregular squares like some scaled-down version of Paris. And on this old, southern side of the town, the terraced hillsides start straight away, almost before the houses have finished. In the Place de la République, at the western end of the main street, there remains the fortified Porte de France, as a gateway into the old town, with, to the right of it, the peeling and dilapidated façade of an old Catalan mansion, much balustraded and festooned and looking ideal for use as the seedy dictator's palace in a film of colonial South America – it is one of those house fronts more effective in their neglect than they could ever be once renovated.

From Céret you can take the main valley road straight to Le Boulou, crossing the river near to, but not in fact by Céret's pride and joy: its fourteenth-century humpbacked bridge. Or else you can take a smaller road through the village of Maureillas and into what is a very Roman part of Roussillon. Just to the south here is the col of Le Perthus, so low, at a bare 1,000 feet, that it presents no sort of obstacle to those anxious to cross the Pyrenees. Hence its use all through history by invading armies and its use today by two almost touching roads, the old N9 from Perpignan to Gerona, and the relatively new motorway that has been created alongside it. This is the route by which Hannibal will surely have entered Gaul, on his way to Italy, and which was later followed by the Via Domitia. Traces of this pre-eminent highway, and of the defence works alongside it, can still be found in the river valley near the village of L'Écluse, and it is supposed that the trophy erected by Pompey in 70 BC, to signify the definitive Roman conquest of Spain, must have stood somewhere here.

Crammed most unfortunately in, on a windy, poppy-strewn oasis of land between the motorway and the N9, is the tiny chapel of Saint-Martin-de-Fenollar, ill-signposted to say the least and open officially for only two hours a day in summer and hardly at all the rest of the year. The chapel is of great antiquity, being mentioned in texts of the ninth century. But what it has, if you are clever enough to get in to see them, are the finest Romanesque mural paintings of Roussillon. My own recommendation of them must be based on reproductions, because I have not managed to coincide at Saint-Martin with the opening of the chapel. Reproductions generally make damaged wall-paintings look to be more legible than they are in fact, but those in Saint-Martin-de-Fenollar, which have been dated to the early part of the twelfth century, retain a colour and vivacity of design that make them something to try and get to.

Unless you have business in Perpignan, or an appointment south of the Pyrenees in Spain, you should now take the road out of Le Boulou which leads due east, straight at the sea. Le Boulou itself, with its attendant spa, is a negligible place, the scene of a considerable victory by the revolutionary French over an invading Spanish army in 1794 but of little else, bar the manufacture of corks, the raw material for which has always been plentifully available in the large forests of cork-oaks in the Albères. By the time you are clear of Le Boulou, the change in the landscape is complete. From here to Argelès-sur-Mer, the country is absolutely flat, and suddenly quite dusty. If you are unlucky, the *tramontane* will be blowing hard, the cold, dry north-east wind that can be a curse in Roussillon.

The two large villages which you pass through on this road, Saint-Genis-des-Fontaines and Saint-André de Sorède, will probably seem nothing, charmless places best ignored. But both have something to show for themselves architecturally. At Saint-Genis this is the sculpted lintel above the entrance to the abbey church, a quite superb piece of decoration on an old but shabby and otherwise forgettable building. This plaque of pale marble is the oldest piece of Romanesque sculpture in France. It is dated very precisely, to the year 1019–20, by the Latin inscription carved into the lintel itself above the figures which it contains, to the effect that it was made in honour of St Genis in the twenty-fourth year of the reign of 'King Robert', and since the King Robert in question was the Capetian Robert the Pious, who succeeded his father Hugues Capet as king of France in October 996, the twelve-month of its making can be calculated exactly. It is a beautiful object, sandy in colour, showing a Christ in Majesty in the centre, attended on either hand by a kneeling angel, and with six Apostles in all, three to the right and three to the left, framed in horseshoe arches. The relief is shallow and the figures, apart from the two contorted angels, are straight and stiff, yet the effect of the whole, inside its border of foliage, is utterly pleasing, not least the harmonious manner in which the Apostles have been fitted into their niches and the variety in the lines of their drapery and the positions of their hands. There is no single work of art I would rather see again anywhere in Roussillon.

Certainly, the comparable lintel over the doorway of the church of Saint-André a few miles further on does not match up to it, even if the actual church of Saint-André – like Saint-Genis, originally a Carolingian abbey – is a considerably more handsome building. The different materials and building styles used in the outside walls here record the history of the church's gradual heightening during the tenth and eleventh centuries. The lintel is sometimes thought to have been made in direct imitation of that of Saint-Genis, although it is much poorer in its design and workmanship. The style is in fact more ambitious, because here the relief is more prominent and the figures of the Apostles – only four of them this time, because two Apostles have had to make way for a cherub and a seraph – are no longer face-on nor full-length, but as if forced into their arcade, with an effect that seems mean compared with the statuesque array of Saint-Genis. Above the doorway at Saint-André there is a splendid window with a sculpted surround of white marble. It is too high off the ground to be easily enjoyed in detail, but the decoration of the band underneath the window is very fine. It shows four medallions, the two outside ones containing a bull and a lion, the two inside ones two pairs of angels, reduced only to their heads, blowing on horns. The medallions are enfolded in the wings of three seraphim. The expert view is that this fine composition is the work of the master who sculpted the lintel of Saint-Genis. The façade of Saint-André also has a *chrisme*, which is modern, and two fine lions sculpted in white marble. Inside the church there is an exquisite example of the decorated marble altar-tables for which the region of Narbonne was famous in the tenth and eleventh centuries.

Perpignan

North from Argelès stretches a flat, sandy coastline which has been hugely developed since the 1960s, and made into a holiday strip. Compared with the scenic vicissitudes of the Côte Vermeille to the south, this northern Roussillon shore is monotonous. Monotonous to look at, that is; as a place to go swimming it has a lot to be said for it, except, again, when the wind is up – on the splendid beach of Argelès once, I spent a jolly hour watching enormous numbers of umbrellas, balls and other volatile impedimenta being plucked from the sand and hurried out to sea to what I assumed was a wasted future as flotsam, until I learnt that they would all eventually be blown ashore again further down the coast, at a sort of natural lost-property office.

The coast road north from Argelès, to Saint-Cyprien and Canet-Plage, is merely functional, strictly for sea-goers. But between Argelès and Perpignan on the main road stands the old town of Elne, a great place once and still today an interesting one. It would be nice to say that Elne stands on a hill, but that would be slightly to exaggerate. It stands on a rise, let's say, 170 feet above sea level, but that modest eminence is sufficient in the surrounding flatness of Roussillon to have ensured this site a distinguished history.

Modern Elne was first the Illiberis of the Celtiberians, and then Roman Helena, a city restored at the beginning of the fourth century AD and named after the mother of the Emperor Constantine – whose feeble son Constans was later assassinated there by mutineers. After being the virtual capital of Roman Roussillon, it passed to being a stronghold of the Visigoths and suffered much in the struggles between the Islamic invaders of southern France and Carolingian efforts to dislodge them. Finally, once Perpignan began to grow, in the eleventh and twelfth centuries, Elne faded out, never to recover.

But it remained a bishopric and thus the ecclesiastical capital of Roussillon right up until 1600. And the considerable cathedral and cloister of Elne are still there, to attest to 1,000 years of religious authority. The present building was begun in the eleventh century and is outwardly unimpressive, being largely of that mixture of large pebbles and rubble-stones set in mortar which is too makeshift to be quite cathedral-like. If you walk round outside to the east end, you can see where they began in the early years of the fourteenth century to replace the apse with a much grander Gothic structure of seven chapels and an ambulatory. The little that was built now appears like a jagged outer wall, enclosing the east end of the cathedral, work having lapsed when discussions began as to whether the bishops of Elne should not move themselves to the upwardly mobile new town of Perpignan. The cathedral has one good tower, of stone, and one poorish, modern one, of brick. Inside, it is sizeable, with a tall, windowless, Romanesque nave, and side-aisles on to which Gothic chapels have been grafted. The intriguing aspect of the nave is the pillars, which are vertical on the outside but lean slightly inwards on the side facing the nave. Which is not their only irregularity, for they show a certain variety of form from one to the next, one on the north side of the nave especially having been very elaborately reinforced.

But it is the cloister, far more than the church, which is truly impressive at Elne. It opens on the north side of the nave and can be quite dazzling to step out into, with so much marble to reflect the sun. The oldest and best gallery is on the south, next to the church. This was built and decorated in the second half of the twelfth century and has some delightful sculptures on its pillars and capitals, as well as some fine funeral stones set into the wall. Here are more griffons, lions and rams, with their attendant foliage, as well as serpents and, unexpectedly, two sirens close together on adjoining capitals, one with a bird's wings, the other with twin fishes' tails, which she is holding up in her hand. There are also biblical (or Apocryphal) scenes sculpted on the pillars in this gallery, in quite high relief and still splendidly legible. They show, first, Christ appearing to St Peter, then, the conversion of St Paul along the Damascus road, and finally a more ambiguous scene usually interpreted as showing Herod giving orders for the Massacre of the Innocents. The style of these sculptures is primitive but the effect wholly engaging. At either end of the gallery is a funeral stone with a full-length figure sculpted on it; these date from the start of the thirteenth century and are curious for the very fussy style of the drapery that shrouds the bodies, which seems to have been made of thousands of tiny, curving folds. Also set into the wall here is the funeral monument of the bishop, William Jorda, who was in office when it is thought that the cloister of Elne was begun and whose death is recorded as having happened in 1186. The other galleries of the cloister are inferior compared with this first one, the sculptures being for the most part incompetent imitations of the superb Romanesque models which the sculptors had to work from in the southern gallery.

From Elne you come into Perpignan through its southern suburbs, past the enormous new housing developments of the Moulin-à-Vent. Just off to the right is the large village of Cabestany, as yet not quite sucked into the urban mass of Perpignan, but separated from it only by the slenderest of green belts. In the church of Cabestany is kept yet one more notable piece of Romanesque sculpture, a marble tympanum from a long-vanished portal that is now displayed inside the building, on a wall. It is worn, but remarkable for the expressiveness of the sculptor's style and the rarity of the subject, which is the bodily Assumption into Heaven of the Virgin. The figures have oversized feet and hands and, with the gentle exception of the transfigured Virgin, the most uncouth faces. These shocking touches of grotesquerie stick in the mind, and it is small wonder that 'the Master of Cabestany', as the unknown creator of this tympanum is known, should have an honourable place in the history of southern Romanesque art.

Perpignan is the largest town of the Pyrenees, having in recent years gone through another of the surges in size and population that have punctuated its long history. It grew unusually fast back in the Middle Ages, increasing in area sixfold between the late tenth and the middle of the twelfth centuries. In this century, it expanded astonishingly during the 1920s, then again after 1939 and the terrible efflux of Republican exiles from Spain after Franco's victory in the Civil War, and for a third time in the 1960s, when many French settlers from North Africa moved to Roussillon following Algerian independence. The population of the town, at 110,000 or so, is now three times what it was in 1914.

Perpignan can thank its old military uses for the fact that it has survived this fierce expansion as a still coherent, shapely town; for up until the early years of this century Perpignan went about its business behind high ramparts. These defence works had often been needed, too, over the centuries, both during the times when Roussillon was being traded between France and Spain, and later, during various Franco-Spanish wars – the town has known some unpleasant sieges in its day, the worst perhaps in the 1640s, at the hands of Richelieu and Louis XIII, and the last in 1793, when the Spanish came over the Pyrenees during the revolutionary wars. Two short and handsome stretches of the old walls remain, on the east side of the town, but for the most part they were demolished in the 1900s, in a final recognition that business and comfort mattered more in this highly commercialized town than security. Where the ramparts once ran, however, there is now a sequence of boulevards, creating a boundary for old Perpignan and preserving its unity. Beyond them the suburbs have taken large bites out of the plain, but inside them is still an attractive city, small enough to be experienced on foot.

The heart of Perpignan is the little Place de la Loge, which is closed to cars, has a paving of pinkish marble and where, sitting at the café, you can just about imagine yourself in Siena or some other northern Italian town. The Italian look comes from the buildings facing you: the Gothic Loge de Mer on the corner, which was begun right at the end of the fourteenth century and later enlarged; then the monumental, court-yarded Hôtel de Ville, mainly sixteenth/seventeenth century; and finally the fifteenth-century Palais de la Députation, with its grand arched doorway and columned windows. These three modest enough buildings, of three different periods, fit together very pleasingly and make the Place de la Loge the best if also the most crowded place to sit in Perpignan. Not that its past as a focal point of the town was always so convivial; once, it was a place of execution and in the 1670s the scene, during a revolt by Catalan dissidents against the unloved royal power of France, of some extremely cruel tortures and executions. The Loge de Mer itself, which was originally built to house a marine consulate, charged with regulating Perpignan's trade, has found uses barely worthy of its

Gothic charms. Once, they stored coaches there, but then, as far back as 1842, it became a café. Today it is a cafeteria – for Perpignan is a modern French town, and you may find that food there has been polarized between the fast and cheap and the slow and expensive.

Most of the best things to look at in Perpignan can be walked to in minutes from the Place de la Loge. Just to the north of the Place is the old fortified gateway of the Castillet, built in the 1360s and graceful much more than warlike with the sun shining on its splendid brickwork and machicolations; more than a century after it was built, the Castillet was converted from a mere gateway into a citadel and another entrance to the town was created alongside it, the Porte Notre-Dame. Past the Castillet on its northern side flows the small river Basse, which is so thoroughly domesticated on its passage through the town, dragooned as it is within concrete banks with grass and flowerbeds either side, that you take it to be some artificial canal. The quays either side are quite Parisian, for the good reason that they were laid out during the Second Empire, in a first, decisive move towards making Perpignan into a bourgeois, tradesman's town.

A brief walk east of the Loge de Mer is the cathedral of Perpignan, begun in 1324, consecrated only in the early 1500s and promoted to the rank of cathedral in place of Elne in 1602. Its façade is attractive, a tall, decorative example of how to mix courses of bricks with stones and mortar. The interior is Gothic, and stately, with a tall, single nave of great width and many chapels between the buttresses along the sides. The dominant items of decoration are the huge baroque reredoses, behind the various altars, and a very fine Renaissance organ. But this is not a particularly distinguished building.

Down a passageway to the left of the cathedral, there is better: Perpignan's oldest church, of Saint-Jean-le-Vieux, consecrated in 1025. Some of it at least has survived the years at the end of the nineteenth century during which it was turned into an electricity power station, with a chimney sticking up through the vaulting as a rival for the bell-tower of the cathedral next door. Nowadays, the passage leading to Saint-Jean-le-Vieux contains a smart restaurant, which has tables outside underneath a rather *ad hoc* arrangement of buttresses – a curious décor for the architecturally alert diner. What is remarkable about Saint-Jean-le-Vieux, and worth seeing, is the first of the two portals, on the south side. This is later in date than it looks to be, having been made in the thirteenth century, out of marble from Céret. On either side of it are the badly eroded statues of Apostles, stuck baldly against the uprights; but it is the tympanum that is oddest, being scooped out where the lintel ought to be into two arches with, on the keystone between them, an extraordinarily rugged, forceful figure of Christ, trampling down a barely identifiable monster and with two less than angelic angels on either side of his head. Because this figure is so low down as to appear almost to fit underneath the entrance, the impression it gives is of waiting to pounce on those entering the church.

If you take only one walk through Perpignan, then let it be in the quarter to the south and south-east of the cathedral, up as far as the Place Cassanyes. This side of the town has much more character than the other, the small streets between the cathedral and the little triangular Place Rigaud especially. Leaving the cathedral by the south or right-hand door, you come immediately to a chapel on the left in which there is displayed Perpignan's most remarkable crucifix, dating from 1307 and in a style of the utmost, impassioned realism – this is a suffering, anatomical Christ. It was carved in fact not by a Catalan but somewhere in the Rhineland. The Place Rigaud is charming, named after one of Perpignan's more famous sons, who went off to become Louis XIV's court painter; his Place has a fruit and vegetable market in it, which is both a pleasure and a reminder to what extent the town's wealth has depended on the tremendous fertility of the country round about. This quarter of

Perpignan has the most elaborate and evocative street-names you could ever ask for from an old town: the Rue Poids de la Fairine, or Flour-Weight street, the Rue de la Main de Fer, or Iron-Hand street; and others.

Between the Place Rigaud and the Place Cassanyes is the popular quarter, 'popular' of course being the guidebook euphemism for poor, or run-down. As in most other old towns, the popular quarter of Perpignan has always been the popular quarter; poverty does not migrate. The fact that there is a Rue des Bohémiens, or Gypsy street, here indicates a tradition stretching way back. Today it is North Africans who have moved in, the new class of marginals in France, immigrants from the Maghreb, and it is their culture which tends to dominate the fine street market in the Place Cassanyes, where there are stalls selling more different kinds of olive, for example, than I ever knew could be grown. More or less beside the Place Cassanyes is the church of Saint-Jacques, which contains what is the most appealing because the simplest of Perpignan's many reredoses, from the late fifteenth century. Next to the church there is also a very pleasant small garden, created among the remains of the old fortifications. You have, up here, as great a sense of altitude as it is possible to find in Perpignan.

The town's most distinctive monument is unquestionably the Palace of the Kings of Majorca, an extensive citadel that dominates Perpignan to the south. For most people it will be a surprise to know that there ever were kings of Majorca. In fact, the kingdom was something of a dynastic dodge, and short-lived, as kingdoms go. It was set up in 1262 by James I, King of Aragon, who divided his considerable kingdom up in order, so he said, to prevent strife between his two sons. The son who became King of Majorca was to rule over the Balearic Islands and the counties of Roussillon and Cerdagne, together with one or two other fiefs in Languedoc. Strife between him and his brother was not as it happened avoided, but James II, the first King of Majorca, was a moderate man in a bellicose age and did

Perpignan much good, even if the kingdom itself vanished again in 1344 after a great deal of murderous rivalry between the twin branches of the Aragonese royal family.

James II it was who had the royal palace built in Perpignan, at the very end of the thirteenth century. It was a first intrusion of the southern Gothic style into these Romanesque regions, and it is possible that the main architect was the same man as took charge for a time of the nascent cathedral of Albi, that sublime church-cum-fortress to the north of Roussillon. The same mature combination of strength and refinement is to be met with in the Perpignan palace as at Albi: this is a most striking cross between a fortress and a courtly residence. The impression of strength you get at once when approaching the palace, which stands well back and up, inside the huge brick ramparts of the citadel, which enclose the whole of the broad, low hill at the southern extremity of old Perpignan. On their western side is a vaulted passage leading up to the esplanades and gardens in front of the palace itself. The fortifications were built long after the palace, at different times and by different kings, notably Louis XI of France, the Habsburg Emperor Charles V, and King Philip II of Spain. Once, the palace would have been rather lost inside them, but now it has been freed from the excrescences which had grown up around it and accurately restored: the rights of residence, if not quite of domesticity, have been given back to it.

The tower over the fortified entrance gate is the perfect viewpoint from which to look out over the town of Perpignan and over the Roussillon plain. What you see *is* Roussillon. To the east is the Mediterranean, curving away northwards into Languedoc – into 'France' as a true Catalan might still want to say; to the north-east are the pale mountains of the Corbières; and then, as you move round towards the south, the two distinct tongues of the Pyrenees which reach out into the plain, between the valleys of the Agly, the Têt and the Tech, with the supreme mass of the Canigou to the south-east; and finally, to the south, the Albères, as the conclusion to the Pyrenees, and to France. Once inside the Palace of the Kings, the finest thing by far is the *cour d'honneur* or principal courtyard, and especially the eastern side of it, which faces you as you enter. This is basically of two storeys, but the variety of levels and of architectural features is enchanting. Along the ground floor is a broad arcade, in which no two arches seem to be of quite the same size, but all are wide and low except for the large central one. The upper storey, reached at either end by elegant and easy sets of stairs, has a row of tall, narrow, Gothic arches at one end and at the other a strong, rectangular loggia. Geometrically, in its mixture of curves, points and straight lines, this is high art. In the centre of this eastern side, but a little back from it, stands the keep, a military element but in this case containing two chapels, one above the other – his and hers so to speak, since the king worshipped in the upper chapel and the queen in the lower. Both are prettily if rather flimsily decorated in a Gothic style, with the local marble again to the fore, and both have a feature I would have thought uncommon, which is false stained-glass windows painted directly on to the walls. Some of the apartments of the palace are splendid enough in their way, especially the vast hall known as the Salle de Majorque on the south side.

To the north of Perpignan, Roussillon quickly ends and with it any guidebook intending to stick scrupulously to the Pyrenees. But I shall make one brief sweep through this remaining fragment of Roussillon. Starting from Canet-Plage on the coast, to get to which, out of Perpignan, you have to pass close by the village of Château-Roussillon, where is the site of the ancient settlement of Ruscino – parts of the Roman town are currently being excavated. Northwards from Canet, the coast-line is no different from that to the south; it is still flat, sandy and frequently blowy. It contains, however, particularly along the stretch between Le Barcarès and Leucate, much new building, because this coast was long ago chosen to be turned into what the more excitable planners called, I seem to remember, the

'California' of France, a new holiday shore created more or less from scratch. In the 1950s it was still quite empty along here: millions of mosquitoes with no one to bite. Now, in summer, it must be exceedingly full, though the mosquitoes have reportedly been sprayed out of existence. Port-Barcarès is nearly all post-1960, built in a style that is an unhappy cross between American Midwest and French Foreign Legion; Port-Leucate, further on, is much better, with its artificial harbours and more imaginative building styles – this is the end to be, I would guess. Between the two is this coast's oddest monument, a substantial Greek steamer called the *Lydia* that was deliberately beached there in 1967 and left for a plaything, some fifty yards from the shoreline. Just to the south of Port-Barcarès, in the dunes, there is a monument of another, more poignant kind, far from consonant with the holiday feelings these beaches ought to engender: an austere stone memorial to 10,000 Spanish Republicans who, in 1939, made the choice here to volunteer to serve with the French army against the Nazis. If you find this a surprising place for such a choice to have been made, then you should know that thousands of those who fled from Spain into France at the end of the Civil War were put into camps along the Roussillon coast. This was camping of a harsher kind than that now practised there in summer by migrating northerners, and not all those exiled campers survived the winter. Indeed, the greatest Spanish poet of this century, Antonio Machado, died in one such camp, outside Argelès, and was buried in Collioure.

Inland from Port-Barcarès and Port-Leucate is the enormous salt-water Étang de Leucate, one of a number of such saline lakes along this coast, full of oysters and, these days, of sail-boarders, who presumably take to it as a good practice-ground for the real sea, because the prevailing winds are boisterous but the water shallow, so that there is no floundering about when you are upset. On the western side of the Étang, at its bottom end, is the town of Salses, a wine town of Roussillon, like Rivesaltes to the south of it, or Fitou just to the north. But rather than its cellars or its vineyards, Salses should be visited for its fort, which is a superlative piece of military architecture, and one of the great monuments of Roussillon (see Plate 10).

Salses commands the passage into Roussillon from France, between the Étang to the east and the foothills of the Corbières to the west, and the fortress was built in its present form by the Spaniards, at the tail-end of the fifteenth century, in replacement of an earlier, too easily pregnable construction made obsolete by the changing technology of warfare. The architect, one Ramirez, did an extraordinary job, his principal concern being to make the construction immune to artillery fire. The ring wall, as a consequence, is some twenty feet thick, and the layout of the defences, as you soon find out should you wander about in them, most sophisticated, with the tops of the curtain walls having been rounded off, for instance, so as to deflect projectiles as well as to make them harder to scale. In the huge inner courtyard or parade-ground, there are signs of domesticity, for Salses had a large garrison and the necessary installations of an independent community. Once it had become finally French, in the seventeenth century, one or two effete frills and ornaments were added to what is otherwise a tremendously severe conglomeration of buildings, such as a now crumbling Louis-XIV clock. Surprisingly, for so strong a place, the fortress of Salses sits down, rather, in its landscape, almost as if it had had to be excavated; but its colouring, in its mixture of pale, reddish stone and bleached brickwork, matches unerringly that of the earth round about and the parched slopes of the Corbières to the west.

Instead of driving straight back down into Perpignan from Salses, turn off to the right outside Rivesaltes, for Vingrau and a brief encounter with the Corbières. The road climbs quite modestly up the Pas de l'Escale, which declares itself to be the *porte des Corbières*. It is indeed the entrance to the delightful valley of the Verdouble. The very name of Vingrau promises vineyards and gorgeous grapescapes are what you find along this road, a patchwork of vines in the flatter places, with grey escarpments and clumps of dark pine trees above them.

But another reason for following this roundabout route back to Perpignan is that it takes you also through Tautavel, a village of which no one probably had heard before 1971 except for those who drank its wine. But in that year, in a cave in the limestone above the village, a French archaeologist discovered what are among the oldest human remains ever found in Europe. Tautavel man, or at any rate his skull, had arrived, to be dated anywhere between 200,000 and 600,000 BP. The site of the excavations is not open to visitors, but Tautavel does now have, thanks to the celebrity of its oldest inhabitant, what is quite the best-arranged and most instructive museum of prehistory in the Pyrenees. There are a great many objects displayed – bones and tools – and a vast amount of information given on the prehistoric environment. There is also a moulding of the skull that began it all.

Leaving Tautavel to the south is a beautiful, lonely road which crosses some very rocky hill country, noticeably less hospitable than the valley you have just left, before you get to Cases-de-Pène in the Agly valley.

The Côte Vermeille

The rocky coastline known as the Côte Vermeille starts in earnest at Collioure, just south of Argelès. Literally translated, Côte Vermeille means 'Vermilion Coast', but vermilion is a very bright red and the characteristic rock of the Côte, though memorably ruddy, is hardly that. So either the *vermeille* is a bit of romantic over-painting of the local geology, or else it comes from another sense of *vermeil*, which also in French means 'silver-gilt'; silver-gilt certainly seems closer to the actual colours you see along this coast. I shall leave this undecided: and say, simply, that the Côte Vermeille is, at its best, a warm and welcoming red-yellow-brown colour.

It runs for twenty miles, south to the Spanish frontier at Cerbère. This was the first piece of Mediterranean France that I ever came to know, back in the 1950s, and I have to be careful now not to see it too much in terms of what it then was, and no longer is. When one thinks what the temptations have been in the years in between for a Mediterranean coast such as this to cheapen and abase itself before the tourist, then I shall say that the Côte Vermeille has looked after itself reasonably well; it is more brazen than before, more built-up, more sea-oriented, but as yet not denatured by its responsibilities as a holiday coast. There are plenty of places on this rough terrain where people either can't or won't be allowed to build, and inland the Côte Vermeille is gloriously prevented from expansion by acres and acres of vineyards, where the wines of Banyuls are grown and which are the most heartening imaginable barrier against an invasion of the hillsides by the apparatus of vacations. And south of Argelès there are in any case no real beaches, mainly rocks, inlets and, at best, pebbles, so that the true holiday coast of Roussillon runs north from Argelès, along the endless sands towards Narbonne, draining much potential nastiness away from the Côte Vermeille.

Collioure is easily the prettiest and hence the best known of the little towns along the Côte. It has a real bay and three tiny, if not terribly comfortable beaches. Its vocation as a true seaport is now hardly noticeable, although once Collioure was the harbour on which the energetic and enterprising merchants of medieval Perpignan relied for the conduct of their export trade. Nowadays, it still has the smell and a little of the activity of a fishing port, but far more of the activity of a summer resort. On the town side the shoreline is interrupted dramatically by the huge Château Royal or fortress, built originally in the twelfth century by the Templars, extended by the Spaniards during the centuries when Roussillon was theirs, and modernized later by Vauban after the Treaty of the Pyrenees. Its robust walls may now be assaulted by nothing more aggressive than pedalos but they are a reminder that Collioure was for long a bastion, with a citadel on the north side of the town and the fortress of Saint-Elme on a hill facing, and that it did not properly become a place for civilians until the latter part of the seventeenth century. Facing the château, at the far end of the beach and the brief esplanade, is Collioure's church and the ancient lighthouse that has been incorporated into it to serve as a bell-tower – this round tower, with its pinkish dome, is somehow the emblem of Collioure, the landmark by which one instantly recognizes it again. To the left of the church is the steep and decorative quarter of the town known as the Moure, full of old galleried houses now mostly renovated. All too many of them seem to have been turned into artists' studios. The pictures painted and sold in these, however, are unworthy of Collioure's artistic past, for in the early years of this century real painters came here, as they did to Céret: in Collioure's case the group of young colourists known as the Fauves, in some of whose paintings – those of André Derain, say – you can soon recognize the colours from the landscape of the Côte Vermeille.

From Collioure it is possible to walk to the next small place along the coast, Port-Vendres, which these days is barely separate from Collioure, both towns having spread along the coastal road. Port-Vendres is a more practical, less hedonistic town than Collioure. There has been a harbour here since Roman times – the Romans called it Portus Veneris or 'The Port of Venus', hence its modern name of Port-Vendres – and possibly for even longer than that, since the Phoenicians too may have made use of this deep inlet for their trading ships. But in the late Middle Ages, when Collioure was doing well, Port-Vendres was in decline and it did not recover until the eighteenth century, when it eventually became the port through which the wines of Roussillon were exported north. Later, in the 1830s, Port-Vendres became the principal port for the passage of the soldiers and supplies needed for the French conquest of Algeria, and this strong North African link lasted for well over a century. When I first stayed here, which was before Algeria won its independence from France, there was a regular, much-used service of boats to Oran or Algiers, ferries that always seemed far too large to negotiate so narrow an anchorage. Port-Vendres is not the place it was, commercially, but it remains a working port, with plenty of fishing boats mixed in with the yachts, and a sense that here, at least, they still take the sea seriously.

Between Port-Vendres and Banyuls-sur-Mer, three miles further south, the open country returns. Towards Banyuls, the grapes crowd in on the sea, filling the terraces of the hills to the west, and Banyuls can claim, unusually, to be at once a wine town and a seaside resort, a rare and virtuous combination. As a town, it is not very striking, nor does it have too many claims as a resort: the main beach in front of the town is stony and stony beaches on summer days as torrid as they may get here can be a punishing experience – I could tell of an afternoon at Banyuls when the pebbles were so painfully hot underfoot that even the healing sea was unreachable.

After Banyuls, there are six more admirably rugged miles to go before Spain, the coastline between Banyuls and the frontier town of Cerbère being the wildest and least habitable of all. The little town of Cerbère is tightly clustered around yet another inlet and it is plain but presentable; the beach smaller but more hospitable than that of Banyuls, and the town rather less bent on the service of tourists. What I do not know is how it came to be named after Cerberus, the monstrous watchdog who guarded the entrance to the Underworld. The question is: which way does Cerbère face, north or south? If north, then Spain is the Underworld and we are being warned not to enter it; if south, the same goes for France. Either way, it is an ingenious name to have hit upon for a natural frontier post. Standing on the little beach of Cerbère, you are, remember, at the very end of the Pyrenees. At the Cap Cerbère, which encloses the bay on the southern side, this noble chain of mountains drops sheer into the sea, and for ever out of sight.

Index

221

INDEX

INDEX